# PHOTOGRAPH AND THE NEW WHEELED ORDER

## BOOK THREE OF THE PHOTOGRAPH CHRONICLES

### MICHAEL BLATHERWICK

Paperback: ISBN 979-8-9867772-5-2
eBook: ISBN 979-8-9867772-6-9

Library of Congress Control Number: 2024917119
First paperback edition: September 2024

Development Editor/Copy Editor: Amy Reeve
Additional Editing and Proofreading: Cleo Miele
Cover by MiblArt


Jackowick Publishing
Trenton, NJ 08620
michaelblatherwick.com

**Also by Michael Blatherwick**


**Photograph Chronicles Series**

*Photograph and the Atomic Juggernaut* (Book One)

*Photograph and the Daughters of Invention* (Book Two)

*Photograph and the New Wheeled Order* (Book Three)


**The Lobster Princess, Apondra's Tales**

*The Lobster Princess* (Book One)

# Prologue

*Lakhini's Juice – Live*

The new ramp, smelling of plywood and pine, creaked under the shifting weight of Jeff Winslow's wheelchair as he propelled himself up the gentle slope. The lodge members had built the ramp, a mismatched addendum to the gray front porch of the building, to accommodate him after the old one disintegrated from lack of use, not to mention the constant freezing and thawing through many Idaho winters. Looking down at his prosthetic legs, he sighed as the front wheels cleared the final section and touched the mostly level deck. The group of men ahead of him looked back and waved before heading inside, avoiding offering help, likely thanks to him admonishing them last month: *I made it out of Kabul. I can make it up a ramp.*

He rolled to the end of the front row, where an open space was always left reserved for him, and positioned himself just as the militia president took his spot behind the podium.

"Welcome, members of the Idaho Liberty Cavalry!"

John Barbosa beamed as he addressed the assembled group, many in fatigues matching his own or in Carhartt and Dickies workwear, fresh from the jobsite. Jeff looked down at his work jacket, stressed only at his elbows and cuffs when they rubbed against his wheels, not by real work. *Meaningful physical work.*

"We have a special guest tonight, as advertised in our email this week."

Jeff scanned the cadre of men next to the podium. A white man, shorter than his own former standing height of six feet, wore a black tactical vest partially covered by a long thick brown beard. He was accompanied by an athletic olive-skinned man with neat black hair dressed in similar gear with but with an assault rifle strapped across his back. Jeff adjusted his Green Bay Packers hat and strained in his chair to see the third man with salt-and-pepper hair—maybe a high-level commanding officer? The older man adjusted his gold tie against his green button-down shirt.

"Gentlemen, please welcome an esteemed patriot, a man who has sacrificed more than we will ever truly know for liberty, Colonel Colin Rhodes."

A smattering of applause filled the hall. Jeff's hat fell into his lap as he clapped. He glanced at the smudged autographs on the brim from four NFL players and smirked. *Meet and greet, then retreat,* he mused of the experience. *Two signatures per leg.* He drifted back to the memory of waiting in line for the photo op in the cold at the practice field, then the bitter taste in the back of his mouth as children asked for the autographs of the players—*not him,* a real hero, who had arrived in a van with a lift instead of a Bentley. He glanced up, noting that Rhodes was waiting for the applause to cease completely before speaking.

"*Men.* Men of the Idaho Liberty Cavalry, as you and I both know, this country is not at a crossroads—it is beyond. We have been forced down the road of submission and have left our liberty behind us, liberty that is now a carcass being picked apart by scavengers. We are no longer *standing* for the Constitution; we are being told to *kneel* to tyranny."

"I don't kneel to any bitches!" yelled a large man in a ripped fatigue jacket. Rhodes pointed at him and flashed a thumbs-up. "Party doesn't matter," the man continued. "They're all corporate bitches!" A round of laughter followed mixed with applause. Jeff held his hands and tongue silent.

"We *will not* kneel." Rhodes lowered his brow and scanned the thirty-odd men seated before him. "We do, however, obey a CO when they earn our respect. Let me tell you about this CO. I was raised by a single mother who worked two jobs. I enlisted in the United States Army at eighteen. I advanced quickly and was tapped to work on some of its most top-secret projects. I used GI benefits to earn my master's degree in engineering. I excelled at the American dream. Then my wife died during childbirth, God rest her soul, but left me with my beautiful daughter, Nina.

"A single father—that was me, trying to provide. I worked on a project so secret and powerful that we were salivating at the prospect of unleashing it on our enemies." He stopped for a moment and looked up at the militia's flag, a simple hawk holding a snake in its beak. "As the bureaucrats chose profit over progress, we were shut down. But I wanted to serve this country. I retired and started a private security and operations company, One Hundred Roads. I see some nods and smiles, so my reputation in the darker parts of the web must be alive and well."

Jeff folded his hands and propped his chin on his knuckles. His recollection of One Hundred Roads from the patriotic message boards bled into a sly smile on his lips.

"The reason I am here," Rhodes continued, "is because I am now, apparently, a traitor in the eyes of our country. I fought for, bled for, and *protected* this country. Through my organization, we did the dirtiest of jobs. We went places where the government needed plausible deniability. We created some of the false flag operations that helped us choke our enemies before they could take a bite." He raised his arms to the crowd. "And what did our country do? They threw me in jail for taking back the pieces of projects I worked on. *My* work. *My* inventions. They punished me for being a capitalist." He lowered his voice. "They arrested my beautiful daughter, who is now being held in an unknown federal facility, crippled and beaten." Another pause. "My *daughter.* This is not my country . . . and I'm taking it back!"

An explosion of applause startled Jeff. His chair lurched forward as the boisterous people in the row behind him accidentally kicked his wheels. He quickly repositioned himself back in line with the front row and pulled the pant legs of his jeans over the plastic shins peeking out from the tops of his boots. Rhodes clasped his hands and briefly glanced at Jeff.

"I am here tonight because I am looking for men. Word on the street may be that I've been to Montana, Wyoming, North Dakota, and a few other places already, speaking to groups just like you. Men who are willing to be the last line of protection to save this country. The house of cards, well," he scoffed, "it isn't a house of cards at all. It's a house of wooden caskets, filled with the bodies of our brethren who have fought and fallen before us. But now, we must *burn that house down* to build a new one."

John Barbosa clapped and strode over to the podium. "Today, Colonel Rhodes is asking for our help, and we are looking for a few great men to join his multistate force. This is not for everyone, and we understand that. Some of you may want to stay and protect your families, your livelihood, and prepare for the coming chaos that we will walk through as victors and heroes of this country." He paused and looked at Jeff. "We accept that others may not be fully capable for their own reasons, and we respect and honor you as well."

"I can handle myself," Jeff muttered. Rhodes glanced at him quizzically.

"What's your name, soldier?"

"Captain Jeff Winslow. Two tours in Kabul. Best damn C-130 pilot you've ever seen. Call sign Dodger."

"Best pilot I've ever seen? Hmph. Not so much now, eh?" Rhodes snickered.

"I *can* fly, but they won't let me, *Colonel*." Jeff shimmied to his full height in his seat. "When my plane was shot down, I laid down the covering fire against twenty insurgents myself until we could evac six wounded soldiers. My legs were shattered on the shallow landing, but I did it. I *landed* that plane." His eyes narrowed as the burning smell reignited in his nostrils, the thuds of rockets returning to his ears. "I sat pinned in my seat and fired out the shattered window with my sidearm. I saved my crew. And now," he said with exasperation, "I live in my mom's converted garage."

Rhodes approached him and knelt next to him.

"I need *able* men. But thank you for your service."

Jeff rubbed the knuckle on his finger that once bore his wedding band. "Do you need men, or do you need cannon fodder?" he grunted. "Because I'm a man. A soldier."

Rhodes looked down his nose and slowly lifted the cap off Jeff's lap. He examined the sweat marks on the brim and traced his finger over one of the signatures.

"You're in a wheelchair. That's strike one. Your outbursts tell me you might have trouble following orders. Strike two." Rhodes reached into his coat pocket and handed Jeff a Glock 22 handgun. He walked back to the podium and placed the hat on his head. "Shoot the hat."

The men standing on the edges of the room fell silent. Their eyes all fixed on Jeff as he wrapped his fingers around the handle and turned the gun from side to side, feeling the weight.

"Go on," Rhodes whispered. "Be a man."

Jeff flung the gun in a spinning motion toward the podium, hitting Rhodes square in the forehead. As the elder man tumbled back, hat aloft and floating in the air, Jeff snatched his smaller Glock 19 from the hidden quick-release holster tucked in his armpit and fired a single shot that pierced the slowly spinning hat in the center of the stitched Green Bay logo. The crowd gasped with appreciation.

Rhodes clutched his head, where a small trickle of blood ran into his eyebrows, mouth drawn into a sneer.

"Here I thought you'd try to fire that empty gun I gave you and that would be strike three, but you just hit a grand slam, son."

"You think I don't know the difference in weight between a loaded gun and an empty clip and chamber?" Jeff barked. "It's just my legs that are gone, not my reflexes. Not my smarts. Not my patriotism." The corners of his mouth foamed as his voice trembled. "*I am still a man.*"

Rhodes reached into his pocket and opened a small notepad. He clicked his pen ceremoniously and began to write.

"Jeff Winslow. Captain." He held the pen up in the air. "Anyone else want to join Captain Winslow? Stand up." He inhaled and surveyed the hands of twelve men. "You will all be standing up for this country's renovation and reinvention, and the rest of you will, of course, be setting the bar high here at home. We need you here to be ready when we rebuild."

Rhodes's associates moved through the crowd gathering names and handing out sealed envelopes to the volunteers. Two men, practically identical, entered the room from behind the podium, each with a shaved head and matching beards, shaggy and long, ending in a knot of red and brown hair. One of them limped slightly as he walked over to offer a bandage to Rhodes, who accepted it with a tiny frown. Rhodes dabbed his head and sat in the chair next to Jeff.

"You made quite an impression. I need people like you in my command circle."

"Sir, I'm not here to join a think tank or an ops center. I'm here to fight." Jeff placed his gun on his lap and folded his hands. "You just got a free sample of what I can do. I can stand up for myself." He lowered his head and studied his legs. "So to speak."

Rhodes chuckled and placed the Packers hat back on Jeff's head.

"You know, I think you *will* be standing by my side . . . so to speak."

# Chapter 1

*Fantasy – Mariah Carey*

Dana Jefferson slid her ragged chewed fingernails into her padded pink-and-black leather gloves. She adjusted her cuffs, the left one barely covering the small tattoo of a cartoonish red pickup truck on the inside of her wrist, and placed her index finger on the front tire of the image and smiled. She breathed slowly, in and out, an exercise she had learned for stress relief in her anxiety and depression group sessions. As her pulse softened to a slow, steady beat, she assumed command of her team. Dana stood at the top of a ramp and looked out at the three other figures: one standing at the top of a ramp to her left, the other on one to her right, and the third figure seated at the far end of the Taos public skate park.

"Ready to roll!" she echoed from the top of the skateboard ramp.

"Look alive, mates! I'm gonna start firing it up," called out the voice at the far end.

Aaron Olsen set down the pocket Bible he had been reading—these days it was always with him—on the ground alongside his cane and his messenger bag, then flicked the switch on the side of a squatty, dented tennis ball launcher. The hopper of dirty yellow balls vibrated as the fuzzy projectiles were loaded, the cannon aimed at the expanse of the smooth surface of the skate park. The dawning sun peeked over the blood-red horizon. A blond almost Amazonian woman raised a hand.

"One more coffee first?" Angela Costanza stood at the ready in her roller derby pads, her zebra-print-striped leggings stretched thin over her muscular quads and hamstrings, almost to tearing. Her golden hair shimmered in the sun, as did her metallic skate wheels, which were revving as she stepped up to the lip of the platform. Dana took her in, remembering how her statuesque figure and stunning beauty were the primary reasons she had worked up the nerve to ask her out after they first met, but also the source of the much unwanted attention Angela had garnered all her life.

Dana and her teenaged sister, Ashley, waved their consent in Olsen's direction, the younger sibling then tucking her light-brown hair back into her helmet. Ashley quickly winked at Dana, her eyes and skin the same light-brown hues. Dana could see her reflection in her sister, albeit through a mirror image about six years younger than herself. They shared not only facial features, but hardened interiors weathered from difficult paths on different roads. Now that they knew each other existed, Dana couldn't imagine being separated ever again.

"And how are we scored here?" Dana asked.

Olsen held up a large whiteboard. Dana squinted and saw each of their code names: "Phoenix" for Ashley, "Photograph" for Dana, and an ostentatiously cursive "Barbie" for Angela. He cleared his throat.

"Are code names necessary?" Angela asked with a scowl.

"Code names enable efficient communication, and they allow you to remove personal attachment during times of crisis so you maintain a level head. Anyhow, each ball *you* catch, *Barbie*, and get into the trash can is a point. Each ball that Photograph or Phoenix intercept and get into their trash cans is a point. Now hop to it!"

Angela's face soured at the nickname. Nonetheless, she adjusted her goggles and shook out the long locks that extended from under her helmet before she rolled down the ramp. The first tennis ball soared across the court. Angela caught the ball in midair, her electric skates grinding and sparking across the smooth pavement. She tossed it underhand into her trash can.

"Where's the challenge in that?"

Dana and Ashley—or Photograph and Phoenix, respectively—jumped off their ramps, their skates exploding as they landed in twin blasts of burning cinders. The cacophony of the three pairs of high-tech skates sawed into the morning silence. Dana shot ahead of her sister and leapt at the next tennis ball. Ashley followed close in her wake, almost within reach of her sister's long black hair, and bodychecked Angela as best as she could with her diminutive frame.

"How you like that, *Barbie*?" Ashley snickered.

"Yeah, we're going to need to change that." Angela pushed the tiny girl out of her path with a grunt. "If you're such a genius, what's my next move?" Angela looped around Ashley and extended her hand into the ballistic path of the next ball. Dana swept under her arm for the intercept.

"Too slow, *Meatball*!" Dana cackled as she smacked the tennis ball to the ground. Angela wrapped her arm around Dana's torso and threw her to the ground.

"First, don't call me Meatball. Second? Next time, buy a girl dinner if you're going to 'take her out' on her new skates." She winked.

"Next time?" Dana gasped as she flipped to her feet and lunged for the next ball. "You never paid for dinner anytime we were on a date!"

"You always offered first," Angela countered, "and if you call grilled cheese and fries at the diner a proper date, it's no wonder we broke up." She swerved around Ashley's incoming charge and skidded as her wheels over-revved.

"Meatball—err, *Barbie*," Olsen barked, "watch your balance!" The words rang in his ears as he glanced at the cane at his feet. "Focus on your center of gravity and velocity management."

Looking up, Dana caught Angela looking smugly at the former soldier. Dana knew his arrogance and authoritarian tone were all he had after the damage done to his body, a finely tuned weapon that had been broken down in many ways, including by her when they fought as adversaries. She slid past Angela and held up a cautionary finger. Angela nodded.

"Yes, sir." Angela mockingly saluted Olsen and regained her footing, then dodged another tackle by Ashley and grabbed a ball out of the air. Dana saw her eyeing the trash can halfway across the park. "Giddyup!" Angela hurled the ball into the can with a violent overhand pitch, drawing applause from her ex.

"Very nice, Ang." Dana sped over to a ramp and spun in the air as she crossed the lip. Her skates clattered as she landed on the downside and swept into an aggressive turn. "You ready for some heat now?"

Dana's prowess as the most talented skater among her teammates was unmatched. She restrained from showing off, but she knew her skill superseded Angela's raw power and Ashley's sprinting speed. She slipped around Angela and shot her leg out as she crouched, spinning around a trash can. Her skates roared as she pressed her toes into the control panels inside the front of her boots and accelerated. With a laugh, she leapt over Angela's head and caught another tennis ball.

"Show-off," Ashley whined, reaching for another ball headed toward the back of the skate park and falling into a heap as it whizzed past her. The sisters were evenly matched in their confidence on the mechanical wheeled boots, but Ashley's size meant she often fell short. She sat up and looked to Olsen for the next instruction as the ball cannon whirred to a stop.

"Bring it in, mates." Olsen pushed his cane against the ground and rose to his full height, his left leg lagging behind his right. Even though Angela barely overshadowed him in her skates, she chose to bend over and rest her hands on her kneepads. Ashley knelt next to Olsen as Dana coasted to a stop and mirrored Angela's pose.

"There is no score," Olsen declared. "I just needed everyone to work hard, to *think* they were behind their adversary. This exercise was to see how you work together and against each other, even when motivated by individual goals. Angela, let me just say, you've really come into your own on those skates."

"Ang, I think you figured out the secret is the fit. The pad placements inside need to match your footprint exactly. Even that ugly middle toe," Dana said with a wink. "It took me a lot of trial and error when I built Laverne and Shirley here." She smacked her left boot, then right, respectively. When she had no one else, she could always rely on Laverne and Shirley.

"Whatever the reason, Angela," Olsen said, "you looked like you could have played wide receiver with some of those catches."

"She *did* try out for the Patriots," Dana said.

"The New England Patriots?" asked Ashley, her eyes widening.

"Somerset." Angela removed her elbow pads and flexed her graceful arms, her biceps inflating into baseball-sized spheres. "Somerset Patriots, a Minor League Baseball team in New Jersey. Two of my three brothers actually played for them for half a season."

Olsen nodded appreciatively. "Do you think they'd want to join TIARA? If they're half the athlete you are, we'd have quite a wrecking crew."

Angela laughed as she unclasped her shin guards and slipped off her skates. "Not a chance. The 'Technology Information Archives Recovery Agency' wouldn't be a good fit for a couple of middle-aged guys with paunches, bad knees, and mortgages." She took off her helmet, leaned back, and shook out her hair. Dana caught Olsen staring at the golden waves in the morning light and sighed. He cocked his head at her, then returned to the focus of the group.

Olsen placed his Bible into his jacket pocket and stood up, leaning on his cane. "Right. Well. I think this went alright."

Dana's pout contrasted with her sister's inquisitive smile that hung on his words. Angela crossed her arms but lifted her brows above her sterling-blue eyes in anticipation of his next instructions. Dana caught herself staring at her eyes, thinking how similar they were to Nick's . . .

*Not the time*, she told herself.

"I know we are unlikely teammates," Olsen continued, breaking the silence. "This is not where any of us expected to be today. And I know I'm the odd man out." He tightened his grip on his cane. "But as the tactical advisor, I need you to trust me, just like I'm going to have to trust that none of you are going to shoot me in my sleep." He attempted a smile.

"Or stab you," Angela interrupted. She lifted her shirt and pointed to the short scar on her abdomen, a souvenir from a time when Olsen had been their enemy and stabbed her and shot Nick. Of course, that was before Dana had broken his back and before he was found by police dying in a ditch at an airport in the middle of New Mexico. There was no time to second-guess asking him to join their team, especially once Rhodes had escaped; the alternative was for TIARA to fly blind while Olsen rotted in a federal prison with his intimate knowledge of the inner circle of One Hundred Roads.

His cane clacked again as he repositioned himself under Dana's judging gaze. "Yes, and I think this is the time to get my daily apology out of the way: I'm sorry, Angela." He inhaled slowly. "Dana, I'm going to thank you someday for breaking my back and dragging me to where I am now. Extreme circumstances put us all here together. What we need to accomplish is not easy, but the stakes could not be higher to stop Rhodes from breaking this country."

Dana let the words simmer in her mind. Every moment since she had built her skates, from the discovery of her parents' military program to the extraction of the Atomic Juggernaut power frame to the dismantling of Colonel Rhodes's operations in New Mexico, had led them here: a ragged band of girls led by a crippled enemy-turned-ally. *I still don't like you*, she thought to herself. Olsen's distracted gaze piqued her attention. "What are you looking at, old man?"

He glanced beyond his teammates at the sun cresting over the far hills of the New Mexico desert and pointed with a slight tremor in his fingers. "The color palette. It reminds me of the Australian Outback. I could barely remember it until I was shot and left for dead . . . you know, before you all recruited me." He squinted at the sun. "And gave me another chance."

Ashley raised her hand to draw his attention back to the group. "This is atonement for you, isn't it?"

*Here we go, big words from big-brained baby sis*, Dana thought to herself.

"Atonement—that's the perfect word, Phoenix." He looked back at the sunrise and inhaled the dry desert musk. "Now then, Barbie, you grab the ball cannon. Photograph, pull the van around. Let's get back to the ranch for a proper brekky. Your mum is waiting, I'm sure."

# Chapter 2

*Our House – Madness*

A little help?"

Dan Sun stood in the driveway of Simone Jefferson's house and extended his arm to Olsen. The former soldier slowly stepped from the white Mercedes Sprinter van down to the packed soil and nodded to his government handler while the trio of girls jumped out the other doors and jogged ahead into the house. He still felt like an interloper at a family reunion when Dana and Ashley were with their mother. Angela, he thought, had the advantage of already being in the circle of trust as Dana's ex-girlfriend and current best friend.

"They'll warm up," Dan said, sensing Olsen's thoughts. "They're still getting used to me, and *I'm* one of the good guys." He raised his thin black eyebrows apologetically. "Rather, I mean, I was always on the same team as them."

"I know what you mean, Dan," Olsen muttered. He took the steps up to the patio and let out a short grunt with each effort. "Do you still have family back home?"

"In the Philippines? My uncles all stayed after my mom came to San Fran. We chat, although not as often as I'd like to. Part of the burden of working for Homeland Security." Dan dropped to one knee and adjusted his ankle holster. "I can't exactly pop in on the weekend unannounced for a pitcher of lemonade."

Olsen held the door open for Dan, a small gesture but one that helped him feel useful as a man once known for his physical prowess. "I had a layover in Quezon City once. I wish I could have stayed longer. Food was amazing, but I had an SIS surveillance team on my tail." He studied the midmorning sun before closing the door. "Hell of a time."

Once inside, Ashley crewed a griddle sizzling with pancakes and eggs. Dana tossed a set of plastic plates onto the counter as Olsen set himself on a stool at the end of the cheap faux marble. Massive painted landscapes of New Mexico and Nevada, all painted by Simone, decorated the dark wood interior of the living area, hanging between three tall bookshelves: one for technical manuals, one for classical fiction, and one a potpourri of art, comic books, and overflow from the other shelves. Olsen reached for a laptop decorated in winged unicorn stickers from across the counter.

"Is this our secure computer?" He paused before opening it.

"Nope," Dana noted. "That's our public access one. Mom took the good computer with the TOR and IP masks out to the barn."

"That's mine!" Ashley yelled over the sizzle of the pan.

"Ah, I should have known by the unicorns. How old are you, again?"

"Seventeen. And they're *horned* Pegasi or *winged* unicorns, neither of which are a real thing, at least as far as documented fictional cryptids are concerned." She waved her spatula to conduct her speech. "Amalgamated mythology."

"Ah." He poked one of the stickers. "Learning something new every day here."

Angela emerged from the hallway in a long bathrobe.

"I split my seams again. I did love those zebra prints." She flexed her leg in midair toward the assembled group, showing off a pair of tiny plaid-print shorts and a cropped tank top emblazoned with a logo of an angel on roller skates, an old souvenir from her derby team in Asbury Park. Olsen found Angela challenging to pin down: so much power and strength, free with her appearance—and fashion choices—and yet disdainful of attention when it was directed at her attractiveness. Dan cleared his throat as he dodged around her with a coffee pot.

"You'll need proper camouflage as we head after Rhodes. I'd suggest loose-fit canvas pants like Dana wears." Dan placed a set of coffee mugs on the counter and began to fill them. "Or, you know, football pants might be good. A little padding."

"Nope, no sports spandex or yoga pants. They don't have pockets," Dana muttered as she slid a coffee mug from under Dan toward Olsen. "Right, koala man?"

"I'm detecting less of your usual sarcasm." Olsen smirked.

"Well, things got more serious." Dana reflected his smirk.

Olsen nodded. Maybe now they could finally have some conversations that needed to take place between them—about her and Nick, about her and her mother. He knew the time and place would come soon when they could clear the air and deal with all the distractions properly, for the sake of the team.

"Indeed, things have gotten more serious," he echoed.

Dana folded a pancake around a scoop of scrambled eggs and headed out the back door. A gray horse next to the barn looked at her in recognition. "Morning, Dick." The horse resumed eating from a hay bin. "Good horsey," she whispered.

She threw herself onto a mesh hammock next to the firepit and chewed slowly on her version of a breakfast sandwich. *Things got more serious*, she affirmed to herself. The hammock swayed slowly as she stared at the open entrance to the barn and her mother's silhouette, barely visible inside as she moved from workbench to workbench. They had barely spoken over the past few weeks, except in an official capacity about mission-critical items. Angela had actually talked to Simone the most, which Dana found ironic, as the two had been completely ignorant of each other's existence until a few months ago despite their significant impacts on Dana's life.

A sudden whoosh behind Dana startled her.

"Hey," Angela said as she stood holding the handle of the open glass sliding door. "Do you want to go into town today?"

"Yeah, I can do that. Maybe pick up some new headphones or something." *Anything to get out of the house.*

Angela sat cross-legged on the concrete next to the hammock, lifting her chin toward the barn. "Do you think your mom will come with us?"

"No. She's in the zone right now, working on her own timetable." Dana's mother stepped out of the shadow of the barn into the light, fully visible with her dark braids twirled over her head into a faux beehive. Flecks of gray in her hair glinted in the sun as she made a terse salute to acknowledge her daughter with one of her tattooed arms. Dana saluted back. "Plus, she's got that whole 'I'm on the run, I'm a criminal' or whatever vibe hanging over her."

"Hey." Angela leaned over and poked Dana in her sternum. "She's your *mom*. She's sick. Don't be so cynical. You don't know how much time you have—or, you know, how much time she has." Angela paused until Dana returned her burning gaze. "You put up walls, you know. I would know."

"I know. Walls keep things out."

"They keep things in, too."

Dana allowed herself a short smile at Angela's moment of vulnerability. She let her hand slide off the hammock and land on Angela's knee. *Things unspoken, everywhere and by everyone around me.* "I know."

The sound of the patio door sliding open again interrupted the two women. Olsen stepped outside, followed by Dan poking his head through the opening.

"Hey," Dan said with a hesitant smile. Olsen pointed his cane at the barn.

"I'm going to talk to your mum, Dana. I have an idea on a new method to find Rhodes."

*Rhodes.* The mention of his name still made the hair on Dana's neck stand up. It pressed on her chest and stung in her ears. Everything tragic in her life, whether directly or indirectly, could be traced back to him. Some of those traumatic moments were also due to Olsen when he had been under Rhodes's command, and Dana took advantage of every opportunity to remind him. Working with Olsen now, she would have to make sure their boundaries were clear.

"Sounds good, Combat Wombat. Go talk to my mom about the guy who used to sign your paychecks before ordering your execution. When you have a plan, come at me. I'm ready to go." She unwound herself from the hammock. "We're going into town for a bit. If you don't have anything new when we get back, we're going boots on the ground the old-fashioned way to find him." She garishly stared at his cane. "*You* can wait in the car."

Dan stepped aside as Dana stomped past him into the house, followed by Angela, who looked back at Olsen and shrugged her shoulders.

"You don't have to be so mean to him," Angela whispered when they got inside.

"I know. But also, in a way, I do."

# Chapter 3

*Rockit – Herbie Hancock*

Olsen and Dan settled onto the workbench stools next to the open barn door silently, watching Simone as she seemed to evaluate the neatly organized tools hanging on the pegboard. She coughed, trying to cover her mouth with her handkerchief. Dan had his head down, distracted by emails and texts on his phone, but Olsen caught Simone staring at the blood-tinged phlegm on the back of her hand. It stood out against her weathered brown skin, much darker and rougher than her daughter's peanut hue.

"You alright, Mrs. Jefferson?"

Simone shot Olsen a sharp look as she wiped her hand with a paper towel. She adjusted the knot in the sweat-soaked neckerchief that hung loosely over her collarbone.

"Don't mind me. I'm just having a bit of a rough morning." She picked up a long metal pipe hanging on the wall and slipped it over the handle of a socket wrench. "Couldn't find it at first. I needed a breaker bar to twist off the shoulder bolt inside the frame. It's just a bugger from being in storage for too long."

"You know," Dan said once he finally put away his cell phone, "you should work on coding if you're not up to anything physical today. It seems to me that you could leave the brawny stuff to those of us who can handle it." The daggers shooting from her eyes elicited clarification. "Objectively, I mean, I'm the only one here without a physical issue. I can help."

Simone huffed and tapped the revolver strapped to her hip. She traced the deep line of the decorative vine pattern engraved in the handle with her finger.

"The day that I can't do any of this is the day I give up." She walked over to a large orange engine hoist in the middle of the barn. Hooks supported a tapered round barrel of segmented carbon fiber panels, shaped like an oversized vest, connected to two thinner leglike apparatuses missing their feet. The arms lay on the ground next to the hoist, one limb split in half at the elbow joint. She extended the socket wrench inside the armhole of the chest piece and put her boot on the engine hoist's frame for leverage, then gripped the breaker bar with two hands. "One more tug," she said with a grunt as the bar shook and loosened an unseen bolt. "Good girl," she told herself, panting. Olsen tapped his cane on the leg of his chair.

"Is that . . . thing . . . going to work?"

"The Protective Emergency Guardian suit? Yes. PEG here was built as a fully functional working prototype. I just didn't have time to add my long-life battery designs and other bells and whistles."

"When did you make this?"

"Well, when Dana's father took my plans for the Atomic Juggernaut to your former boss, I started working on the second generation. PEG was meant to be a more advanced, lightweight version—smaller, slimmer, and with fewer power-plant requirements. It's the type of thing a couple of soldiers could toss into a Blackhawk and drop off in a minefield or forest fire to get someone in and out." Simone reached her arm inside the housing and retrieved a broken bolt. She held it up and squinted through her examination. "I need about a dozen of these," she said, flicking the bolt in Dan's direction. "Tell your boss—*our* boss—we need titanium ones."

"I'll ask Director Jameson tonight to have some mailed to our PO box."

A pile of what appeared to be auto parts in the near corner of the barn drew Olsen's eyes. "And those?"

"Catalytic converters. I have a stockpile for the platinum, palladium, rhodium, and the other bits I need for the skates. It's how I was able to finish Angela's skates so quickly." She raised a defensive eyebrow. "And yes, I did obtain some of these illegally. But that was before Dana arrived." She swung the wrench mockingly like a baseball bat. "I'm going to need more palladium for PEG. You can't just pick that up at the Piggly Wiggly."

"I'll tell the director to add 'theft and vandalism' to your rap sheet when she asks how the team is doing," Dan added dryly. "But the main reason we came out is on the bench. Can we get on the secure laptop for a moment? I need to see if any intel dropped overnight."

Simone pointed to the computer, and Dan leaned over to retrieve it. He logged in through her Onion Router software onto the dark web browser. Olsen craned his neck to glimpse the screen.

"Is that an off-the-shelf browser download?"

"Of course not," Simone said, a hint of irritation in her voice. "Nothing I do with software isn't first modded by myself or Ashley. We remove all of the ghosts."

"Ghosts," Dan echoed. "Interesting way to put it, coming from someone who has at least two dead aliases." He flicked through a series of screens until his eyes lit up. He jabbed a triumphant finger in the air. "Something *did* drop overnight!" He presented the screen to Olsen first. "Check this out! Rhodes got sloppy, finally."

Olsen scanned the screen. "What am I looking at here?" He was familiar with the type of content found on the dark web from his own misadventures into obtaining specialized weapons during his tenure at One Hundred Roads.

Dan continued. "Per some militia boards, Rhodes is hitting up groups as an in-person guest speaker. He's not even disguising himself."

"How do we know it's really him?" Simone asked. Dan clicked into a link and uncovered a photo of Rhodes and three men shaking hands in front of an inverted United States flag.

"I don't think he meant to pose for that one. Someone broke protocol and put this on their newsletter. The facial recognition trackers I have nabbed this against his former GI ID."

"You have facial recognition software? Why has it taken this long to get a hit, then?" Olsen asked, annoyed at his continued helplessness in running this mission.

"It's not software," Dan replied. "My *trackers* are people. I pay them with crypto—hired them on another board. I told them who I wanted, sent them his ID photo, and then they run the scans and do the legwork." He smirked. "And my cousin back in Manila, he's a bit of a conspiracy nut, so he jumped at the chance to work on this. Off the books, of course."

"Hmph." Olsen hopped off the stool and landed with a thud. He puffed out his chest, still thick from isometric exercises and body-resistance weight training. His legs were getting better, but it was a race against muscular atrophy as the nerve endings rebuilt themselves. His left leg was lagging behind his right leg's progress, and he feared it was as good as it might ever get. He extended an arm to Simone to offer help.

"Nope. I told you before, I'm good." Simone groaned as she adjusted the pulley holding up the suit. Olsen surmised that out of everyone, she felt the most uncomfortable with the current arrangement—not just because her secluded ranch was being used as an operation base, but because of the years she had spent on the run trying to hide from the government and other factions. Now, she practically ran a bed-and-breakfast for an ex-government contractor and a fully licensed federal agent.

Simone rotated the body of PEG and leaned it forward, its chest toward the ground. "You and me, Olsen, we may not be the most perfect physical specimens at the moment, but we both got our brains, right? Dan, you put Olsen to work on that militia thing. Maybe we can get into a meeting covertly?"

Olsen raised his hand to object. "Not you, ma'am. Bluntly, your skin is too . . . *dark* for some of the more bigoted groups. And Dan, same for you, and for Dana and Ashley too. That leaves me and Barbie as the only fair-skinned folks who could slip in undetected, until I accidentally open my mouth and unleash a bit of Aussie speak."

Dan ran his fingers through his jet-black hair. "I could dye this blond and wear sunglasses." He chuckled, and Olsen scowled. "Just throwing it out there."

"I don't think Angela is ready for this type of thing . . . let's table this for now. Dan, do we know what city Rhodes is in, or where he was last seen at a meeting?"

"Actually," Dan said, typing quickly, "it looks like he's circling a few states. Once his picture was tagged, my contacts could cross-check the boards. Boise was this week. Before then, it was Helena, some dirt pocket outside of Cheyenne, and a couple spots in the Dakotas. He started there and keeps going back."

"Can you get me those sightings, all of them, and we'll take them to the map in the main house?" He glanced over to Simone. "I think Rhodes is up to something."

"Obviously," Dan said, shrugging as he typed the locations into a note on his phone.

"What I *mean* is that I think he's showed one of the cards in his hand."

"If I may," Simone said, interrupting the conversation, "we should make sure to cover all the bases. I have a tiny armory here, including the Barrett fifty caliber. But we need some other things, too. Jameson said it's a challenge to get us the comms and other gadgets without a potential mole for Rhodes in her department being tipped off." She glanced at her workbench. "And I keep some things hidden on a need-to-know basis. I've got my Desert Eagle and a pair of flash grenades here in the barn—which the girls don't know about, by the way. There's a false panel on the exterior of the house by the porch with a small cache—"

"Simone," Olsen interrupted, "does that Jeep behind the barn still run?"

She bit her lip. "Yeah, although I haven't used it in a couple months. Everything here is functional: the armored Sprinter van, the compact car, the Jeep. What are you thinking?"

"Just planning. If we're going to have to wait for information, we might as well bide our time with some other activities, keep the girls' spirits up." *Maybe I'm being too hard on them, too soon.* "Let's dust off the Jeep and fill the tank." He rubbed his thumb over the palm of his hand. "I can use the girls on something."

"Alright, but that's on you, old man," Simone snickered. "I got my hands full with PEG." She leaned over a milk crate and slowly pulled out a half sphere the size of a serving bowl and tapped it with her fingers. A pair of lights flickered at her touch, illuminating PEG's face. "You know what? I have something the girls could do for me, too. Get the Jeep ready and tell Dana she has to run to Alamogordo."

# Chapter 4

*This Photograph Is Proof – Taking Back Sunday*

Well, I'm just saying it would have been more fun to skate our way here. Sure, it would have taken a few hours, but I could use the practice."

Angela leaned her head into the direct path of the Jeep's air vent, closing her eyes. The sun burned through the windshield but was diffused by the air conditioner running on full blast, which rippled the ragged and hole-pocked soft-top. She tolerated Dana's driving as best as she could—not the best, but also not the worst. As they approached the Alamogordo Navajo reservation, she took in the lonely flat and serene desertscape, occasionally glimpsing the tiny faded orange and brown peaks of the distant mountains. The change of scenery was a nice perk in agreeing to join TIARA, she mused.

But the changes she observed weren't only in the landscape; they were in Dana, too. She wasn't the carefree, often sarcastic spirit she had met back in New Jersey. Now, she was a more serious woman involved in some very complicated circumstances. This Dana always seemed preoccupied with some immediate task or "the mission." It seemed that almost every conversation they had—even about which burrito joint they were going to for dinner—always mutated into a discussion of Rhodes, how to find him, how to catch him.

"You know," Angela said, breaking their current silence by bringing up the topic first this time, "maybe revenge isn't enough of a motivation to catch Rhodes."

Dana adjusted the toothpick dangling from her lip. "Hey, does this make me look tougher? I got the leather jacket and the aviator sunglasses thing going, but there's something extra about chewing on a toothpick." She flashed a smile, toothpick still adhering to her lower lip. "Cool, right?"

"You totally avoided the question."

"It wasn't a question. It was a statement."

"Okay, fine. Do you think you're too focused on revenge right now?" Angela knew all about revenge, the gnawing feeling of being wronged and finding an outlet for that quiet, smoldering anger. The Jeep slowed as they approached a trailer that acted as the reservation's planning office.

"We're here," Dana announced. "And maybe revenge is keeping me focused on anything at all. Or at least focused on things other than my mom's cancer, Ashley's school applications, my own applications—"

"You applied? Where? And for what?"

Dana parked in the first space. The two travelers hopped out and began to approach the office's porch, but Dana halted.

"I'm thinking about psychology. I saw online degrees and some community colleges here in New Mexico. Maybe I'll do counseling. I dunno. I feel like . . ." Dana paused and spread her arms wide. "Like maybe I'm going through all these things for a reason. I was really digging my support group sessions. I could run one of those, you know. Maybe I'm going through all of this to find myself."

Angela nodded appreciatively. "That makes two of us." As she raised her hand to knock on the office door, it swung open. A middle-aged man with reddish-brown skin and jet-black hair laced with silver smiled at the visitors.

"Dana! I'm so happy to see you, lady friend!" He hugged her, and she hugged him back ferociously.

Angela smiled and extended her hand. *No hugs.* "Angela Costanza."

"Frank Irons at your service," he said with a lilting voice, reciprocating Angela's handshake.

Their host waved them inside and pointed to two plush chairs across from an old metal office desk. He sat in his chair, a professional gamer's luxury rig, and folded his hands on the blotter next to his laptop and a glass dome enclosing a shining ingot of silvery metal.

"So, what's the occasion? Oh, wait, how rude of me!" He reached behind him to the mini-fridge on the counter and proffered each of them a water bottle. "Angela, you know Dana is a *very* special celebrity here."

"Oh, is she?" Angela said, crossing her arms in a mocking gesture.

"Yes, she is. If it wasn't for her, this place might have been burned to the ground by One Hundred Roads. They're a terror group. Used to be government contractors."

"So I've heard." Angela looked over at Dana, who winked at her.

"What brings you here today, Dana? You didn't mention when you called last night."

"I have a request that I didn't want to make over electronic communication."

"Oh?" Frank leaned back and crossed one leg over the other, his pant legs creeping up to reveal a pair of spotless, ostentatious cowboy boots embroidered with yellow and red thread connecting the brown and white dyed leather pieces. Small strips of turquoise-colored embroidery enhanced the intricate floral patterns. Angela was impressed with the style and subtle sign of wealth they implied.

"Frank, I need to get some of . . . this." Dana tapped the glass dome display. "Palladium."

"How much?"

"Eighteen ounces."

Angela didn't know what such a thing would cost, but she assumed it was not just something you could pay for with a quick trip to the ATM. She sat back to watch the bartering in action. Frank rubbed his chin and clicked his tongue. *He's going to bluff,* she thought to herself.

"That's a decent amount. I'm guessing there's no chance you have the cash on you for the figure I'm going to throw at you."

"How do *you* know?" Dana's eyes were flat, narrow, and unblinking, offset by a goofy smile and her dimples. "I'm a very good bartender."

"Not from what I've heard! You ghosted your last job, which, need I remind you, I helped you get."

Angela watched Dana slide her hand into her jacket's inside pocket, retrieving a thick envelope that Dan Sun had brought the previous day. Dana peeked inside, then placed it flat on the desk blotter. She tapped it once with her index finger.

"We took the sixty-day high price for spot futures for palladium on the New York Futures Exchange and added five percent to ensure a good offer."

"You are reading from a script." Frank wagged his finger at her and laughed. "You have no idea what that means."

"Come on, Frank, no more dog and pony show. You're going to help me out, right?"

He picked up the envelope and counted the bills, every single one, in what felt like an excessively long examination. He ran his fingers over the mustard-colored bank straps around each bundle of hundreds. Then he sniffed them, which Angela found rather peculiar, before placing the envelope into a drawer and folding his hands. "Go ahead."

"Go ahead and do what?" Angela blurted.

"Take that one."

Dana pointed to the glass dome. "This one?"

Frank erupted into laughter. "Yes! That one! Here!" He slid off the dome and handed her the heavy chunk. "That's about half a pound. And here." He slid open another drawer and brought out two more ingots. "This should be a pound and a half, easily." He handed her a reusable shopping bag from the local mini-mart chain. "If you don't use it all, just bring me back the remaining ore, and I'll give you your deposit back."

"Deposit?" Angela asked.

"I can't charge you for this. Dana, you *saved* this reservation," Frank said. "I owe you."

*I do, too*, Angela thought. She was astounded that her sometimes careless, sometimes selfish ex-girlfriend really had done some of the things she talked about. It made Angela want to make a bigger impact herself.

"Frank," Dana said as she grabbed the shopping bag, "you are a prince."

"If I was *the* Prince, I'd be an awesome guitar player. And I would dress a lot cooler." He clicked his boot heels.

"Yeah, you would," she said with a laugh. Dana handed the bag to Angela. "Pleasure, as always."

"Pleasure, indeed. Nice to have met you, Angela."

"Same here, sir." She shook his hand again.

"Oh, Dana," Frank interjected as they walked through the trailer door, "say hello to Nick for me!"

"Have a good one," Dana said with a wave.

The two friends returned to the Jeep and started their long journey back toward Taos. Angela respected the silence, hyperaware that Dana had made no acknowledgement of Frank's mention of Nick. As Dana changed the radio station, the signals droning in and out of range, her patience appeared to ebb. She switched channels more frequently as they drove, fickle to which songs came on. Angela withstood her chaotic DJ session for an hour until she couldn't take it anymore.

"Hey, just pick a station. I'll change it when we lose the signal." She put her hand on Dana's as it clutched the radio dial.

"Angela, I just . . ." Her voice trailed off, and she released her hand from the dial. "I was just really hoping to find some Prince right now."

"I get it. Prince would really hit the spot."

They exchanged quick glances, then both refocused back on the road. The unspoken was just as valuable between them as the spoken. Dana shrugged.

"I miss skating."

"You can still go back to the roller derby team here. I'm sure they miss you."

Dana lowered the AC by one click. "No, I mean I just miss *skating*. Not derby competition, not racing around on Laverne and Shirley preparing for a fight. Heck, I've spent more time on skates fighting than I think I have on my bare feet." She huffed. "Like, back in the day, at boarding school. Getting my skates, a bus ticket, and going to the skating rink on a Friday night by myself. The DJ would play some house and freestyle music, maybe some disco. And I just . . . skated. No cares in the world . . . I miss that version of me."

Angela tucked a piece of hair behind her ear. "I never really met that version of you, but I think I'd like that person, too."

"Different paths."

"Different lives."

"Yep."

The crackling of static over the radio prompted Angela to change the station. "We still going out tonight with Olsen and your sister?"

"Yep. The chaperone and the chaperoned." Angela saw the edges of Dana's smile tilt downward. "This is my life now."

# Chapter 5

*She Likes to Party – Kris Rodgers*

Dana lifted herself off the barstool and brushed a piece of hay off the seat of her jeans.

"How much of this crap is still in the Jeep?" She looked past Angela at Olsen seated at the end of the bar, reading his ever-present Bible, even here. He took a small sip from his glass before answering.

"All I did was make sure it could run. I didn't know you wanted it washed, waxed, and detailed. I figured the wind would blow the dust and cobwebs out." He smiled back at her sour expression.

Dana appreciated his attempts at camaraderie, but their relationship would not be mended over a pint and a cheeseburger at Bernie's. True, they all needed a night off after the days and evenings filled with training, scouring the internet for clues, and listening to Dan's thin reports on Rhodes's whereabouts. But Dana would not give Olsen any fealty beyond their mission to find Rhodes.

Angela, who Dana saw taking on the role of physical and verbal mediator between the two, walked over and leaned in close to Dana's ear. "Whitney's playing, let's dance!"

She grabbed Dana by the wrist and pulled her to the sparsely populated faux-wood dance floor. The neon beer signs reflected off the dented tiles. Dana absently imagined the local high school holding their reunions here. She felt the eyes of the other patrons, huddled around their tables or at the bar, observing them, likely wondering if they were from out of town. The girls danced and shouted song lyrics off-key, eliciting a few smiles from some young men, with Angela drawing their primary focus.

"They're staring, Ang!" Dana shouted. Angela placed her hand on Dana's hip and swayed with her in time with the pulsing bass.

"Let them," Angela replied with a giggle. "We deserve a night out, right?"

Dana swung her head, her black curls bouncing with the momentum. Each time she turned toward Angela, Dana felt the eyes of her ex-girlfriend peering into hers, trying to discover what was going on inside Dana's mind. *Can she tell I'm trying not to think about Nick?* She gently removed Angela's hand.

"Let's take a break for a sec!" Dana yelled. "I feel like I have old lady knees today."

It was a valid excuse to take a pause from dancing; the mileage on Dana's body was piling up from her recent adventures. Repelling down the side of the Hoover Dam in roller skates had easily added ten years to her knees, she reasoned, although without any medical examination. Or maybe she was just too tired, too paranoid, to enjoy the moment and was looking for any excuse not to enjoy herself.

Olsen pointed to two glasses of water once they were back at their seats. "I don't want to act like your parent, but just make me feel a little better and rehydrate." Dana nodded and gulped down half of the beverage in one swallow.

"Fine. Thanks, *Dad*. Where's Ashley?"

"Hedy Lamarr is over there charming those gentlemen and simultaneously making a fool of them," said Olsen, pointing to the pool tables.

Ashley was hustling a pair of middle-aged bikers with her amazing ability to determine every angle and hit each pocket with precision. It had been Dana's idea to bring her along, despite Ashley being underage. Ashley did have a fake ID, thanks to the skills and resources of their mother, but fortunately she preferred to drink at home, and really only when her mother pressed a bottle into her hand.

"She's more like Minnesota Fats out there," Olsen remarked. "She's amazing."

"In more ways than one, that's for sure."

Dana was grateful not to have to babysit her sister on a night when she already felt forced to enjoy recreation. She was about to put in an order for a plate of buffalo wings when movement caught her attention from the corner of her eye.

"What's up, girls?" A tall blond man wearing a tight gray tee, work pants cuffed over cowboy boots, and a yellow trucker hat leaned in next to Dana. Another man, dressed almost identically except for a backward red hat, stood next to Angela.

"Hey, are you also here for the herpes recovery group meeting?" Dana deadpanned.

Yellow Hat ignored the joke and crossed his arms on the bar, brushing against Dana's arm and making her physically recoil.

"You girls looked good out there. You want to look good somewhere else?" He smiled and flashed an unnaturally white set of veneers. "My name's Dino. And that guy is Wings." The man next to Angela flexed his bicep mockingly.

"Guys," Angela interrupted, "I'll get right to the point: We're not interested."

Dana felt a small wave of goosebumps on the back of her neck. She knew

Angela better than anyone, and not only did Angela have no interest in men, but this type of obnoxious behavior really set her off. The story that Angela had told her in confidence so many years ago . . . it made Dana shudder and instantly put her on high alert. Dana quickly considered how to deescalate the scenario before things got out of hand.

"Come on, girl," Wings cooed. "How about the four best-looking people in here head out to the back patio?"

Dino placed his hand on Dana's forearm. "You're not usually my type," he whispered, way too close to her ear, "but you're pretty hot for a Black chick. I know you're down with this."

Her plans to deescalate forgotten, Dana slapped his hand away and knocked her stool onto the floor as she stood up. She saw Olsen stretch his arm below the bar and grip the handle of his cane. Dana shook her head once in his direction.

"We don't all have to go out back," Wings announced. "Just me, Dino, and you, big girl." He placed his hand on Angela's lower back.

*Oh shit.* Before Dana could do anything to stop her, Angela whipped her arm up and backhanded Wings in the face with her bare knuckles.

"Don't touch me, trash!" Angela spun off her stool and stood at her full height, an inch above the brim of his red hat.

"I like that—you got a little fight in you. You're a wild horse I'd love to break in." He reached his arm around Angela's hip.

Dana's danger radar exploded. *Oh no, no, no—*

Angela reached behind Wing's head and abruptly slammed his face into the bar.

*Shit, shit, shit!*

"Whoa! Ladies!" Olsen bolted upright.

"Bitch, you're done!" snarled Dino as he shoved Dana out of the way, trying to get to Angela. Dana seized the opportunity to firmly plant her knee in his crotch.

"Ashley, get the Jeep!" Olsen yelled, flinging the keys toward her as she ran past him.

Wings straightened up, blood smearing the front of his face. "You broke my tooth!" He spat a bloody wad at Angela, his body suddenly jerking with the impact from Olsen's cane at the back of his knees.

"Girls, let's go."

Ashley appeared in the doorway, whistling with two fingers. "Jeep's running outside!" she shouted in a singsong. "Mom's going to be so pissed when she hears about this."

"You're damn right!" Angela shouted, backhanding a moderately drunk combatant in a formal boxing stance. She dropped to her knees and flipped him onto his back with a short smile.

Dana just watched the scene around her unfold, reeling as her chest tightened, her heart pounded, and gold flecks filled the corners of her eyes.

*Oh God, not now, please not now . . .*

The neon lights bled across the faces of the angry patrons as Dana's head swam, the panic attack blooming. A meaty hand suddenly grabbed her shoulder and pushed her toward the exit.

*Olsen.*

"We're leaving now," he shouted above the row. "Barbie, come on!" Angela let go of the torn shirt of the man she had pinned against the floor. Olsen scowled. "Jeep, *now*."

The bartender rose from behind the cash register, hands shaking as he pointed at the group. "I . . . I don't need to tell you that you're not welcome back," he stammered. Olsen nodded.

Even with a broken back and fumbling legs, Olsen's steadiness and confidence in moments like this filled Dana with . . . was it admiration? Something like that. Whatever it was, she was glad he was here in this moment, although she still did not accept his perpetual presence as leader.

"Let's go," Dana commanded, regaining a modicum of her leadership role back. She looped her arm around Angela's as they headed out into the dirt-covered parking lot.

"What the heck was that about?" Ashley pleaded from behind the wheel. Olsen pulled himself into the passenger seat as Angela and Dana scrambled into the back. Olsen adjusted the side mirror as the Jeep pulled onto the highway in a cloud of dust.

"Angela," Olsen chided, "you can't fly off the handle like that."

Dana shot him an angry stare. "Not the time for a lesson. Not tonight." She wanted to explain things to him, but these were not conversations for her to have on behalf of Angela. It was not her place to explain the night that made Angela into the confident woman she knew and loved, even though it had shattered her and left her in the darkest of places. Dana believed that ex-lovers should always respect the confidences shared in intimate moments.

"It's okay, Dana. I apologize, Olsen," said Angela. She turned to watch the bar disappear behind them, her blond locks now a mess and dotted with tiny flecks of red. Dana placed the back of her hand gently against Angela's cheek.

"Hey. Angela-la-la."

"Hey. Dana-na-na-na."

"I'm not mad." The corners of Angela's mouth turned up in a recalcitrant smile. Dana smiled back. "People suck. We'll always have to deal with that."

"Yep, I know. People suck."

# Chapter 6

*Good Enough – Sarah McLachlan*

The morning sun peeked through the gaps between the weathered wallboards of Simone's aged barn. The quiet slurping noises as Dick chomped his hay were interrupted by Dana's grunting. The horse paused to observe her as she dragged two small bales, one at a time, just inside the open barn doors. She picked up a six-foot length of pipe and shoved one end into one bale and the opposite end into the other, her makeshift deadlift bar complete. She stopped and allowed herself to watch the horizon release the sun into the new day.

"Well, Dick, time for work. Again." She squatted and grasped the bar firmly with an overhand grip. For the first five repetitions, she focused on the perfection of each movement, the activation of each muscle in her legs, back, and shoulders, as the weight of the bales yielded to her strength. In the mornings—and only then—she allowed herself to wear shorts and a tank top. She wasn't ashamed of her body, but Dana had spent so many years being discreet about her bruises and road rashes to avoid suspicion; life on the ranch blessed her with a freedom she hadn't anticipated. A set of rhythmic footfalls broke her concentration at the end of her third set.

"Photograph!" Dan called out, giving a terse wave. He jogged up to her workout area, looking out of place in his white polo shirt and bland straight-legged jeans, sidearm on full display in its nylon holster. She tried to ignore him as she readied herself for another set.

He tried again. "*Dana*. How are you doing?" His tone was reserved, less gleeful than usual when he did his regular rounds with the group. Dana didn't mind the interruption, but she never looked forward to seeing him. Every time, it was a stark reminder that his partner, Joshua, had died trying to protect her.

"Fine. Just working out," she said in a monotone voice. "I'll be done in a few."

"I, uh, need to talk to you. You might want to stop and check this out." He extended his cell phone toward her. "I got an email."

"This can't wait until breakfast?" She removed the pipe from the bales, then lifted the pole over her head in a shoulder press movement, moving slowly through each rep to feel the resistance. Five seconds up, she counted, then five seconds down.

"No, this is *important*." Dan waved the phone in front of her face again. "The email is from Nick."

She gripped the bar even tighter and exhaled slowly, extending her arms again, trying to touch the sky with the bar. *Just breathe, Dana.* Once her elbows locked, she reversed the motion, this time bringing the bar to rest on the back of her neck. She opened her hands and let the steel pipe thud onto the barn floor behind her.

"Hey, Dick?" she yelled. Dan turned, startled, as the horse lifted his head and began his slow plod over to Dana. "What do you think would be the appropriate reaction to this?"

The horse snorted and huffed before lowering his graying face to her extended hand. An old horse, a good horse, and a very smart horse, Dick amazed her. Every time her mother talked to him, Dick seemed to listen to her tone and react to her, intuitively. He did it with Ashley, too, and Dana only recently realized the horse knew who was and wasn't kin.

She continued addressing Dick. "What do you think Nick wants? Maybe he wants me to apologize? Or do I go catatonic again with more of my PTSD bullshit?" *Or maybe he wants me to admit I did what I did to keep him out of danger?* She raised an eyebrow toward Dan. "I mean this politely: stay out of this."

Dan crossed his arms and tucked the phone into his armpit. "Dana . . ." He exhaled slowly, very slowly. "Mr. Andrews passed away. Nick emailed me to let me know his dad had a heart attack."

"*What?*" A lump rose in her throat; she felt like she was choking. Her brain took in the words, she understood them, but there was a dullness as she tried to attach any emotion to them.

Dan tapped one of the hay bales with his boot. "Funeral is on Friday in New Jersey in Hammonton. I thought you should know. And I'm sorry. Nick's my friend, too, you know. I can't take time to go." Dan gave her a sympathetic look and headed back to the house.

Dana sat on a hay bale and pulled her knees into her chest. She let out a long, low sigh as the dullness faded, replaced by a menu of emotions for her to choose from. Mitch was the closest she had ever come in her adult life to having a father figure. An imperfect man, but a caring dad who had raised Nick to be a good guy. *A great guy.* All her admiration of who Nick was could be directly attributed to the way Mr. Andrews had nurtured him. He had been stoic in the face of losing his wife, Nick's mother, but he confronted his demons and conquered them when he had every reason to give in to them.

*He was my friend,* she thought. But her loss was nothing compared to Nick's: The person who had stolen a piece of her heart, fought by her side, and supported her had lost his father. And she knew how that felt.

"Shit." She stood and rubbed her eyes as they began to well. "Goddamn it, Nick." She walked to the barn door and leaned on the frame, watching Dan pace in a small circle next to the house, glued to his phone. He caught her gaze and slowly receded around the house.

Dick whinnied and brought his face to Dana's shoulder. He nudged her.

"Well, Dick . . . I guess I'm going back to New Jersey."

# Chapter 7

*Mama Said – The Shirelles*

You're *not* going back to New Jersey."

Simone clutched the edge of the kitchen island and coughed hard. "Dana, it's too big a risk, you know that. We're safe here while we work on a plan."

Dana stomped out of the kitchen and grabbed her backpack from its storage cubby by the front door. Everything—at least outside of Dana's bedroom—had its place in her mother's rancher. Being organized had kept Simone alive and nimble as she lived on the run, and even a semipermanent house could not make her relinquish obedience to her methodical system that had allowed her to leave anywhere in under five minutes. Dana rummaged through the interior of her bag and dumped a pile of burrito wrappers, fast food sauce packets, and used napkins into a pile on the faux-wood vinyl flooring. From her seat on the couch, Ashley noisily slurped a spoonful of cereal from her bowl.

"Mom, I think she should go."

"Thank you, Ash, but this isn't up for debate." Simone's eyes fixated on the tiny garbage pile next to Dana. "We need Dana here so if we get a lead, we can rally into action and put Rhodes six feet under." She reached into the fridge for her shaker bottle, a concoction of vegan protein powder and pulped greens. "This tastes like ass," she noted after a swig.

Olsen emerged from the hallway sans cane, dragging his left foot slightly and loudly clearing his throat.

"I think Dana should do what she needs to do. I need her to have a clear head. I can't have her skating into danger with regrets or clouded thoughts." He gestured for the shaker bottle. Simone let him smell the drink, and he winced. Dana raised her hand.

"I think *we* should stop talking about *Dana* in the third person and treat *her* like an adult!" She grabbed a pair of pink-framed sunglasses and perched them atop her head.

"Alright, let's think about this for a minute." Olsen lowered himself into the couch next to Ashley. "Current plan: Ashley is working on a project for school as well as the software updates we need to install into PEG."

"Yeppers," Ashley confirmed. "It's my language-learning algorithm used to decode voices and grammar to identify original authors against ghostwriters and apocryphal contributions to revised manuscripts." Olsen blinked vacantly. Ashley pointed her spoon at him. "AI language learning that we can *also* use to synthesize the voice commands in PEG's controls for adaptive learning. It's also going to be my doctoral project, hopefully. I'm kind of a big deal in the online college world, even if everyone thinks I'm a thirty-five-year-old woman with ten cats."

"Right," Olsen mumbled. "What I'm saying is, Ashley needs time to work on that while I obtain the backup for Rhodes's network."

"Say what now?" Dana jammed her phone charger into the front pocket of her pack.

"Rhodes keeps his backup servers at the safe houses." He paused as Dan stepped back inside and put his phone in his pocket. "I assure you, every communication gets logged and backed up via satellite relay to his servers at the safe houses in a handful of remote locations."

Dana nodded as she slung her bag over her shoulder. She would gladly defer to Olsen's strategic and tactical prowess if it would get her back to Nick. Olsen continued on as Angela entered the room.

"One of the safe houses is in Wyoming across the northern Colorado border. We used it as a relay point on rare occasions when we needed a place in or out of Denver International. I can go up there while Dana is in New Jersey. Rhodes thinks I'm dead; no one will be looking for me. I'll see if the server is still in the cabin and get anything else I can pull out of there—guns, tactical gear, anything we can use."

Dan raised a hand to join the discussion. "We can get you anything you need from Director Jameson."

"Not while there's still a possible mole from One Hundred Roads lurking in DC. Requesting supplies for a mission could signal to them that we're on the move." Olsen jutted his chin at Dana. "Dana's trip to New Jersey could be a good distraction for my mission, since she's the one in their sights."

"So I'm bait?" Dana responded with a huff. All she wanted to do right now was get the keys to her mom's compact and drive to the airport. She was once again losing control of her own decisions. What was next, she thought? Would she be told which greasy diner to eat at in Jersey? She grew more and more tired of being told what to do.

"I'd certainly rather you weren't found out, but if you are, that gives us more time to get to and back from the safe house," said Olsen.

"Who is 'us,' may I ask?" Angela interjected, her first comment of the discussion.

"Well, you and me." Olsen smiled at her. "I need some muscle if we're going to potentially carry anywhere from thirty to eighty pounds of ordnance and hard drives out of the woods." He nodded over his shoulder to Simone. "She certainly can't go. No offense, Simone, but with your illness . . ."

Dana felt dissatisfied with Olsen's logic as well as his candor in discussing her mother's cancer. His enthusiasm for planning was appreciated, but she still held his participation under perpetual suspicion. *The enemy of my enemy is my friend, but I don't have to like it.*

"Are we taking the Jeep up to Wyoming?" Angela inquired. "Six, seven hours?"

"For sure. The van's not quite built for those back roads. Let's add another hour to our ETA for the off-road portion," Olsen countered. "We should be able to get within just a couple miles of the cabin, but we'll have to hike on foot for the final approach." He massaged his knees and examined his thighs. "Mostly flat ground at that point. I can make it."

Dana stepped forward and stood over him. "So, I guess I have your *permission* to go see my friend's dead father?" she asked sarcastically, regretting her tone somewhat but holding her composed, slightly angry face.

"You need to go." Olsen raised his eyebrows.

Dana saw a flash of compassion in his expression, perhaps the first time she had felt any form of true empathy from him. She had sworn she would not allow him any emotional latitude in front of the group. She read the rest of room one face at a time: Ashley looking eager to get back to her work; her mother scowling a dissenting vote from behind the kitchen island; Dan nodding silently and stoically. Lastly, she turned to Angela, who was picking at her fingernails as she leaned against the wall, her gaze fixed on an invisible spot on the floor—body language that Dana knew too well implied passive disagreement. Dana had experienced this posture when she insisted on the wrong movie for date night or when she chose not to stay overnight at Angela's back in Asbury Park. This time, she knew the elephant in the room was a blond boy back in the Pine Barrens.

"Hey, Ang, I'll be safe out there."

"I know you will." Angela straightened her posture and blew a strand of hair away from her cheek. "Don't worry about me. I'll have my hands full babysitting our resident senior citizen on his trip to the park."

Dana felt relieved to hear her sarcasm. *Okay . . . she's okay with this.*

"I'm right here, *Barbie*." Olsen reached down to his boot and placed his small pistol on the coffee table. "I am pretty confident I'll be the one babysitting *you* on this mission."

Dana walked over to her mother as Simone glared from under her eyebrows, shaking her head slowly. "Dana," she said in a low voice, "I'm just thinking about how this personal trip clashes with our tactical goals, but I don't need to lecture you about being careful and doing stupid things. You already put Nick through the ringer once. That's all I'll say about it."

"I'm not going to do anything stupid, Mom."

"Love can make people stupid," Simone replied with caution. "Be safe. I love you, Star."

"I love you, too, Mom."

# Chapter 8

*Innuendo – Queen*

Angela's skates lay on the concrete back porch next to an empty beer bottle. A tiny black spider, no bigger than a ball bearing, crept toward them, legs skittering in tandem pairs into the shadow cast by the bottle. Angela extended her finger toward the arachnid; she remained motionless, calm, as the spider touched her fingernail timidly, then scurried up to her first knuckle. Mindful of the breeze, she pivoted to protect it from blowing away. She walked to a large wooden planter box on the lip of the patio and placed the spider on the dry dirt.

"Needs watering," Simone said, emerging from the house with a fresh beer in each hand. She placed one bottle next to the empty one. Angela nodded.

"I will water those later, Mrs. J."

"Thank you," she replied, followed by what seemed to be a perpetual cough. A humming from her phone distracted her. "Dammit."

"What is it?"

"Driveway cameras. Better not be a tourist." Simone unbuttoned the holster to her revolver and stormed through the house. Angela followed, feeling like a tourist herself these days, living a temporary life in a beautiful villa in the desert—if you didn't factor in the paranoid innkeeper, the Australian mercenary, and the robotic suit hanging in the barn.

Simone flung open the front doors. Angela looked past her and saw a small red convertible Mazda Miata. A woman with short silver hair wearing a black pantsuit stepped out.

"Sorry about the lack of notice," announced Carmen Jameson.

"Carmen," snarled Simone, holstering her gun. "If you don't give me a heads-up, I might accidentally shoot you, you know."

Carmen dusted off her slacks and grabbed a large black messenger bag from the passenger seat. "Sorry, I have urgent things to share that can't be typed. Hello, Angela."

"Hello, Director." Angela straightened her posture in an effort to look more professional.

"Carmen is fine."

The trio set themselves up around the coffee table. Angela sat on the floor as the two older women took the couch. Once again, Angela felt like an observer in this cloak-and-dagger world she was now a part of. Carmen arranged her laptop, a cell phone, and a notebook on the table, then folded her hands.

*Something is wrong*, Angela thought.

"Is Olsen here?"

"He's out back," Simone replied. "He's working with Ashley on something."

"Good. Probably better to discuss this first with you so we can break the news to him."

"What news?" Angela asked. She was already worried about Dana's trip; this would just be one more thing.

"I got a call. From Silver."

Simone laughed, then pivoted to a sneer. "What the hell are you talking about? Why would Silver call *you?*"

Angela raised her hand. "Silver?"

"Yes," replied Carmen. "How much do you know about Silver?"

"Bad guy, makes weapons, Olsen hates him."

"You're one for three," corrected Carmen. "Silver is not a villain, and he is a technocrat who makes expensive equipment and devices, not weapons. But yes, Olsen does hate him, although I'd argue it's a bit of an unfounded grudge."

Simone rubbed her eyes. "Okay, she's all caught up. So, why did he call you?"

"Specifically, his assistant called me to let me know he wanted to meet. Apparently, he had a recent job for Rhodes that he thought I should be aware of."

"Is Silver playing both sides, you think?" Angela inquired, feeling proud of her contribution.

"Angela, Silver plays one side—his own," said Carmen as she pulled up a map on her laptop dotted with dozens of orange beacons across the globe. "These are all the places where Silver has done what it is Silver does. You'll know some of these from the news: little revolutions, natural disasters, outlier events like a near meltdown of a nuclear power plant.

"Silver, as I've said, is a technocrat. When government agencies and ruling bodies are too slow to act, Silver takes it upon himself to do what he deems is right for the 'betterment of humanity,' or so he likes to think. Sometimes that manifests as helping to overthrow the dictator of a banana republic, or, say, instigating a labor strike for workers' rights by grounding an oil tanker. And sometimes, this means hiring One Hundred Roads for a couple of missions." She looked from Angela to Simone. "Silver does what Silver wants. And we don't stop him because ninety-nine percent of the time, he makes the right call that ultimately benefits the United States. And he does it on his own dime."

Angela felt a flash of excitement in her gut, then a growing nervous energy. Weeks of skating and doing chores and babysitting Olsen were finally going to pay dividends.

Carmen continued, "Whatever Silver is up to now, he's decided he wants my help, along with Dana, Ashley, and Olsen. I assume he is aware that you are alive, Simone, thanks to his godlike powers of surveillance, but I'm not going to freely offer that up yet."

"Well, this is a nice little coincidence," Angela interjected, "because we need information on Rhodes, too. Just tell me what you need me to do."

Carmen's lips pursed slightly. "Dana, Ashley, and Olsen only. Sorry, Angela."

"Oh . . . okay then." Not hiding her disappointment, Angela stood and brushed imaginary dust from her leggings. "Then I'll just go out back and clean my skates. Again."

Carmen stood and gave the cell phone she brought to Simone. "This is a secure satellite phone. Have Olsen call using this when they're ready to meet tomorrow. Penny, Silver's assistant, will arrange everything. Tell Dana to be on her best behavior."

Angela scoffed. "Tomorrow? We don't even know when Dana is getting back."

Carmen tilted her head, mouth partly open. "Getting back from where?"

"She's in Jersey," Angela replied. "Agent Sun didn't tell you?"

"I've been on a plane, another plane, and a helicopter for the past twenty-four hours." Carmen pulled another phone from her pants pocket and scrolled through the screen. "Shit. I have to make a few calls. Simone, can I trouble you for a non-alcoholic beverage?"

"You may want something stronger," Simone replied dryly. "Olsen's walking up to the patio door."

"You talked to Silver?!" Olsen whacked his cane against the counter. "That lying sack of shit! We don't make deals with the devil—not now, not ever."

Carmen held up her hands in appeasement. "I know you have your issues with Silver, but that was simply an incident that went sideways, as things sometimes do."

"*Sideways?* Do you remember how many innocent people died?" He paced behind the couch, the stomp of his cane maddeningly arrhythmic, his breaths coming in short huffs pushing out spittle. "No. Absolutely not."

Angela had never seen him this enraged. The only thing that came close was the scolding in the Jeep after the bar incident, but that was a calming lullaby compared to now. She wasn't sure who to trust, but Olsen had been the one coaching and training her every single day since they had arrived. Carmen was, for all intents and purposes, a stranger she had only met a handful of times for background checks and paperwork slathered with nondisclosure agreements. Angela looked to Simone, but she retained her casual posture, relaxed on the couch with a beer in hand. Carmen took a seat, motioning to Olsen to calmly join her.

"Olsen. *Aaron.* I'm aware of what you went through on that mission, and I'm sorry. I know Silver is . . . he—"

"*He* wasn't boots on the ground. *He* didn't hear the screams, didn't watch those people die because he backed the wrong horse for the 'betterment of humanity.'"

Carmen leaned forward, hands on her knees. "I'm going to ask you politely to sit down and listen, or I'll have Angela pin you to the chair and make you listen."

*Well, at least then I'd be useful,* Angela thought.

Olsen turned to Angela, who flashed a smile of acquiescence, then sat. He placed his cane over his shoulder like a baseball bat.

"What is my role in this?" he asked.

Carmen relaxed. "When Dana gets back, you are going to call Silver, arrange a meeting, and take it from there. And of course, Silver will not do this without a quid pro quo to be determined. He was explicit with me about that."

Angela interjected herself into the conversation once again. "How do we know it's not a trap? I can go always go as backup."

"Angela," Carmen said, "that's not how Silver works."

"And how do we—how do *you*—know that?"

"Because this is how we've done things every time the United States has asked Silver for help."

# Chapter 9

*Ordinary World – Duran Duran*

The thick oaks lining the cemetery gave Dana a place to conceal herself while she observed a smaller group than she anticipated—only about a dozen—huddled around the hole in the ground. Everyone stood with their heads bowed as the priest spoke prayers and devotions that were erased in the breeze before they could reach Dana's ears. She spotted Nick immediately, even with his back to her: his lean build and sandy hair, his slightly slumped shoulders that were more prominent in his grief. Dana slid her pink sunglasses down her nose, trying to discern the details of the two people standing closest to him. One was a woman, older than Nick's father had been. *Maybe his aunt, or a close coworker?* The other woman looked familiar, a bit stocky, and appeared to be middle-aged. She grasped Nick's biceps and then bear-hugged him, nearly lifting him off the ground.

*Mary Beth!*

As if she could sense Dana, Mary Beth looked her way and winked. Dana pivoted behind the tree and pressed her back into the bark so hard, the ridges pricked her shoulders through her jacket. The sound of cars starting and then pulling away filtered through the sporadic chirps of birds. It was such a sad moment and a tragic end to the life of a good man, but the day and the place were simply beautiful, which she felt, in its own weird way, was the least Nick deserved as he faced the most tragic event in his life.

"Dana?"

With a little jump, Dana turned as she felt a gentle hand on the shoulder of her jacket.

"Hey, MB." Dana tightened her face but failed to hold back a wave of tears. "Mama Bear," she said warmly, clutching her substitute mother, roller derby mentor, and friend. "I should have been here . . . I wasn't here. I screwed up." She exhaled, an almost shivering sob slipping past her attempt at restraint. "I should have been here."

"Hey, kid, you're alright. It's okay."

"I'm sorry, I'm so self-absorbed—how are you doing? Mitch was your guy."

"Well, sweetie," Mary Beth said mournfully as she released her hug but kept one arm around Dana's waist, "I never called Mitch my anything, but yeah, he was my guy. More than friends, for sure."

"Oh, God, you saw Nick's dad naked." A giggle escaped between sobs.

"I'll spare you the details, okay? But yes, I've lost a new piece of my life far too soon."

"You're so goddamn wise." Dana looked around her to see if Nick was still in her sight line, but he was gone.

"I can't turn it off, as you know." This was true. Dana could not count how many times Mary Beth had been a counselor as well as a coach for the girls on the Asbury Angels roller derby team, getting them through bad breakups, single parenthood, even domestic abuse. Mary Beth knew that the precious time on their skates gave them the strength to carry on.

Dana wiped her cheeks with her leather sleeves. "So, should I go talk to him? Is there one of those reception-type things afterward, where everyone goes to some Italian restaurant and tells bawdy stories of 'remember when Mitch did that thing'?"

"Absolutely not. Nick said no to that. He's probably halfway home already. He's been processing it all, but . . ." Mary Beth paused. "He has a lot on his plate and he's trying to micromanage it all, as he does." She rubbed her chin with a large calloused hand and locked on to Dana's inquisitive gaze. "Dana, I'm not sure how to put this, but you may want to, you know, lower your expectations if you go see him. I mean . . . I'm not good at saying the right words."

Dana's heart skipped a beat, something she thought only happened in doo-wop song lyrics or in the chests of old men with bad pacemakers. *Geez, Dana, what is wrong with you?* "Okay. Just tell me—will he open the door if I knock?"

"Yes, he will. Just, you know, be cool."

*What the hell does that mean?*

# Chapter 10

*Midnight Blue – Melissa Manchester*

The envelopes addressed to "Mr. Nicholas Andrews" lay in a neat pile on the counter. Nick opened the one on top, a card that looked like the many others he had received decorated in pastel flowers, washed sunsets, and watercolor crosses. After he read each one, he wrote down the name of the sender in his notepad for future thank-you notes and placed the envelopes into the recycle bin that had taken up semipermanent residence under the kitchen table.

He finally waded through the cards and moved to a new pile, starting with a bill from his father's insurance company. Nick placed it in a pile of similar requests. He would have to reconcile the checkbook again. Thankfully, the mortgage was paid off, but the regular utility bills on top of medical bills and Nick's college bills chewed at the declining balance faster than he could infuse it with paychecks. He gave a long, deep sigh as he walked to the refrigerator.

Ginger ale had become a staple of Nick's over the past week. Irregular eating and stress had left his stomach with a lingering malaise and a feeling of being full even when he forgot to eat. The frying pan—his father's favorite kitchen tool, a gift from Nick on Father's Day the year his mom had passed away—sat unused on the cold stove. A memory came to him: His father washing it after breakfast and then handing it to Dana, who dried it carefully with a faded floral dish towel, smiling and laughing at Mitch's jokes. The promise Mitch had made to teach her how to make his famous French toast would go unfulfilled.

*Dana.*

He sat down in a slump at the kitchen table. Why hadn't she called? Or texted? Not just now, but ever? He understood—at least now—that her self-imposed exile was for his own protection. At the same time, he had thought, he had *hoped*, that one day she would just call and check in, ask how things were. He was grateful for the sympathy from his coworkers, his classmates, even people who barely knew him, but he missed *her*—her jokes, her sarcasm, her smile.

A knock at the door drew him back to the cold reality of the empty house.

Dana rapped her knuckles on the front door of the Andrews family's white rancher. She heard the gravel churn behind her as the Uber driver pulled out of the driveway onto the two-lane county road. The gentle breeze caressing the pine trees sounded like the most beautiful symphony she had ever heard after so much time away from New Jersey. She adjusted her backpack—which was lighter without the presence of Laverne and Shirley, left back in New Mexico thanks to airport security restrictions—and knocked again.

The door swung open silently and Nick stepped out and sagged against the doorframe, almost in relief. He was clean-shaven, his hair just slightly tousled, but his eyes were still that glacial blue that hid nothing. He smiled and bit his lip.

"Hey."

"Hey."

Dana's lip began to quiver. His father had just died, a genuinely good man who had raised this quiet hero, and yet Nick was still able to smile. A patient young man with a heart of gold, the person she admired more than anyone she had ever met. All she wanted to do in this moment was tell him she was sorry, sorry for everything. She let her backpack slide off her shoulder, tears bursting from her eyes as she threw her arms around him and knocked him backward into the living room.

"Nick," she sobbed, "your dad was . . . I'm sorry. I loved Mitch, he was such a good dad. And he was so nice to me, and I just feel awful I punted you away at the airport, and I am such a shitty person, and I really, really, really have missed your friendship . . . I'm rambling."

Nick gently pushed her a few inches away from his chest. "How was your flight?" He smiled as he sniffled.

"Really?" she said with a playful laugh as she wiped her runny nose on her sleeve. "I just, I mean, um . . . I don't know what to say."

She glanced over at the couch where she and Nick had taken turns sleeping while the other one used his bedroom, back when they had first met. Everything in the house was just as it was. She saw the photo of Nick's mother—rest her soul—the coffee mugs on the counter, the frying pan on the stove, the work boots still neatly organized, or dare she say *displayed*, next to the couch. She didn't expect Nick to be in complete disarray—that wasn't how Nick's mind worked—but she at least thought she'd find a beer bottle without a coaster, or perhaps a video game controller left out on the coffee table. He gestured toward the kitchen, where they had once shared many plates of toast and eggs with his dad.

"Drink?"

"Sure, yes. Water. Or beer—I'm not driving." She bent her wrist, pulling her cuff over her tattoo.

"I've got beer in the garage."

*Right.* She momentarily forgot that Nick didn't keep alcohol in the house to respect his father's ongoing victories with sobriety.

Dana followed him out to the detached garage. Again, everything was still in its place. His tools were neatly arranged and hung on specific hooks on the wall, the floor was swept clean of pine needles and dirt, and the bench vise where they had huddled together and worked on her skates was smooth and dust-free. Nick's organizational, borderline anal-retentive habits had prepared him well for the meticulous details of being an electrician. Just one more thing she loved and respected about him: He took care of things. And people.

"Here."

She accepted the cold beer bottle he handed her from the fridge and reoriented herself.

"Hold on, let me guess." She smirked as she pointed the bottle in front of her like a scanning device. "Something. Is. Missing."

"Well, the truck is . . . at the shop, getting new tires. I would do it myself but, you know, I've been a little busy."

"Was that almost a joke?"

"I'm trying. I can't get my head around all of this at once. It's like . . . bits and pieces." He hopped onto the workbench and opened his own bottle. "I think in some ways, when Mom died and I didn't process it fully for almost a year, I must have been thinking, 'What if Dad dies?' and just . . . you know." He mimed his hand rocketing out of his head and exploding. "I don't know. I can grieve a little every day, but I can also remember the happy memories every day."

His face shifted to a more serious mask. "This is all so surreal sometimes. Until yesterday, the house was covered in mail and flowers, and my clothes were all over the floor. I hadn't showered for three days."

"My God, who are you and what have you done with Nick?" Dana teased gently before walking over and clanking her bottle against his. "To Mitch, the second nicest man I've ever met." She followed the toast with a wink.

Nick cleared his throat with a deliberate cough as he blushed. "You still haven't figured out what's missing."

She knew he was changing the subject. Classic diversion.

"Okay." She spun around and immediately spotted that the tarp that usually covered his dirt bike was in its place against the wall, but draped over something . . . bigger?

"It's under there, isn't it?"

Nick bit his lip and smiled. "I traded up. Go ahead."

Dana grasped the edge of the worn plastic tarp and slowly peeled it back. The front wheel emerged first, a single slick tire crowned with a black fender under a pair of sinister headlights in the fairing. The short windscreen preceded two black antlers on the beast, handlebars with clean grips. The sloping glossy black fuel tank blended into the leather seat pad over the chrome-covered engine. Two side compartments at the waist of the motorcycle straddled the rear wheel, sitting above two large chrome exhaust tips. A black helmet with a clear visor rested on the passenger seat, perfectly aligned with the body, looking like the turret of a tank.

"Dana, let me introduce you to my baby, my Honda NT1100. It's got all the bells and whistles, from trim package to touring saddle bags. Now I don't have to worry about being able to keep up with Laverne and Shirley." He traced his hand along the seat. "It's nice to be able to go out, just me and my thoughts, and just get lost on the roads."

"I can relate." She felt a pang of longing for her skates. "Does that even fit in the back of your truck?"

"Diagonally, sure. It's a tight fit. Do you really think I wouldn't check? Dad was out here one night with a tape measure, checking every single dimension just to be sure." He smiled at the thought, and his face was overtaken again by sadness.

"Do you want me to go? I mean, I know I just barnstormed my way into your time of mourning. And your beer supply."

"I think I could use the company until . . . my truck is done." He dragged his boot across the floor. "Do you want to go for a ride?" He extended his hand toward the inky black, almost mirror-like helmet. She was so fixated on the beautiful machine that she didn't see Nick had already grabbed his old helmet, now cradled in the crook of his arm. She grabbed the new helmet with both hands and grinned.

"I would love to."

# Chapter 11

*White Houses – Vanessa Carlton*

The late afternoon sun draped long shadows in ragged stripes over the edges of the front lawn. Nick pushed the bike from the driveway onto the thin blacktop and got on, then smacked the seat behind him.

"Hop on."

Dana straddled the motorcycle and, unsure of what to do, placed her hands on Nick's shoulders.

"Grab the edge of the seat behind you, or just, you know." He shrugged his shoulders. "Grab my hips."

Dana felt her face turn hot under her helmet as she placed her fingers delicately on the edge of his jeans. The engine purred and vibrated under her as Nick began to speed up. She rocked backward at first before firming her grip on his hips, clacking her helmet against his.

"You alright, Dana?" Nick said into his helmet microphone, his voice suddenly in her ear.

"Yeah, I'm good." She inched her hands up so that her index fingers rested on his belt. The position felt almost intimate to her now, much more so than the playful punches and shoulder pokes they were used to exchanging. "I'm good."

The bike whined with Nick's acceleration. A break in the trees ahead indicated the blueberry farms were quickly approaching. Dana lifted her head and tried to inhale inside her helmet, a feeble attempt to take in the aroma of the sweet crops. On the horizon, white blustery cumulus clouds dotted the sky, each lined by a dark ivory shadow on the edge furthest from the sun. The wind nipped at Dana's neck and whipped the hair that extended below her helmet.

"This is nice," she said to no one in particular.

"Yeah, it is. Is this your first time?"

"Yes. First time. Virgin alert." She laughed self-consciously, then swallowed and realigned her grip at his waist. Under her hands, she could tell he had shed a few pounds, or at least had lost a layer of baby fat. Or maybe he just *felt* different to her somehow.

The bike accelerated again and lurched forward. "Sorry, I'm still a little less experienced at higher gears. Trying to make a smoother transition."

"You keep doing what you're doing." She felt the increase in vibrations and a twitch in her thighs as she instinctively flexed her feet to adjust her speed. She realized she was used to being the one in control, directing Laverne and Shirley at high speed, but having Nick at the helm and sitting back as the passenger instead of the driver . . . it felt okay.

The Honda slowed as Nick approached a side road. "Okay, when the bike goes right, *gently* lean like I do," he instructed her. "Like you're trying to stay in line with me. Don't lean out. This keeps our center of gravity more stable. Lean into me—I'll lead."

Dana pressed her chest against his back and slid her hands around toward his stomach. His untucked shirt flapped up, and her hand grazed his skin as the bike swooped into the turn. Dana pushed her thighs into his and pulled her hands back down to his hips.

"Can you go faster? Open it up a bit?" Her nervous energy metastasized into a bubbling burst of endorphins.

"I thought you'd never ask," he replied. She could hear the smile in his voice, only overpowered by the roar of the wind and whine of the engine. His hands moved effortlessly on the handles as she watched him change gears again. She had definitely sped much faster on her skates, but the lack of control on her part and the blind trust in Nick's navigation and piloting drove a rush of blood to her head, creating a mix of fear and excitement.

"Faster?" Nick asked.

"A little faster."

The bike weaved slowly from side to side as Nick laced the wheels between tiny ruts and debris in the road, serpentine and smooth, but ferociously fast.

Dana leaned back and saw a familiar road sign approaching. Faded lettering indicated Hardwicke Lumber and the road for the sawmill ahead, the place where they had first ridden together with his dirt bike and her skates.

"Can we go down there?"

"Not today—they're repaving it. The mill was finally sold, and there's a housing development going in there."

Dana felt a twinge of sadness. She turned her attention back to the road ahead and pressed her body against his, curling her arm around his torso and resting her hand on his chest. *I like this,* she thought. *I* really *like this.*

"Hey Nick? I want to enjoy the view a bit. Can we slow down a little now?"

"Sure. We should probably head back home." He made a gentle U-turn and began to retrace their path toward his house.

"Are you trying to get rid of me before your mistress comes home?" Dana asked, laughing into her earpiece.

Nick didn't answer but instead downshifted, and the bike jerked. Dana's hands slipped before landing again on his hips.

The shadows continued their invasion of the road. Nick's house approached in the distance. A series of large white blobs were now visible in front of his house, and Dana squinted to try to make them out. She bolted upright and hammered him on the shoulder.

"Nick. Nick! Don't slow down—keep going."

"I told you, I have to get home . . ." His voice trailed off, affirming he saw what she did: two white pickup trucks parked akimbo in his driveway, a third on the lawn.

The bike roared past the rancher as Dana jerked her head around to see as best as she could. She thought she saw a pair of shapes through the large front window.

"Shit, shit, shit." Someone had figured out where she was. Had she been followed? Had Rhodes suspected she would come back here? Was Nick the target? The bike began to slow as her mind accelerated. "Nick, why are we slowing down?"

A red pickup truck approached from the oncoming lane—Nick's truck. *Huh?*

Nick slowed the Honda and braced it perpendicular to the lane as the Ford rolled to a stop. He planted his feet on each side of the bike as the driver rolled down the window and leaned her head out. It was a woman wearing lavender medical scrubs, pretty even without makeup, her eyes as blue as Nick's own. A claw clip held her chocolate-brown hair in place.

"Nick, is everything okay?" Her eyes searched his with true concern before she looked over at Dana, giving her a cautious but welcoming half smile. "Hi, I'm Jennifer."

"Jennifer, we got a problem," Nick interrupted before Dana could respond. He glanced back at the house. Two men now stormed the driveway, shouting and pointing, while a third leapt into the driver's seat of the closest truck and rolled into reverse, spitting gravel across the driveway.

Dana dismounted the Honda and ran to the truck bed, flinging open the liftgate. "Hi, I'm Dana. And *those* are bad guys. Get the bike in the truck, Nick." Nick followed Dana's instruction and pushed the bike over to where she had already extended the wooden plank ramp. Jennifer got out to help, and the three grunted together as they rolled the bike into the bed, barely fitting it in diagonally with the front wheel turned.

"Nick!" Jennifer shouted, attempting to wrap a bungee around a plastic gas canister in the corner of the bed. "What the hell is going on?"

Nick hopped into the driver's seat while Dana jumped in through the passenger side and slid to the center of the bench, Jennifer getting in after her. She slammed the door shut as Nick spun the Ford around into the opposite lane and stomped on the gas pedal.

"Uh, Jennifer, this is the friend I told you about. Roller skates, robots, weird Australian dude, all of that stuff?" Nick slammed the brakes and made a hard right down a side road. "Dana, Jennifer is kind of my girlfriend."

"*Girlfriend?*" Dana blurted.

"*Kind of?*" Jennifer retorted.

"Can we put the semantics in a shoebox for later?! I think they're following us," he said, twisting the steering wheel to avoid rear-ending a sedan in their lane. "I see three pickups behind us in the rearview. Dana, you see them?"

Dana hadn't been paying attention, the term "girlfriend" loudly bouncing around in her head, but Nick's question snapped her back into focus. She slid the cabin window open and surveyed the trucks weaving through traffic behind them. With another swerve, the motorcycle in the back thunked against the sidewall. "That's going to leave a mark." Dana winced, guessing that the chrome and paint on his new bike were no longer pristine. "Yes, I see three."

Dana turned back around to find Jennifer staring at her suspiciously. The word "girlfriend" started replaying in her mind again.

"So, Jennifer, why is it you had Nick's truck?" asked Dana before she could stop herself. She was genuinely surprised by the realization that the sudden swell of threats had failed to trigger a panic attack, but this Jennifer person was disarming her on a completely different level.

"I picked it up on the way home from work. I wanted to do a favor for him, you know, considering everything he's going through."

"Yeah, I know. I was at the funeral." Dana crossed her arms, perhaps intentionally elbowing both the heroic driver and his confused girlfriend flanking her. "I didn't see you there."

"I was in surgery, saving a *life*."

"Of course you were. Who was it, the Pope?" Dana asked sarcastically.

The truck swerved into the right-side shoulder as Nick abruptly turned onto an entrance ramp. Dana caught the word "Philadelphia" on the large green sign as they skittered past.

"It was a boxer. *Freckles*." Jennifer ignored Dana's raised eyebrows. "I'm a veterinary technician, and Freckles was a service dog that got hit by a car pushing his owner out of traffic. And what do *you* do?"

"Uh, bartending, skating, and secret government ops."

"Dana, Jen, I'm glad we're all getting to know each other, *yay*," Nick growled, "but I really need some help. Eyes ahead, eyes behind." Nick jerked the truck across three lanes and hammered the gas pedal. "Shout if you see an airport sign."

Dana turned her head back around and willed herself to focus on the road behind them.

# Chapter 12

*City and the Ghost – Bedlight for Blue Eyes*

The driver and his passengers remained in stony silence until Nick suddenly whooped and pointed toward a sign.

"Philly is getting close."

His hands were cramping from gripping the wheel so tightly as he continually swerved the truck, trying to outmaneuver their mysterious pursuers. Dana bounced into his shoulder, eliciting a faint "sorry" from her lips.

"No need to apologize," he said. He hoped she sensed the subtext there, that he was grateful she was here. But for now, everyone's safety was at the top of his mind.

"Who are these guys?" Jennifer asked, her arms crossed over her scrubs.

"Honestly, I don't know. Just keep your eyes in front, please."

She nodded. Nick wanted to reach over and hold Jennifer's hand in reassurance, but reaching across Dana would have been the definition of awkward, albeit oddly symbolic of her being the unspoken thing that always came between them.

Jennifer had asked him once to be candid about his complicated relationship with Dana. He had obliged with the truth, although it resulted in him suffering through many hours of silence after. Jennifer loved him—she had told him so—and he was fairly confident that "love" was a word he wanted to say to her as well.

Again, he pushed the thoughts down deep and let his care and concern for both women turn to action as he jerked the steering wheel again. He glanced at the large green sign ahead and felt relief. "Finally, Walt Whitman!"

Dana raised both her eyebrows at Nick with a quizzical smile. "Um, Emily Dickinson? Are we playing some kind of game where we yell out the names of poets while being chased?"

"No, the sign! The Walt Whitman Bridge! We're almost to the Philly International Airport."

The Ford pickup careened across the lanes of the entrance ramp as the bridge rose into view, silhouetted against the rose-colored sky of sunset. Dana turned to look over her shoulder through the cab's rear windshield and saw the three white pickup trucks still in pursuit, only a few car lengths behind them. One began to accelerate and inch closer via an opening in the left lane.

"Nick, I'm going to need a lot more information," Jennifer grumbled. "Why are we going to the airport? Why aren't we calling the police?"

"Because we *can't* call the cops," he replied as he maneuvered around another car on their approach to the bridge. "The plan is to take these guys to the airport so they think we're leaving town in a hurry. The airport complex is a zoo. They'll have a harder time tracking us, especially if they think we jumped on a flight at any one of the terminals. Once we lose them, we can slip out." He crossed two fingers and hoped he was making sense, although in his head he wasn't sure he knew what he was doing at all.

"It's as good a plan as any," Dana replied.

Dana shook her head and couldn't help but let out a brief chuckle. Nick, on the fly, coming up with a risky plan to get them out of trouble? Improvising was usually what *she* brought to the table on their adventures. Without her skates, she felt sort of useless in the effort to shake the three trucks.

*Three trucks.* An idea flashed in her head.

"Nick, what do you have back here?" Dana snaked her arm behind the driver's seat and yanked out a cylindrical stuff sack. "Do you mind?" she asked without waiting for an answer as she dumped it out onto Jennifer's lap and parsed out a first-aid kit, a socket wrench, a portable USB battery for cell phones, and a long avocado-colored thermos that was likely older than any of the car's occupants. "Mitch" was scrawled on the side in faded magic marker. It rattled when she shook it.

"Those are road flares," Nick said, his eyes widening. "Yes! Road flares!"

The pickup surged as it climbed the bridge's ascending roadway. *Inhale, exhale. Inhale, exhale.* Dana zipped up her jacket and looked at Jennifer.

"Jennifer, roll your window down and hold on to me until I say to let go, got it?" *Please like me enough to not let go.*

A flash of uncertainty flashed across her eyes, but Jennifer nodded. "Got it." Her firm hand tightened on Dana's jacket.

Jennifer pressed the button for the passenger-side window while Dana leaned across and waited until the opening was wide enough to push her torso through. The crosswind of the bridge whipped her hair into a frenzy, the slowly illuminating skyline of Philadelphia behind her.

"Nick, stay straight!" The tug at her jacket let Dana know that Jennifer still had a firm grip.

Dana leaned out more than halfway and grasped the wall of the truck bed as a white pickup from the pursuing pack snapped around a van and crept closer. *I sure do miss my skates.*

"Let go! Jenny. I got this." With a silent count to three, Dana swung her legs out the window and into the bed as the truck sped along at sixty miles per hour. The force landed her next to the Honda, now lilting on its side. She reached up to the open window slot of the cabin's rear windshield.

"FLARES!" she yelled against the wind and road noise.

Jennifer handed her two red tubes through the window.

"Nick! Count to three! ON THREE, BRAKE, THEN GAS! READY?"

Nick knocked on the glass to indicate he heard her. "One . . ."

Dana popped the first flare. Hot embers danced around the truck bed and fell onto her jeans.

"Two . . ."

Dana popped the second flare and leaned back to load her legs for recoil.

"Three!"

Dana shot up into a standing pose. The sudden braking flung her back against the cabin as she released the flares. The white pickup closest to them squealed as the front tires locked, and the two airborne flares landed in the gulley of the windshield wipers. Dana felt her body surge and tumble toward the liftgate with Nick's rapid acceleration.

"Shit, shit, shit!"

She soared over the bike and her shoulder rammed into the liftgate, which she suddenly remembered had a temperamental latch. It fell open with her impact, and she slid further down the truck bed until her fingers caught the chrome tailpipe by the Honda's rear wheel. The bike slid a few inches but stopped as it was caught by the wheel well against the front tire and handlebars.

"NICK!"

As the small red plastic gas canister tumbled out of its bungee and toward the lip of the open truck bed, Dana intercepted it with her free hand. The white pickup truck snaked back and forth a few yards behind, attempting to smother the cinders erupting from the flares.

Her breath felt short and shallow. *Not now. Not yet.* From the pulse in her temple, she knew her heart was racing, but time seemed to be slowing. Another short breath.

*Not now. Oh God, not now.*

The headlights of the white pickup dashed back and forth as it continued its fight against the flares.

*Breathe in . . .*

The air around her, cold and smoky, stank from a mix of sulfur, exhaust, and burnt rubber.

*Breathe out.*

Dana rolled onto her stomach and loosened the cap to the gas can. "Not today, Satan!" she mumbled. "Dana's in control."

With an upward heave, she flung the gas can through the air in the direction of the truck. A thin glistening line of fuel backlit by the bridge's freshly ignited lights landed on the flares at the base of the white truck's windshield, and the immense heat from the flashing fireball reached Dana's face. She covered her eyes and pushed her body back up the truck bed, crawling toward the cabin window.

"Oh God, my eyebrows! Do I still have eyebrows?"

A gentle hand touched the top of her head. "Yes, they're intact," Jennifer yelled through the rear window. "Nice job, by the way!"

Dana adjusted her stance, accidentally kicking the handlebars of the motorcycle. She grabbed at empty air as Nick's bike unwedged itself from the wheel well and slid the rest of the way out of the truck bed and onto the bridge, smashing into the front of another pursuing white pickup.

"Oh no, no, no!" Dana watched the wreckage in horror. "Nick, I owe you a motorcycle!"

"Oh my freaking God!" Nick yelled.

But there was no time for Dana to think about it. Nick barreled through the toll booth at the end of the bridge and yanked his truck into a sweeping turn for the exit ramp that led to the airport. Dana could see the growing silhouette of a plane descending against the dying sky. "We must be close, right, Nick?"

"Five minutes!" he shouted back. "I only see one truck now."

Dana looked back to see he was right. What had happened to the other two? Were the drivers injured severely, or worse? What about other drivers on the bridge who had been in the wrong place at the wrong time? She never really thought about the repercussions of her actions in these situations until after the fact, her adrenaline usually smothering any moments of self-reflection. So why were these thoughts nagging her now? She would mull it over later, eventually. She forced her attention back to their escape.

"Dana," Nick barked, "we're heading for the international terminal—that's the first one up on the loop! When I slow down and yell 'run,' you and Jennifer jump out and head into the parking garage. I'll lead them to the next terminal's drop-off."

Dana gave a thumbs-up through the window in acknowledgment. For a second, there was no sign of the remaining pursuer until she saw a white form swerving out from behind a pair of shuttle buses further back on the ramp.

Nick cut off another shuttle bus slowing to a stop for the passenger drop and hit the brakes. "Run!"

Dana rolled over the rear fender and began to sprint toward the garage, darting between cars. The sound of heavy footsteps behind her signaled that Jennifer was on her heels. She extended her hand and felt Jennifer's firm grasp.

"Jennifer. Stairwell! Second floor so we can see out."

"Got it."

The two women ran hand in hand under the flickering yellow lights of the poorly maintained concrete structure. A wordless sign with a zigzag illustration indicated the second floor's entrance. They swung into the stairwell.

At the second-floor landing, Dana whipped around the doorway and collapsed next to the retaining wall overlooking the terminal drop-off. The growl of cars starting and stopping, horn bleats, and muffled announcements echoed in the structure.

"That was some insane shit back there," Jennifer said, panting as she collapsed next to Dana. She drew a long, stuttering breath. "I have a lot of questions. So many questions."

"Me too." Dana felt her phone vibrating in her pocket and saw Nick's number on the screen. "Nick, we're on the second floor. I see a sign for D2 about two rows away from us."

"Okay," he replied. "I parked the truck at the curb and now I'm across the street crouched behind a parked car. I saw a white pickup park a few cars behind me, and some guys dressed like paramilitary duck hunters ran out and got into a shouting match with TSA. One hopped back in the truck and the others ran inside." Nick paused. "Okay, the white pickup just backed up and the other guys ran back out and got in. They're taking off. I'm going to grab my truck." He hung up.

"Nick, wait! Shit." Dana stared at the phone and slumped against the concrete.

"What's going on?" Jennifer peeked over the wall.

"I don't know. I think he's going to get his truck back. He thinks they might have left."

Dana looked down at her phone and studied the black screen behind the single crack along the middle that she kept promising herself to get fixed. She stared at her reflection, skewed by the damaged glass. Her eyes were shifted slightly above her nose where the crack intercepted her image. "Shit."

"What?"

"My phone—I booked my trip out here on my phone. I used it to order the car to take me to Nick's house . . . shit! Do you have your phone?"

"Yeah." Jennifer dug it out of her purse slung across her body. Dana flicked her own phone's screen on and scrolled to her short list of recent calls.

"Take a picture of my screen. Now, here," Dana urged, scrolling to her contact list. "Take a picture of this number, and hers, and his, and hers. And this one, too." Angela, Olsen, her mother, Ashley, and Jameson. She hated what she had to do next. "Did you get them all?"

"Yep."

Dana picked up her device and scanned the parking lot. A nearby SUV had left the sunroof cracked open. She jogged over and slipped her phone through the slit, then ran back to Jennifer.

"Someone's tracking me. I think those guys were trying to capture me." *Or something worse.*

Jennifer crossed her arms over her scrubs and pushed her chin into her chest. "Nick told me the stories, but it was just, you know, too fantastic to believe. I thought he was exaggerating." She locked eyes with Dana. "Please tell me you can get us out of this, Dana."

"I'm trying." Dana spotted a flash of a red truck between the cars in the next aisle. "Nick's here. Jennifer, I promise you, *promise you*, I am not going to let anything happen to you or Nick."

The familiar Ford rolled to a stop next to Dana.

"Is everyone okay?" Nick leaned over and opened the passenger door.

Dana ignored him and kept focused on his girlfriend. "Jennifer." Dana stretched out an empty hand. "You can trust me." Jennifer reached out, grabbed her hand, and pulled Dana close. She placed her lips near Dana's ear.

"Fine, but I'm not going to let anything happen to Nick, either. I love him."

Dana felt a pinch in her chest. Her cheeks tensed as her brain boiled. She didn't hate Jennifer—just that she existed, and that she was the kind of person Nick wanted to date. She swallowed and attempted to speak. Nothing.

Jennifer released Dana's hand. "Let's get the hell out of here, find someplace to regroup, and sort this out, maybe get some food. Did I mention I came from surgery before this whole shit show started? I'm starving." She smiled, and Dana forced a smile in return.

"Well, we can't go home, at least not right now," Nick said. Dana saw a flash of an idea in his eyes. "How about we head west?" he asked as they both settled into the cab. "Maybe Amish Country? Can't beat the food there."

Jennifer typed something on her phone. "After I let my folks know I'm going on an impromptu getaway with Nick, I'll look up some places." She shot a sideways glance at Dana. "How far away do you live? Maybe we can crash there after a bit?"

"Too far," Dana sighed. "At least on a single tank of gas, that's for sure."

# Chapter 13

*Can't Hardly Wait – The Replacements*

Olsen brushed the wiry hairs on Dick's neck and shoulders. He tried to remember all the steps Ashley showed him for taking care of Dick: feeding him, inspecting his hooves, and brushing his mane and flank. *Was it fur or hair? Hair.* The time spent on the ranch had taught him a welcome lesson in how to slow things down to match his new pace. That and his rereading of the Bible had done wonders for his psyche. He hadn't made up his mind yet on what he should get out of it, fact or fiction, but the overarching lessons and mantras calmed the storm in his head.

He finished and went back to the house, greeted by another aromatic dinner prepared by Simone and Ashley with the table set by Angela. They were only missing Dana, but the group felt so much smaller when assembled around the table. He always tried to choose a spot directly across from Simone, if available, so that he could continue to study her expressions and mannerisms. She was still an enigma to him—a brilliant scientist, an experienced mother, a broken woman. Before he sat down, he pulled his Bible out of the back pocket of his pants and sat it next to his plate. Conversation tonight was minimal, so he decided to open up a new topic.

"Simone, are you at all religious?"

She let her fork drop and glared at him. "Are you going to try to convert me in my own house? I see you carrying that book around with you everywhere."

"I meant no offense. I was just looking to—"

She burst into laughter and picked up her utensil. "I'm messing with you, big guy." Ashley launched into her own laugh while Angela smiled and nodded. Simone placed a hand on her arm. "You can laugh, Ang. That's allowed!"

At that, Angela broke into a bigger smile. Olsen saw how much Angela always tried to fit in, not stir the pot; her fit of anger at the bar was an outlier. Perhaps, he surmised, she was using the calm moments to offset the furious ones, or really putting in an effort to not get into a situation where she might be put on her heels or blow her top. In this, he saw a moment to pivot and prod.

"I was just curious, Simone. I've come across some people out in the field who use religion as a coping mechanism or a crutch to get them through some really tough times." He slid his glance over to Angela. "Religion's not for everyone, but some people never try it."

Angela lowered her eyes. "Some things just don't make sense."

Olsen put his hand on the Bible next to his plate. "There's a lot of stuff in here I can't make sense of."

"Actually," Ashley interjected, "it's completely subjective. There are so many variations based on translations, and translations on top of translations. There are some very simple sentences that are completely upended by changing a single word, or changing the tense of a word."

Angela stood and gathered the plates from the table, bringing a clear end to the conversation. "Thank you for dinner again, Mrs. J."

"Thank you, Angela. And again, you can call me Simone, you know."

"Yes, ma'am."

Olsen found himself at another intersection of admiration and inquisitiveness toward Angela. She was a physically formidable woman yet usually kept quiet in the background, even when placed in a small group. She was also a considerate person, not just clearing plates to do her share after dinner, but also picking up Dana's socks off the floor or folding Dana's towel after she left the bathroom. When they had all moved into the rancher, Angela had helped Dana put her things away first before unpacking her own. This was behavior he had seen from leaders—the *best* leaders—in some of his mission camps: people who made sure everything else and everyone else was taken care of before attending to their own tasks or needs.

"Olsen, hey," Simone whispered, snapping him back to attention. "Have you heard anything from Dana?"

He shook his head. "Nothing."

"She was supposed to check in."

"She might be out late, hanging out with Nick, reconnecting and such."

"Yeah, well, it's the 'and such' that makes me worry."

"Let her have her fun, if you think that's what's going on."

"Well, *her* kind of fun isn't always well thought-out."

"Noted." He walked over to the sink, grabbed a dish towel, and held out his empty hand to receive a clean wet plate from Angela. "Are you ready for tomorrow?"

"Ready. Should be an adventure."

"Hopefully not." He saw a flicker in Simone's eyes as her jaw tensed. "Hopefully it's boring as hell."

# Chapter 14

*Interstate Love Song – Stone Temple Pilots*

God, I hate truck stops."

Dana dawdled at a table covered in poorly folded stacks of tourist shirts emblazoned with various logos for Hershey, Pennsylvania, and a mix of local colleges. She decided on a gray shirt with the outline of the state, remembering that Nick floated between a large and extra-large. As she waited to pay at the counter with her credit card, suppressing any thought of its accelerating balance, she grabbed a handful of beef jerky sticks from a display box. "Screw it. I'll take the whole thing." She poured the contents onto the counter and handed her card to the catatonic cashier. He counted the sticks and ran her card.

"Thank you, miss. Have a nice day."

"I'll try to. There's about thirty minutes left of it that can still go wrong."

She stepped through the automatic doors and jogged across the parking lot. A short leap over the landscaping berm landed her next to Nick's truck, parked in front of their room at the motel. Jennifer stood in the open doorway with a towel wrapped around her head.

"Here you go, doll," Dana said with a toss of the bag. Jennifer caught it and poked through the contents.

"Which shirt is mine?"

"Not the gray one."

Jennifer held up a pink shirt emblazoned with the Hershey logo and cursive script underneath.

"'Live, Laugh, Eat Chocolate.' Really?"

"It was the only one in your size," Dana lied with a shrug.

"Funny." Jennifer slung the shirt over her shoulder and walked back inside as Dana followed, closing the door behind her. Jennifer pulled the towel off her head and tossed it onto the bed. She peeled off her scrubs and slid the gaudy tee over her sports bra, striking a model pose in front of the mirror. "Thank you. It's horrible. I love it."

"Yeah, well, mine's no better." Dana held up a blue shirt with the words "Chocolate Lover" in flowing white letters.

"That *is* awful. I'm now very happy with mine."

Dana dumped another bag on the bed: a three pack of men's white briefs, another three pack of nearly identical women's undergarments, and a six pack of plain white crew socks. "Not really a lot of choices."

Jennifer nodded to a plastic bag on the faux-maple laminate-topped dresser. "That bag is for you. The guy at the front desk sells pay-as-you-go phones. I figured you might need a burner."

"I'll pay you back when I can find money."

"Forget about it."

*Dammit, don't be nice to me.*

Jennifer flopped onto the edge of the bed and pulled her knees up to her chest. "You know, you kind of saved our lives back there."

"Least I could do since it's my fault this all happened."

"Forget about it." Jennifer picked up her phone and started typing. "Just wanted to say thanks."

Dana glanced around the room, listening to the quiet rattle of the bathroom fan. "Where's Nick?"

"He went out to get some air."

Dana looked out the window and saw Nick on the other side of the parking lot on a concrete berm between two lampposts. He sat with his back to the hotel, facing the black distant profile of rolling hills. Dana put her new phone down. "I'll be right back."

"Dana." Jennifer stood up and stepped in front of the door. "Give him a little time. He's . . . decompressing. He's still grieving."

Dana had forgotten in the unraveling chaos that Nick's grief was still so new, so raw. Keeping it under the surface was his way. She remembered shortly after they first met when he had told her about his mother's death: his pragmatic strength in facing the loss, followed by his father's admiration at first that then turned into concern for his son. Dana herself was still processing Mr. Andrew's death, following Nick's lead and hoping to deal with it later. It still felt like Mitch would be waiting back in New Jersey whenever all this ended, always there to cook them breakfast and brew them coffee.

She sat on the side of the bed and winced as her jeans rubbed against the scattered tiny burns from the road flares. Jennifer reached for her purse.

"Hey, off with your pants. Let me clean those up." Jennifer knelt in front of Dana and dug into her handbag. "I have magical things in here."

"Fine." Dana shimmied her dirty, damaged denim down to her ankles and surveyed the wounds. A smattering of scabs and dried blood dotted her thighs, adding to her collection of road rashes, scars, and recently acquired bruises. Jennifer blotted a tissue with alcohol.

"This will sting, but I'm sure you know that."

"Yeah, I know, it's—OH MY GOD, NOT TODAY, SATAN!" Dana yelled as the cold stinging liquid touched her skin. "I'm not a *horse!* Be gentle!"

"Horses are better behaved," Jennifer said, winking. "Seriously, I love working with equine patients. Sadly, all the horses I've handled so far in Jersey are mostly washed-out surrey racers and malnourished pets of rich people."

Dana sensed Jennifer had a real connection with her animal patients—another admirable feather in the cap of the girl who had won Nick.

Dana picked at a hole on her hip where the elastic separated from the cotton. "My mom has a horse. If we make it out there, I'm sure you'll find something wrong with him. He's older than my underwear."

Jennifer finished applying bandages and antiseptic from a tube. "Good enough. I'm going to go check on my boyfriend."

"Wait! Can I go, please?" Dana blurted as she yanked her jeans back to the appropriate location on her hips. "I need to talk to him for a minute." The flash of a scowl crossed Jennifer's face. "Please."

The doorknob turned, breaking up their tiny debate. Nick pushed open the door, his eyes swollen and pink.

"It's fine. I'm here." He reached for the gray shirt on the bed. "Thank you for the shirt."

Dana decided to let him be for now. Pointing to Jennifer's phone on the nightstand, she asked, "Can I have that for a sec? I need to copy those numbers from your photos into the burner."

"Uh, one sec," Jennifer replied, a small frown on her face. "I'll spare you from accidentally seeing some gross veterinary pics on there. Let me find them for you."

Dana tried not to scowl as she waited for Jennifer to find the photos. At last, she showed the screen to Dana, who punched the various numbers into the burner phone's contact list.

"Thanks for that, and for doctoring me up. I'm going to step outside."

Gently closing the door behind her, Dana stepped into the warm still night and tried to find the scent of the cornfields that surrounded the rest area plaza. She dropped the tailgate to the Ford and sat, legs dangling like a child.

She sent her first text:

NEW PHONE IT'S DANANANANA

She immediately regretted using her old nickname. The screen lit up with an immediate reply:

HI IT'S ANGELALALA

Tears immediately sprung to her eyes. *Damn it, I'm just lonely.* She typed back:

I'M OK. IN HERSHEY PA. TELL THE OTHERS. I MISS YOU BESTIE. CALL YOU LATER.

The reply came in a few seconds later:

I MISS U 2 XOXO.

A tear fell onto the screen. Dana lay back in the truck bed, hitting her head on the wheel well.

"Shit."

# Chapter 15

*Rooster – Alice in Chains*

Angela startled awake.

"What the . . . ?"

It took her brain a few seconds to recognize what she was hearing: the jostling of the Jeep as it maneuvered over an uneven dirt path covered in a veiny lattice of exposed tree roots. From the splinters of sun through the woods, she guessed it was early. With a quick glance at her phone, she saw the time was 7:00 A.M. as well as a small volley of unread text messages from a group chat with Dana and Ashley. She looked over at Olsen in the driver's seat.

"There's some cold coffee in that cup," he growled as he wrestled with the steering wheel. "Beware: the bottom is probably a sugar bomb."

Angela chugged the cold bitter beverage until a wad of thick grainy syrup hit her lips. She would not have guessed Olsen took his coffee any other way than black, maybe even burnt. She tried to imagine him flicking a sugar pack at a deli, making small talk with the cashier, and stirring the granules with a wooden stick, right before stabbing a would-be robber in the eye. She admired his controlled rage, remembering the first time they had met in the bunker of New Jersey as enemies.

"It's fine," she said, trying to moisten her dry lips. "I've got some protein bars if you want one."

"Already had one, thank you."

He pulled the Jeep to the side of a wider section of the path and swung the vehicle around to face the trail they had just taken into the woods.

"We're here. First piece of advice: plan your exit. Part of any plan should be how you want it to end." He set the emergency brake. "That's why I'm facing the car in the direction of our egress."

"Noted, boss."

He swung open the door and stabbed the ground with his trekking pole before disembarking. Angela hopped out, grabbed their mostly empty rucksack, and secured it squarely to her shoulders. She understood her role was simply to be the mule for whatever Olsen intended to bring back from the safe house, but she was happy for the meager task and the chance to be his tactical apprentice. He studied her for a moment.

"The beanie," he said as he tightened his black leather gloves. "You might want to put that away."

Angela slid off her pink knit cap with a matching pom-pom and shook out her blond waves. "Done."

Olsen smirked. "Here." He handed her his paracord bracelet. "Pull it back so your peripheral is wide open and free of distractions."

"Have you had many women on your teams?"

"Mostly men. But a good solider is a good solider, period."

"Noted."

He stepped into the woods without any indication of following a trailhead or beaten footpath. Angela secured the bracelet around her hair and followed, jogging up to his side. He used two trekking poles, grunting at random intervals as they continued into the forestry. The silence was broken only by their footfalls, a single bird call, and finally, Angela's voice.

"So, how do you know the way in? Is there some kind of secret trail marker or blaze on the trees?"

"Memory and internal compass. The established trail is about half a mile back, but it's a shorter trek on foot the way that we're going in, although a little more up and down. Not ideal for my legs, but we'll come up on the weak side of the cabin. The front trail is still wide enough for a vehicle to wind through."

"Are we walking into a trap?" She listened for phantom noises of imaginary engines and shouts.

Nothing. The woods were as quiet as the desert in New Mexico.

"We're not expected, so there won't be a trap. But we're also not going to ring the doorbell with a bottle of cabernet and a coffee cake." He paused, turned his head back toward where they had come from, "No chatter from here on in until I give the word."

"Yes, sir."

The duo continued onward for an hour, pausing more frequently than Angela expected for Olsen to stretch his legs or rotate his hips in a stretch against a tree. She knew he was uncomfortable, and possibly in pain, but also that he would never show any sign of weakness while he assumed command. She didn't mind; she knew he was going to keep her, Dana, and the rest of TIARA alive as best as he could, and his experience was not to be underestimated.

His brief stories and anecdotes of coverts missions, obscured by generalities like "somewhere in Indonesia" or "it was a Middle Eastern country," had engaged her imagination. Before getting tangled up in all of this, Angela's biggest adventures had been on family vacations and at a few roller derby expos. She had often mused what life would have been like if she had made that baseball team and was crisscrossing the country to various Minor League Baseball stadiums, but somehow this life—even just this walk in the woods—was more exciting and rewarding. Having her own pair of motorized roller skates, of course, was an added bonus.

They began a short gradual ascent that leveled off with a view of a small square log-sided cabin about two hundred yards away. Olsen held up his hand to signal a stop and pointed toward the top of a nearby tree.

"I mounted that camera myself. We're in its blind spot right now," he whispered, a brief smile crossing his face. "I figured if I ever had to get out of Dodge while I was here with OHR, I had to create my own exit route that wasn't under any surveillance." He repositioned his poles and leaned forward on them with one arm, using his free hand to produce a small monocular tube from his jacket's chest pocket. "We're going to be here for a few minutes. Just standard surveillance to make sure no one's here now, even though I don't think anyone's been here in quite a long time."

Angela observed Olsen take a careful sip from the straw from his water bladder, custom sewn into the back of his tactical jacket. Everything he did was a lesson in preparation, caution, and a readiness for violence, if necessary. He was the foil to her own father and brothers who had always been too scared and polite to physically protect her from harm, preferring to negotiate and debate when things happened. She knew that every moment with Olsen was an opportunity to learn how to keep herself safe—to keep Dana safe—from harm. He tapped a text message into his phone and sucked his teeth.

"You have a signal all the way out here?"

"This isn't exactly an iPhone," he said, staring into the distance. "Okay. Let's go."

Their short walk led to a set of simple wooden porch steps. Olsen ran his fingers over the drab olive door, paint flaking off the steel underneath. Carefully, he slid a piece of the door trim to the side, revealing a hidden number pad, and punched in a sequence. He exhaled with relief as the door responded with a click.

"So far, so good. I thought they might have changed the code."

The interior of the cabin was not what Angela had expected. Corrugated steel panels lined the bottom half of the walls below sheetrock painted a light gray. A space above the simple fireplace mantel was adorned with multiple guns: a shotgun, two .22 caliber hunting rifles, and an AR-15, well-worn with a noticeably crooked barrel. A pile of folding cots was stacked neatly against the far wall next to the fireplace. A small square table surrounded by four folding chairs stood in the center, and to the side was a simple metal desk topped with a bank of tiny closed-circuit monitors and a large computer tower. One corner provided a makeshift kitchen, complete with a full-size refrigerator. Olsen opened it and placed his hands deep inside.

"Here," he said as he flipped Angela a plastic bag containing several bank-wrapped packs of hundred-dollar bills. "We'll take this to start. Next, I'm going to need to copy everything from that server. Rhodes was a bit paranoid, and I'm confident he's still using encrypted satellite uplinks."

"For what?" Angela asked as she lifted the AR-15 off its rack and pretended to track an imaginary target across the vaulted ceiling. Two ladders, one on each side, provided entry to a set of lofts.

"For everything. Rhodes is notorious for keeping every electronic communication he receives: text messages, emails, trail camera photographs. Anything he ever sent or was sent is data to him, and this is just one of many backup locations fed via satellite." Olsen placed a thumb drive into the computer and began to type on the dusty keyboard on the desk. "That gun you're holding—see that bent barrel?"

"Yep."

"I used that to pry open an armored car once. Kept a hostage alive."

"Another vague story from your past, rescuing some kidnapped VIP?"

"No." Olsen tapped away at the keys. "He was *our* hostage."

Lines of text streamed across the monitor as the files began to transfer to the thumb drive. Olsen tapped on the closed-circuit monitors in sequence as each one hiccupped with static at his touch. "These still work. The solar panels on the roof and the power cell under the floorboard provide the power, but without anyone coming up here for maintenance, electronics can still wear out . . ." Olsen paused. "That's odd."

The top right screen, providing an aerial shot of one area of woods, flickered twice as it came to life. A large black rectangle immediately came into view and continued out of frame only to appear on the next monitor. A third monitor from a camera facing out from the porch revealed a total of three black shapes coming into focus. Olsen saw them all at once: three bumpers. Three grills. Three trucks.

"Shit!" He heaved himself over to the table without his trekking poles. "Push this against the right window. Open both front windows. Get the shotgun and the rifle above it."

Angela froze as she stared at the third monitor. The three trucks came to a stop and two men emerged from each, wearing various combinations of camouflage, fatigues, and denim. The first two each appeared to have an assault rifle of some sort. Olsen broke her focus by tossing a box of shotgun shells onto the floor.

"Ever kill a man?"

She knew the answer in a heartbeat. "I can kill if I have to, sir."

He grabbed the shotgun himself. "Load the shells, like this. Then cock it." *Click.* "I'll call out the positions. We're home plate." He pointed out past the porch in several directions. "First base, second base, shortstop, third base."

"Yes, sir."

"You just need to fire in the direction I call out. I don't expect you to hit anything. Don't worry about that—just get the shot off as fast as you can in the general direction. You're going to get them to pop out for me."

"Got it." She rapidly opened and closed her fists. "Yes, sir."

"Just do as I say and stay on plan, and you'll be fine."

Olsen looked Angela deep in her eyes. She saw a reflected calm that anchored his ferocity. *He's got this. I got this.*

"Stay on plan. Say it."

"Stay on plan."

"Attagirl."

# Chapter 16

*Let's Go – Trick Daddy*

Angela inched to the edge of the window and peered through the hem of the translucent curtain. The mystery men crept along each side of their vehicles, arms drawn. The apparent leader stood up from his cover, held up his hand, and made a circular gesture in the air. A crack and a short hiss preceded the bullet that flew through his shoulder from Olsen's rifle.

"Angela," Olsen barked. "Shortstop!"

Her adrenaline bubbled as she popped up and fired the shotgun into the area between the center of the yard and the left edge. She rolled back to her cover area, glancing at Olsen as he sought his next target. He exhaled softly as he pulled the trigger, and a loud pop erupted outside her field of vision.

A barrage of semiautomatic gunfire rattled the armored front door of the cabin in retaliation. "Olsen!" she called out. "What did you hit?"

"I got a tire that time, rear vehicle. They'll need to cut wide around it to get out of here. First base!"

Angela popped up again and fired at the right side of the yard. The shotgun pellets tagged a man running to a tree, dropping him to the ground. "I got one!" *I can do this.*

"Stay focused," Olsen calmly responded, "and good job."

The cabin shook again with a staccato blast of bullets, still held in check by the plating inside the walls. She added another shell and crouched, ready for his next order. She felt the sweat lining her palms.

"Second base!"

She sprang up and fired again. A movement beyond the invader's vehicles distracted her momentarily. *Something else is out there.* Angela sank to the floor. "Olsen, I think I saw something—movement beyond their line."

"Their reinforcements," he said flatly. He inched his rifle to the left and fired another shot. The explosion outside was followed by a sharp scream. "I got the gas tank. Finally."

"Where to next?" she asked, wiping a new sheen of nervous perspiration off her forehead. Her fingers tightened around the handle and barrel, instinctively mimicking the grip of her warmup swing when she was on deck during a softball game. She looked over to see Olsen tapping away at his phone before he placed it on the table and pivoted his gun.

"On my mark, get three shots off to first base. First shot, second shot, *pause*, then the third. Each one just few yards apart. We need to pin down the men running up to that spot." He exhaled slowly. "One, two, pause, three. Now!"

She leapt up again and followed his cadence. When she paused between her second and third shots, he fired. The next volley of gunfire at the cabin cracked the safety glass of the window above her. Olsen's phone vibrated on the table with a notification.

"Hey, old man," Angela yelled, "who the hell are you texting at time like this?!"

"*Our* reinforcements." He smiled. "You might want to get a good view of the show."

Olsen beckoned her to crawl over to his position. He grunted with discomfort as he shimmied toward the window and pressed a piece of wood under the frame. It clicked and swung open to reveal a slim twelve-inch block of Lexan through which they could observe the battlefield.

Angela leaned her head against his to get a look. The invaders were continuing to march toward the cabin when a sudden blast of machine-gun fire erupted from the left side. A man, large and thick with dark skin and a white beard covering his neck, sprinted from tree to tree, his gun looking like a toy against his massive arms. He grabbed a grenade strapped to his tactical suspenders and hurled it into the parked caravan.

"Holy shit, he's huge! He's on our side?" Angela whispered.

"His name is Odemo," Olsen sneered, "and the one you *can't* see is Perry."

Olsen pulled back from their observation slot and placed his gun back on the table, the barrel facing the chaos. He glanced through the sight and fired four evenly timed shots, then held his palm toward Angela, indicating she should stay down. She held the shotgun against her body and peered back through the window slot again.

Odemo worked rhythmically, felling his targets one at a time. A rustling pile of leaves between two tree stumps rolled like a wave toward another one of the attackers and erupted as the man underneath in a ghillie suit assailed him with gunfire from a compact machine gun. The pile of leaves whooshed around him as he tossed the ghillie poncho into the face of another aggressor and followed it with a burst of bullets. The man had now fully emerged, confident and handsome, his tanned face cut with the angular lines of a lead actor in a Hollywood movie. He bleated a pattern of whistles toward Odemo.

"*That* is Perry."

Olsen nonchalantly fired again. Angela now noticed the shells from his rifle amassing on the floor as they rolled off the table.

"Why didn't you tell me we had reinforcements coming?" She began to crawl back toward her window. "That would have been useful information!"

Olsen staggered to his feet and braced the rifle against his shoulder.

"Can you get the door, please? And don't stand directly in front of me."

Angela scrambled toward it, grabbed the handle, and pulled it open. A rumbling of footsteps rattled the porch planks as one of the militiamen, unarmed, sprinted into the cabin.

"Down on the ground!" Olsen yelled as the man, startled that the door had opened for him, spun around with a pistol now in hand. Angela dropped to one knee and swept his legs out from under him, then delivered a smash to his head with the butt of her gun.

Olsen lowered his rifle and raised his eyebrows. "Good girl."

"Good soldier," a deep voice added. Odemo had entered the cabin and extended his hand to Angela. "Odemo. Sergeant Odemo Ndidi." His thin accent was from somewhere overseas that she couldn't place. She shook his hand.

"Um, Angela Costanza. Hi. Thank you?"

"You're welcome, ma'am." He patted Olsen on the shoulder, nodded, and turned his attention back to the doorway. "Perry's just cleaning up the remains." He smoothed the sides of his beard and glanced at Angela. "He's grabbing the wallets, keys, IDs, all of that. Anything that tells us their point of origin or exit, like plane tickets, parking stubs."

"Smart. Sure." Angela relaxed her grip on her shotgun and frowned at Olsen. "Again, when were you going to tell me we had backup?"

Olsen used his rifle as a cane to find a seat at the table in the center of the room. "I was going to tell you once I knew I was wrong about this not being a trap." He winced, and Angela saw that the pain had finally caught up to him physically, and mentally, after the period of exertion. "We got set up. Someone knew we were coming here."

Angela looked back outside at Perry adding another wallet from a dead body to a large plastic bag spotted with blood. She moved across the room and sat down next to Olsen while Odemo remained on guard at the door.

"Olsen? *Aaron?*" she whispered. "How do I know we can trust these guys?" She adjusted her grip on the gun.

"Odemo and Perry turned down a chance to join OHR."

Odemo snapped the closure on his holster, and she realized he was listening. "We're still pals, so to speak. When Olsen called me, I knew it was something much more important than a paycheck." He tightened the straps on his tactical suspenders. "Not everyone works for money."

Olsen breathed a deep sigh. "What about the others? Anushka, Sunny, Boo-Boo?"

"Boo-Boo?" Angela arched her eyebrow.

Odemo smiled. "Boo-Boo is finishing up his other gig. Sunny didn't reply, and Anushka is . . . on another mission." He nodded to Angela. "But we were enough today."

Angela walked to the door and surveyed the lifeless bodies of the mysterious militiamen strewn across the leaves. Perry moved quickly from vehicle to vehicle, emptying the glove compartments and firing a single shot into each one's serial number plates by their windshields. Angela pulled out her phone, squinting at the lack of bars. "I have to call Dana."

She looked back to her mentor. Olsen, on his feet again, scurried around the back of the cabin, unfolding two duffel bags. He jammed a handful of hard drives into each sack.

"We can't waste time trying to copy these at this point. Odemo, you and Perry finish outside, then head back the way you came in." He lifted a floorboard and began pulling various supplies from their hiding place. "Angela, help me load this up. It's mule time."

# *Chapter 17*

*Someday – Glass Tiger*

T his burrito tastes like shit."

Jennifer tossed the half-eaten remains of her dinner onto her plate and scowled. "Can someone flag down the waitress? I'm just going to load up on chicken fingers."

Nick sighed and raised his hand. After a solid day of driving he was exhausted, even with Dana and Jennifer taking turns so he could nap, but he still put on a brave face for both his girlfriend and his best friend.

Dana reached over slowly and placed her fingertips on Jennifer's plate. "So . . . you're not going to finish that?"

"Go ahead, girl." Jennifer held her hands up and smiled at Nick. "It's like we adopted an eight-year-old with a bottomless stomach."

He lowered his hand as the waitress approached the booth, smiling politely, and then pointed at the chicken finger special on the chalkboard without speaking.

Outside, the sky behind the St. Louis Arch faded into a deep blue, flecked with gray clouds. Dana knew the playful interaction between the women across from him was a small victory over the past thirty-six hours, but she knew more issues lay ahead once they got to New Mexico. She was painfully aware of the fact that he had dodged talking to her about their time apart, not to mention their reticence to speak to each other. The death of his father only compressed his mood into an even deeper funk. Dana realized she might need a hammer to break through his walls.

"So, how did you guys meet?" Dana chimed in, breaking the silence. She stuffed her face with another bite of burrito so she wouldn't say what else she was thinking: *I used to live with Nick. You guys are dating. We've both kissed him, so you might as well talk to me.*

Jennifer coughed somewhat uncomfortably and placed her hands flat on the table next to the warm plate of chicken fingers and fries that had just arrived. "Well, we met in class, unofficially," she said with a smile, "but actually we first really talked about a week afterward at the Stroudsberg."

"You were hanging out at my old bar!" Dana jumped in. "That's where we first met, too. Officially, that is." Nick replied to her wink with a sour face.

"Anyway, we ran into each other there. Nick was looking a bit like a sourpuss, like he is now," Jennifer said, wagging a chicken finger at him, "sitting at the bar alone. And I remember—wait, he was eating a bacon bleu cheese burger and studying some engineering diagrams, and I just, you know." She snapped her fingers. "Struck up a conversation."

Dana snapped her fingers. "And just like that."

"And just like that."

Nick snapped his fingers at each one of them. "Yeah, I remember the day a little differently. I was sitting at the bar just trying to . . . work out some things."

He gave Dana an almost imperceptible side glance that she understood to mean he had likely been thinking about her and their abrupt separation, wallowing at the place where he was most reminded of her.

"I brought printouts of some old diagrams from . . . an old project. I was so absorbed that I missed Jennifer's 'hello' when she sat down next to me. But she was persistent even though I was just, you know, in the zone."

Dana knew Nick to zone out when he was looking at the plans they had retrieved from the bunker where her father died. She wondered how he saw the world, following circuitry diagrams and mathematical formulas the same way her sister saw sentences and paragraphs like a magical matrix. Dana, although she had built her own skates following her mother's blueprints long ago, still felt challenged just ordering from a takeout menu, and now she sat, once again, in the company of geniuses.

"Jen and I had a computer science class together. She was taking it to learn how to create databases she planned to use to 'revolutionize veterinary science,' while I was just sleepwalking through it for the credit requirements. She asked me if could tutor her, and that was the start of things."

"That's cute," Dana responded, trying to mash down the jealousy brewing inside.

"So, we became study buddies," he continued. "And then we just kind of started dating." He looked over at Jennifer for reassurance to continue. "She was in the right place for me when I was in a bad place."

"Understood" was the best Dana could come up with.

"Jennifer just really made me feel confident. I mean, that is, after I lost my confidence after . . ." His voice trailed off, and he looked a bit helpless.

*Because of me,* Dana thought. She wanted to reach over and hug him, but before she could, he placed his hand on top of Jennifer's.

"I'm in a good place, thanks to you. With the obvious exception of the fact that I'm on the run from unknown murderers and my father just died."

Jennifer returned his grip and pressed her lips against the back of his hand. Dana was about to leave this torturous conversation when Jennifer grabbed a few bills from her wallet and placed them on the table.

"I got this. I'm going to the hotel to get a head start on sleep. I'll drive first tomorrow." She looked over to Dana. "And I know you two have some things you probably need to talk about." Standing up, she squeezed Dana's arm as she walked away.

Nick waved goodbye and began to sip the remains of his soda through his straw. Dana waited till she could see Jennifer cross the street before speaking again.

"Why do I feel like I'm in some kind of horrible rom-com right now?"

"Dana, you're my best friend."

"That you didn't talk to for months. I had to hear secondhand that your father died." Her throat tightened as her lip quivered. "Your dad was *my* friend, too. If I'm being completely honest, I deserved to hear it from you." She reached out her hand to grab his, then thought better of it. "It's me, *Dana*. I wanted to be there for you."

"I get that. And you coming to New Jersey for his funeral was amazing. You don't know what that meant to me." He tightened his jaw to affirm his composure. "I couldn't just *ask* you to come out, though. I just couldn't drop that bombshell on you out of nowhere, ask you to come and then follow that up with, 'Oh, by the way, seeing anyone? I am, and she's amazing!'"

Dana crossed her arms and looked away. She didn't want to get into things in the middle of a noisy restaurant. "Let's get out of here and take the long way back to the hotel."

The St. Louis skyline flickered to life gradually as lights came on across the high-rises. A white glow emitted from the baseball stadium at the heart of the city. Dana jutted her hands deep into the pockets of her mother's jacket, reminding herself to call Simone later to check in. Nick zipped up his coat as they turned down a street perpendicular to their hotel.

"Dana," Nick sputtered, "when you kissed me, at the airport, my head nearly exploded. I wanted so badly to just . . . find the right thing to say. And right now, I feel like I'm back in that moment. I don't know what to say."

"That makes two of us."

"So, we both had feelings for each other. We've established that."

Dana kicked at a broken bottle on the sidewalk and watched it clink and clunk toward a trash can. Sighing, she carefully picked up the brown glass and placed it in a nearby recycling can. Next to the bin, she spied another bottle that she also placed inside.

"Nick, truth?"

"Always truth."

"I feel like I'm back in that moment . . . sometimes. I just don't know what to do about it, about how I feel . . . sometimes." *Yes, you do. Kiss him.*

"Dana, can't we be friends like we were?"

"Yes. Well, *no.* I don't want to be friends quite like we *were.*" She huffed. "Like, I don't want to be jumping from one crisis or adventure to another—that's not normal. I just want us to be regular friends. Someone you call when you have an extra concert ticket, or you need a ride to the airport."

"Maybe not that last one," he replied, chuckling.

"Okay, fine. But you know what I mean. Normal friends. Normal people. And for now, nothing will be normal until I find Rhodes and stop him once and for all." She stopped to look back at the skyline.

"You will, Dana, you will. And I'm here, and I'm still along for the ride." He lightly touched her wrist. She suddenly felt heat radiate from her tattoo under his hand.

"I missed you, Nick." *And I love you.* Her stomach ached from what she wanted to say, exacerbated by her now regrettable decision to finish Jennifer's burrito.

"I'm right here—there's no one to miss. Hug it out, come on, Dee."

Nick placed his hand behind her head and cradled her against his shoulder. She rubbed her hands across his back. Her heart fluttered in her chest, simultaneously flying high in his presence and plummeting into the earth knowing he was with someone else.

"You are my best friend, Dana Jefferson."

"Ditto." *Ditto? Did I just say "ditto"?*

Dana relaxed her arms and let the embrace between them fall away. "Nick, do you love her?" She looked into his eyes, glowing in the streetlights and speckled with the reflections of the windows behind them. "I'm just, you know, asking how things are going."

"I think so. I mean, I do—but I don't want that to come between us. Dana, I still need your friendship. I've missed it more than you know." A lone tear fell down his cheek. "I'm a better person, a better me, ever since I met you."

"And since you met Jennifer, apparently. She's oddly okay about our relationship."

"Emotional honesty is something she always talks about. I've found the ability to better articulate my feelings since I met her. And I also owe a big part of that to you. You and me, we talked about everything. Anyhow, she's mature enough to not be threatened by my friendships, or my past." He smiled. "She's a big upgrade from Lindsey."

"*Big* upgrade." Dana still hated Lindsey, his girlfriend back when they first met, for taking advantage of Nick's kindness and loyalty, and she hoped Jennifer was everything Nick had framed her to be, despite Dana's own budding jealousy. She turned and started walking toward the hotel. "Come on, let's head back."

"Dana?" She turned on her heels, hoping he wouldn't notice the water pooling in her eyes. "Can we just walk one more block before we go back?" He sighed and ran his hand through his hair. "I have a feeling tonight is the last time we'll get to catch our breath until we get Rhodes." He held out his hand.

"Is hand-holding cheating?" she asked with a smirk.

"Not if we're truly just friends."

With this affirmation, she placed her hand in his.

"Emotional intimacy is still intimacy. I think I heard that on a talk show."

They shuffled across the street together. At the corner, Nick released her grip to pick up a crumpled can and lob it at a recycling receptacle, but it hit the rim and ricocheted back into the street. Afterward, he tucked his hands into his coat pockets.

# *Chapter 18*

*Til I Hear It from You – Gin Blossoms*

"THIS IS NOT A BED-AND-BREAKFAST!"

Dana winced as her mother's words pierced the dry New Mexico air, a stark change from the last leg of their trip through Kansas and Colorado. Simone charged off the porch and stomped toward Nick's truck just as Dana hopped out.

"Hi, Mom, I'm home?" Dana opened her arms for a hug but was met with her mother's crossed arms and a bootful of dust kicked onto her feet.

"Dammit, Dana—" Simone suddenly drew a deep breath followed by a raspy cough.

"Hi, Mrs. J." Nick stepped in front of Simone, saving Dana from her mother's lecture.

"Nick." Simone extended her arms and hugged him gently. "I am so sorry to hear about your father."

"It's alright, Mrs. J."

Dana watched Jennifer hesitantly step out of the truck and walk over to Nick. Her hair danced across Nick's face as she pressed against his shoulder.

"This is my girlfriend, uh, Jennifer. We've gotten into a bit of a mess." He glanced from Simone to Dana to Jennifer. "Kind of par for the course."

"So I heard," Simone huffed. "Hello, Jennifer."

One by one, everyone gathered on the porch behind Simone: Angela first, then Ashley, followed by the lumbering frame of Olsen on one cane.

"What's all this, then?" Olsen boomed. "Is that Nick?"

Dana sighed. "You guys remember each other, right? Olsen, this is the guy you shot because he paintballed you. Nick, this is the guy who shot you." Olsen crept down the steps toward the driveway. "An apology would be appropriate."

Olsen glanced back and forth between Nick and Jennifer. "Yes, an apology is in order, mate. I apologize over what happened when we were adversaries." A small smile crept across his face. "But to be honest, if I'd really wanted you dead, I wouldn't have aimed for your shoulder."

The color ran from Nick's face. "Say what?"

"You were using nonlethal arms, *paintballs*, so I only needed to incapacitate you." He held out his hand, palm up. "Sorry again, mate. Glad you're here, and I'm glad to have a second chance to do better."

Dana watched Nick grasp Olsen's hand and shake it once. A wave of relief washed over her as Nick smiled, as did Olsen, for once. Simone placed a hand on top of the apology gesture.

"Right. Now that everyone is all sunshine and butterflies . . . Dana, you're going to bunk with Angela and Ashley. Nick and Jen can have the spare bed in the study for their room. *Temporarily.*"

Dana had failed to notice that Angela had sidled up and placed an arm around her. Given the circumstances, Dana felt it was the safest place to be for the moment.

"Dana-na-na-na."

"Angela-la-la." They embraced. "I need a shower."

Dana tossed a plastic bag of toiletries onto the extra cot set up in the study where Jennifer and Nick would be sleeping. They were outside touring the ranch, so Dana took a second to decompress, flopping down on the stretched canvas. She looked up to see Angela standing in the doorway. She stepped in, closed the door behind her, and sat cross-legged on the floor. Dana shut her eyes, waiting for her to speak.

"Dana. *So.* Nick and his girlfriend are here. Now."

"Yep."

"And you're feeling a bit overwhelmed."

"Yep."

"Because you have feelings that were reawakened when you saw him."

"Yep."

"But you know you should be happy for him and support him if you truly care for him."

Dana opened her eyes when she felt Angela's hand pat her knee. "Ang, if you're going to make some kind of proclamation that you're still in love with me, just get it over with."

"Scooch." Angela pushed her to the side and sat on the edge of the cot, and the contraption promptly collapsed under the weight of the two women with a crack and a thud. Dana couldn't help but laugh despite the stinging pain in her tailbone.

"This was probably my mom's favorite cot from her prepper stash."

"Can't she just pick up another one from IKEA's apocalypse collection?"

"Can you see my mom shopping at a store where they paint directional arrows on the floor? Or any store, for that matter?"

Angela laughed and reset herself back into a seated pose on the floor. "I was going to make a nice little speech. Don't break my train of thought."

"Okay, fine." Dana settled herself across from her and placed her hands in Angela's. "Talk to me."

"When you asked me to come out here, I know you wanted me to be your muscle, your second set of eyes to keep tabs on Olsen. And it didn't hurt that I kicked his ass once before."

"Before he stabbed *you*, you might recall."

"I was winning before he cheated, you know."

"Ang, I was coming off horse tranquilizers. My recollection's a little fuzzy."

"Anyway, do you know why I agreed to come out here?" Dana opened her mouth but was shushed immediately by Angela's middle finger pressed to her lips. "I know you think I was tempted by the thrill of the adventure, 'finding my purpose,' or some other trope, but that's only part of it. I came out here because I *do* love you. As a friend. As a best friend." Angela paused and looked down. "Because you saved my life once—twice, really, and I will never repay that debt to you."

This was true. Dana had met Angela during the start of their tenure on the Asbury Angels roller derby team, but it was a leap-of-faith phone call that had led to their romantic bond.

"Ang, you don't have to—"

"It's okay. I know I don't talk about it, but that's why right now, I need to." Angela tightened her grip. "That night, when I had the pills on the counter, I just thought I wasn't worth anything to anyone."

"Angela—"

"And then you called me." Her voice broke. Dana felt her own throat tighten as Angela recalled the details from long ago: Dana had decided to call Angela late one night during one of her first lonely months in New Jersey, but she didn't realize at the time how important that call would be. Reliving this moment was like awakening a recurring nightmare.

"I was going to kill myself, but then this stupid, gorgeous girl with light-brown eyes asked me out to eat. And that's the moment I knew I didn't want to die, because I meant something to someone. And because you saved me that night, I would die for you."

Tears began to roll down each of their faces. They sat in silence amongst the footsteps and muffled voices from the rest of the house. Dana smiled through her tears as she remembered all the good things about Angela that had made her fall in love, back before giant robots and men with guns became her "new normal": her exuberance, her wit and sense of right, her sometimes misdirected anger that manifested at odd moments, like when a vending machine got jammed and was met with a glass-shattering punch.

If Angela wanted to talk about her true tragedy, the deep and dark memories, Dana would allow it, but it was a story that was not hers to bring up. She let the silence hang until Angela was ready to resume speaking.

"Dana, what I'm getting at is . . . you can love and care for Nick because he's your friend. You want him to be happy. And to succeed. But you also have to realize that when someone isn't perfect for you or when your lives won't go on together, that's okay. We're sisters now. And that's how I love you." Angela sniffled and giggled. "Even if you are a gorgeous idiot."

"And you're an ill-tempered, gorgeous mess." They leaned together and hugged, leaving tears in each other's hair. "Come on, let's clear out of here. And my God, girl, you're gorgeous even when you're sobbing. Your hair smells stupidly good right now."

"Your mom has great shampoo."

"She makes it herself with cactus and horse manure."

Angela shoved her back and skewed her face. "WHAT?"

"I'm kidding. But would it surprise you if she actually did?"

# Chapter 19

*Hallogallo – Neu!*

Nick changed the channel on the television, searching for something mindless. He had hoped to find sports, any kind of sports, but it turned out he had been mistaken in thinking that being closer to the West Coast meant more games would be on at this time of night. That was probably better anyhow, he reasoned. Even though Jennifer was happy to tag along when he went to a Minor League Baseball game, she had never watched any of the big network sports; instead, she had grown up a soccer fan. She walked into the study now—their temporary sleeping quarters—with her hair almost dry from a shower, wearing a pair of borrowed shorts and a classic rock T-shirt from Ashley. As she tossed her dirty clothes onto the cot across from the bed, he turned off the television.

"Hey, Nicky." She sat on the bed next to him, draped her arm across his chest, and kissed him lightly on his neck. "How are we doing?"

*We.* She always said that when she meant *him* but wanted to open the door to talking about feelings. Tonight, he had too much going on to want to share.

"All right. Just . . ." he said, placing a heavy hand on the top of his head, "a lot going on."

"Anything weird about being here? I mean, in this house."

"No, it's okay. I didn't really spend much time here. Our other house . . ." He caught himself saying "our," but it was too late. "That place that was more like home."

"Well, I'm thinking we might as well take advantage of the getaway, enjoy the ranch and all of that. If you want to talk, we can talk." She traced her fingers across his thigh. "And if you don't want to talk, I'm here. We can just, you know, make it a night in."

He gently placed his hand over hers and relocated it to his knee. "I'm not exactly in a good place."

"Oh." She fell back against the bed and let her hands fall on her stomach. She lifted her shirt to drum a rhythm on her bare skin. "Is it . . . her? Be honest."

"No." Although that wasn't completely true; of course it was Dana, but it was also a matter of respecting a house where they were uninvited surprise guests. His dad had always told him to be polite inside someone else's home, to be available to help out if a host asked.

"Let's just get some sleep, then. At least when we wake up, we don't have to run somewhere new."

The lamp on the nightstand clicked as Nick shut it off. The noises of the house in the background quieted, except for the occasional *tap-thud-thud* of Olsen lurking from room to room. Jennifer's breathing whistled in his ear, her arm thrown across his hips as she fell asleep. The ambient light from the New Mexico sky poked through the curtains. He didn't know how long he stared through the slit, but it was long enough that he observed a star moving slightly through its nighttime path, crossing from one side to the other. Jennifer stirred, her hand sliding up to his chest as her breath rolled across his cheeks.

He had never felt so alone in his life.

# Chapter 20

*Make Yourself Comfortable – Eydie Gormé and Steve Lawrence*

The laptop hummed and whirred as the accelerating fan speed cooled the processors. Ashley lifted it off the kitchen table and slid an overturned plate under each side to increase the ventilation.

"Running pretty hot." She tapped the many tentacles of USB cables linking the computer to the disk drives splayed around her, some linked to external power cords that ran across the floor into the outlet next to the sink. "I didn't expect this much data."

Olsen uncrossed two of the power cords and examined the setup.

"We got lucky. The backups Rhodes sent via satellite to the safe house were as fresh as last week, which gives us an up-to-date timeline. Given not only the volume but the conditions of our arrival and exit, it wasn't going to be very efficient to just copy them onto the drives I brought with me." Olsen slid another hard drive, untethered, across the tabletop. "This one. That's the last of the batch."

"This guy really did document everything." Ashley tapped at the spinning clock icon on her screen.

"*Everything.*" Olsen sat in the chair next to Ashley. She glowered over her shoulder.

"You don't have to literally look over my shoulder. I can do all of this myself," she said, sliding the laptop slightly to the right for his viewing, readjusting the plates underneath.

"Sorry. Well, not sorry, actually." He grabbed the table and pulled himself closer to her side. He found himself once again in awe of her intelligence, forgetting that she was just a teenager. "Anything else we can feed your beast?"

"It's technically not *my* beast, since I borrowed some of the code from an undergrad I met online. Well, not *borrowed*, but asked him to write some sections to clean it up." She smiled as the spinning clock icon disappeared and the fan rotors began to slow. "I think we're past the worst of the overclocking now on the processor. It's starting the index."

A black box with cyan letters manifested on screen. A single pixel in the middle of the box began to expand in a veinlike pattern, some arteries changing color as they filled out.

"This is 3D, actually, and technically quantum." Ashley used the mouse to drag the shape, rotating it and then clicking on various sections so that the veins blinked off and on in new shapes. Olsen marveled at the image, a constantly changing rainbow-hued crystalline structure made of text, a sentence diagram exponentially expanded across millions of words.

"How are you supporting this on just the laptop?"

"My friend, the coder? He set this up on a locked cloud server. I'm just grabbing little bits at a time. Here." She typed "Aaron Olsen," and immediately a bolt of blue lines surged through the patterns. "That's all of your emails and texts from the sources." She picked up the unconnected hard drive from the table. "Except this one."

"That can't be correct. I've never used my full name in any correspondence."

She clacked on the keys, and an email transcript popped onscreen. "That's you, right?"

"Aye. How did it do that?"

"It's text profiling. Anything you've said, allegedly, in these transcripts is confirmed and iterated through the way you speak, the way you type, the way you've relayed an order or direction from party A to party C. That's how my software was originally intended to work, to use 'influenced writing' to assist in verifying old letters and ghostwritten documents." Ashley held up her fist and pointed the knuckles at Olsen, who only stared back. "Way to leave my fist bump hanging. Anyway, this is technically reverse-engineered AI, a large language-learning model but highly trainable on specific individual language. That's kind of a big deal."

"So it is." He at last gently bumped her fist. "What can we do now with it?"

"I can crawl the dark web and start looking for contextual matches, see if Rhodes pops up, and then target where he lurks as soon as he makes any updates. The risk of using most of the off-the-shelf AI programs is that once something is added to the algorithms, it's 'out there' on the internet. This thing works like a tethered switching station. The data we feed it goes out but is immediately purged from the code as it returns the results."

"I'm trying to follow, Ashley, I really am." He narrowed his eyes to try to scan new lines of text exploding on the display.

"It just makes sure that anything we put in doesn't then reside on the internet or the dark web accidentally."

"Aye." Again, he was impressed. "That's still some massive computing power. And nearly impossible in real time."

Ashley frowned. "It starts slow, but every time it gets a hit, it adds to the AI logic and then tethers the source. As it moves along, it autocorrects and gets faster."

"How fast?"

"I can't say. I've only done this with scans of essays from Lord Byron and letters from Tom Clancy. It's pretty funny to see when Tom's lawyer was replying to Mrs. Clancy about the Orioles instead of him." Her stone face met Olsen's gaze. "What? He had part ownership in the team!"

"You're a remarkable girl." Her potential was limitless, and he felt a small tinge of envy at her wide-open future. She had choices he would never have again. "I'm assuming there's a reason why you're still here in New Mexico and not at Oxford. Or Langley."

"I am here until I am eighteen, and then I plan to go to Princeton," she said with a smug smile.

"Your father did some work there, I hear, in concert with the Plasma Physics Lab. Allegedly, he was running models of genetic markers with their computers. I'm not sure how that works—not my field of expertise." He looked down at his lap. "Of course, you probably knew that."

"Mom told me." Ashley unplugged a completed scanned drive and inserted the last one into the squid of cables. "Last text load. Man, this guy even had his fax images scanned and stored. Here's the warranty and instruction manual for a hot water heater—"

"Our main focus is to find any repeat correspondence *not* on the list of One Hundred Roads agents I gave you. And anything involving Silver."

"She's an old woman, right?"

"No, a technocrat arms dealer, white male, maybe in his forties or fifties."

"There's problem number one," Ashley said as her shoulders slumped. "Silver's a sixty-year-old woman, according to the text patterns I'm seeing so far."

"That's a pretty big bug in your software."

"It's not. These phrases are all matching lingo and linguistics of a female who was either raised on pop culture from about fifty to sixty years ago or was *born* fifty to sixty years ago. I could be a little off with the age, of course, but Silver's definitely a woman. You can't unlearn that type of bias. Even a trained actor can't be in character twenty-four hours a day. Except maybe Andy Kaufman."

"And he was insane." Olsen scratched the day-old stubble on his chin. "How would *you* know about Andy Kaufman?"

"I like professional wrestling. He's part of the history."

"You really are a remarkable girl, Ashley."

"And apparently, so is Silver."

# Chapter 21

*Land of Confusion – Disturbed*

Dana dipped the dishes into the soapy sink water as Simone clicked on the television for the evening news. Simone had thrown together dinner for this newly assembled army, but once they had all sat down, Dana observed the distance in her mother as she spoke in short, sometimes curt phrases and glanced repeatedly at her smartwatch to keep an eye on the house monitors. After dinner, Ashley had retreated to the bedroom to continue to work on her research, and Angela snuck off to take a shower before the hot water was all used up. Dana was wiping down the counters when she noticed her mother standing frozen with the remote.

"Mom?"

"Everyone out here, *now*. Sit down. And I do mean *sit down*."

Simone rewound the DVR of the broadcast a minute or so. Dana flopped onto the couch as Olsen, Nick, and Jennifer each took a seat.

"Good evening, everyone, I'm Jill Joyce. News Four opens tonight with breaking news of what is being described by the Department of Homeland Security as a pair of terrorist attacks, one at a power station in Garden City,

Kansas, and another at Sioux Falls Light and Power Hydro Plant in South Dakota. Police in both cases were alerted to a group of people in military fatigues on motorized roller skates—Is that right? Yes? Okay, then—who were attacking and destroying the main power distribution at each site. We're being told as many as twenty public service employees may have been killed in the two incidents. We go now to Ross DeBois from our sister station who is on-site in Kansas."

"Thank you, Jill. It is absolute chaos down here as police and emergency services are struggling in the darkness to treat the victims and recover those who did not survive. We've been told that at approximately ten P.M., an organized group of about ten individuals—some who were described as having mechanical limbs and all on some type of self-propelled roller skates—swarmed the three power stations here, including this main hub behind me, injuring and even killing employees who were simply doing their job.

"Beyond what is happening here, with the grid completely blacked out, the entire area is facing tough conditions. While we await word on whether the National Guard will be deployed here, a local civilian military group, the Kansas Roads Freemen, has been assisting in keeping the peace. We spoke to one of them earlier tonight. Here's what he had to say."

"I think people have many misconceptions about what a civic organization like ours can do. We train for crisis assistance, command and deployment structures—many of the same things first responders do. I think we even do a better job than the local sheriff's office and the other services funded by elected officials. The National Guard isn't here, but we are. You can count on the Kansas Roads Freemen to be here for the community."

"Thank goodness for these patriots. Back to you, Jill."

Olsen drove his fist into the back of the couch. "They're a goddamn militia! Say the word! *Militia!*"

"*Aaron*, hush," Simone hissed.

". . . in Sioux Falls, it appears a devastating set of explosions were set off. Local authorities have confirmed several have been killed, and the entire county has been left without power. We cut now to the local law enforcement briefing there, currently in progress."

Dana looked over her shoulder at Olsen, his eyes glued to the screen. When she turned back, a plainclothes officer stood at a podium, dabbing sweat from the thick moustache on his round ruddy face.

". . . we believe these men are part of a concerted, coordinated effort but currently have no distinct information on their organization. We did not receive any threats preceding this attack and have not received any regarding additional attacks. The National Guard has already been authorized by the governor to assist, but in the meantime, we are fortunate to have the already mobilized Liberty Roads civic defense organization assisting us by standing guard in the commercial districts to prevent looting. Food and water are already being provided by Liberty Roads, as well as portable generators to critical care facilities for the elderly."

"Have there been any outbreaks of civil unrest?"

"We are aware of at least three injuries involving altercations with Liberty Roads. I have no further details at this time."

The report ended. Simone turned off the television.

"Son of a bitch!" Olsen slammed his cane against the floor. "This is what Rhodes has been up to: dismantling infrastructure. It's the same bullshit we used in backwater towns in third-world countries! Create a crisis, showcase the inability of the government to help, then provide the false flag saviors. In this case, *the militias*." He leaned forward to gather his cane and fell to his knee. Jennifer shot up and helped him to his feet.

Olsen leaned on his cane, his jaw tensing as he ran his hand through his hair.

"Dammit. We need to know where he'll strike next."

Nick raised his hand. "It's just been power supply-related so far. We can start to make a list of targets based on that."

Olsen didn't respond. He slunk over to the mantel and turned away from the group, tapping his fingers in silent contemplation.

Dana refused to let him shut down. She didn't want him here, but they *needed* him to stop Rhodes. She stood up and walked up behind him. *This is my team, not his.*

"Speak up, Aaron! What's next?"

He turned to face her. At this moment, he didn't look like the stiff-jawed, cold, calculating militant leader she knew, back when he was her nemesis. His eyes were soft, his brows raised.

"I don't know." He struggled to straighten up to full height. "He's recruiting in and around the Rockies. He's hit the Midwest." Dana saw a flash of an idea in Olsen's eyes. "It's a test run."

"This was practice?" She grabbed the TV remote and turned the set back on. "We're talking about *practice?* Rhodes just killed several people!"

"All power stations and infrastructure nodes should go on full alert based on this. But they can't all do it like *that*." He snapped his fingers. "The Eastern Continental United States is dense. He won't go there. The Midwest is sparse—good to hit and run, so to speak. So . . . west."

"West? He's going west? That's your conclusion as our tactical advisor?"

Nick crossed the room, his thumb tucked under his chin. "Actually, Dana, it makes sense. Look at the Colorado River. It's a gigantic extension cord for water and power, basically, feeding through several states. You hit any point on there and it creates serious downstream issues." He glanced at the TV, where a newscaster on mute spoke in front of a photograph of an artificial leg with a skate attached. "Looks like they got a good close-up on one of the security cameras."

Dana swallowed. "They look just like our skates."

Nick nodded. "Hold that thought. I'm still working through this 'go west' theory . . . Oroville, Folsom, Shasta—I know those. Power stations."

"You know them?" Olsen said.

"Well, I know *of* them. Remember, I work for an electric company, and I studied these in class. There are a few dozen hydros in California alone. But what if Rhodes is going bigger?"

"How so?"

"Cut the power. Choke the water. Start a forest fire. I mean, it's California. You can make a real mess." Nick turned back to the TV and the shots of ambulances and firefighters scrambling onscreen. "A real mess."

"He'd need a lot of manpower, and firepower, to pull this off." Olsen looked up, lost in thought. "I know this is all very broad speculation, very broad, but it's better than nothing." He continued gazing up at the high ceiling, holding silent as the group waited for him to continue.

"When we would work an op, to sow civil unrest to seed a rebellion, we'd take out the infrastructure first: power, water, medical. But to get the local population to cross the Rubicon to revolution, you target the most vulnerable people. Those with nothing to lose—the poor. He's recruiting from the poorest areas of the country, and if, *if* he attacks California, the most vulnerable and most affected will be the farmers, the migrants, the reservations that rely on legacy land and water rights. Rhodes knows it's easy to bait a battle along racial lines." He closed his eyes. "It's what we've done. Before."

This was not what Dana had expected to hear, but she knew Olsen spoke the truth. Dana slowly recoiled and turned to gauge the reactions around the room. Simone was looking down, hands on hips. Jennifer cupped her hands over her mouth. Nick was staring directly at Dana.

"Okay, then, there's no time to waste," Dana replied. "Where does he go next?"

Nick interjected again. "We look up the power plants, the big and old ones where security and maintenance might be the weakest." He turned to

Jennifer. "What do you think?"

Dana jumped in. "With all due respect, she's not part of the team." She was not going to involve another innocent person who could be put in harm's way; she had done enough of that already since she first became entangled with One Hundred Roads. "Nick, neither are you. Not anymore."

Before he could respond, Simone interrupted. "Dana, I vote Nick stays. Jennifer is free to choose." Mother and daughter stood on opposite sides of the couch. "This is a *team*, Dana."

Jennifer nodded to Dana. "I'm staying. I can help—just tell me what you need. You don't have any other people, do you?" Her lips parted, awaiting Dana's answer. "Anyone?"

Olsen shook his head ever so slightly once at Dana.

"There's just Dan," she blurted. "He's the only resource we *know* we have, our federal agent liaison. He's out of town right now, right, Mom?"

"Errand boy running errands," Simone answered. "When he comes back to town with my supplies for PEG, we can give him the rundown. I'm sure he'll know more details about the two terrorist attacks."

"Who's Peg?" Jennifer interjected. Ashley and Angela entered the living room, each wearing pajamas and sweatshirts.

"PEG is a robot," Ashley volunteered. "Mom's fixing her up. She's like a power suit but also can be autonomous." Simone shook her head. "Well, not yet. But she's, like, seven feet tall, and if you wear her, you can lift heavy loads and enter fires—stuff like that."

"You have a robot suit? Here?" Jennifer's jaw slacked.

Olsen clacked his cane twice against the hardwood to get everyone's attention.

"Focus, please? We need to plan. *Now.* Nick, start mapping out California—every power plant, the flow of water and power there and in the surrounding states. Ashley, give him a hand and then compare the list with your software. If Rhodes has talked to any local contacts—plant managers, cops, senators, anyone he can manipulate or blackmail—they go on the list. Then we send the list to Jameson, but only when we're absolutely ready. We still assume Rhodes has someone on the inside, somehow." He plodded to the kitchen. "I'm putting on coffee."

"Olsen," Dana said, "no coffee. We're not going to save the country before dawn. We need sleep. *I* need sleep. Anyone who wants to stay up for extra credit, go ahead, but I'm going to bed now. *Photograph* says we attack this in the morning."

Jennifer, Angela, and Ashley took her advice and walked past her to their respective rooms. Dana started heading to her room as well. She felt sick— sick of all of this, sick of Rhodes, sick of the invisible string pulling her wherever he was sowing death.

She stopped where the hall began and turned back. Nick was now seated in the kitchen with the laptop and Olsen was opening a bag of coffee beans. Simone remained in the center of the living room, motionless, staring out the patio doors into the backyard.

"Mom?" she called out.

"Go to bed," her mom replied with a breathy sigh. "Get some sleep. I'll be in the barn with PEG a little longer."

With a flippant shrug, Dana turned to Olsen. "And what about you?"

"I'm going to help Nick." He looked away from her, staring out the window over the sink into the black. "But truth be told, we may only have one true option. Tomorrow, I think I have to do what Jameson asked and call Silver."

# Chapter 22

*Steady, As She Goes – The Raconteurs*

Chillier air than Olsen expected seeped through the open patio door. The steam from his coffee danced in the breeze, sifting its black aroma over the kitchen table where his phone lay dormant. He tapped the screen to activate the dial pad, then paused, swallowing the bile in his throat brought up by the call he was about to make. Ashley sat next to him and tapped her spoon on her cereal bowl to get his attention.

"Do you want me to call? Are you nervous? I really don't mind."

He allowed himself a smile. He couldn't always pinpoint when Ashley would shift from cynical, sarcastic child to wunderkind genius, but her feedback and guidance were always appreciated. At this moment, she was speaking like a helpful parent—albeit one dressed in a pink knit hat with cat ears and a tank top advertising some pop band he had never heard of.

"I can do it. I just need to get my game face ready."

"That's not a phrase you use. At all."

"Thank you for the observation." He tried to overanalyze Ashley as practice, a necessary reassurance to himself that his mind was as sharp as possible before speaking with Silver. "Ashley, what's the deal with you and cereal? You eat a very high volume of it. Even though your mother is a very good cook, you know."

"Nutritional efficiency," she deadpanned. "Easily transportable, easy to prevent spoilage, quantities are precisely measured for consistent nutritional value, tastes great, and Mom says that back in the day, they used to put toys inside the box. That's kind of charming, in an old-fashioned way." She licked her spoon and folded her hands under the chin. "You're avoiding the call. Just do it. It can't be worse than asking someone out on a date."

"And you have how much experience in that realm?" He immediately regretted poking her a little too hard with that comment, given Ashley's clear interest in any conversation involving Dana and Angela, Dana and Nick, Nick and Jennifer. Simone had also made subtle references to Ashley being stranded in their isolated kingdom without any suitors knocking down the castle doors.

He sat back for a moment and folded his arms. "Sorry. I am a little nervous because of the high stakes. And my general dislike and distrust of Silver, of course."

"Apology accepted." She turned the phone to face her, dialed the number left by Director Jameson, turned on speakerphone, and spun it back toward Olsen before hitting the call button. "Go for it."

The speaker barely registered a single ring before the party on the other side picked up. A monotone female acknowledged, "Aaron Olsen, you've finally called back."

"Hello, Penny." He bit his lip and rolled his eyes. "And how are you today?"

"Please," she replied dismissively, "don't waste time on pleasantries. You've had more than enough time to admit you can't move forward without Silver's aid."

Olsen spied Ashley quickly typing into her phone's notepad, her lips quivering as she recited the conversation quietly to herself and transcribed it in real time. *Good girl.*

"You've got me there, Penny. But I think Silver would be interested to know that I have some information that may . . . interfere with his own plans."

"This is about Rhodes, correct?"

"Correct. He has a militia, or rather a consortium of militias that he has been gathering to create a domestic civil uprising. I'm sure you've seen the media reports about organized groups of skaters attacking infrastructure."

Penny took a moment to answer. "We have. Unfortunately, we had a hand in building the technology those skating rogues are using. Rhodes provided a pair of prototypes to us. A simple contract job, obscured and gone sideways thanks to his betrayal."

Ashley waved for his attention and mouthed, *Those were my skates!* He nodded.

"Penny, the prototypes he brought you were created by Simone Jefferson," he said, holding up a finger to Ashley. "I'm sure you are familiar with her work, and her husband's as well."

"Yes. We are quite aware of the Jeffersons." More silence followed.

"Penny, I believe that Rhodes is just warming up for something big, like a critical infrastructure failure, maybe in California. For the entire state of California. I know his tactics. You know his tactics. *Silver* knows his tactics." Anger stirred in his stomach. He leaned in closer to the phone. "I'm quite frankly surprised that Silver *allowed* this domestic situation to manifest."

"It was not something we conceived. You are probably correct on Rhodes's next course of action, given his—and your—prior history. I agree." Another silence, then a deep sigh. "And you want Silver to fix this mess. Need I remind you that we are not a military organization?"

"I know you are not. That's why you manipulate others into doing the dirty work of your grand agenda." He forced himself to sit back in his chair, lest his temper cloud his words. "I need to find and stop Rhodes."

"I agree. It was a terrible lapse in judgement, thinking he was going to take this work, our work, overseas. He came to us with a false premise, but now we're seeing the execution of his plan on domestic soil."

"Surely you knew he was arrested and escaped, and that he was not exactly doing the Lord's work here."

"We had inaccurate information. He has a very good network of informants and information distortion agents. Look, Olsen, let's cut past the exposition here. What do you want from Silver? If you knew where Rhodes was going to attack, you would have called the proper authorities or be planning your own, I don't know, countermeasures?"

"Correct."

"You certainly don't have the funds to hire Silver's expertise and technology."

"Correct." He glanced at Ashley and smiled. She returned a slightly confused look. "But Penny, Director Jameson told me you need something from me, too." *Checkmate.*

"We cannot have Rhodes going rogue and setting back our ideology. You and your ragtag group are indeed the closest and best group to help obscure our involvement and reset the playing field. Now that we know your location"—Olsen placed his palm over his face. *Of course you do now*—"we will contact you for a tête-à-tête in person. And tell the Jefferson *girls* we look forward to meeting them." The screen of Olsen's phone went blank as the call ended.

Ashley finished typing and let out a short sharp exhale. "Phew. I got all of that." She scrolled through her transcript. "I have questions."

"I'm sure you do, but I don't know if I'll have all the answers."

"First, who is Penny? Is she the handler or secretary or part of Silver's board?"

"Silver is a man, not a board. Penny is the go-between."

"I'd disagree. She seems like she's got a lot of chutzpah. Second question: What's this deal with Penny's agenda?"

"*Silver's* agenda," he corrected, "is world-building. Silver believes that governments are too bloated and self-interested to move globalization forward, so it falls on the elitists to make the world a better place. Something about the 'moral burden of success is sharing it with the world,' I believe is how Silver puts it."

"I disagree with that," she said, "but we can discuss global politics later. Third question: Have you personally ever killed any children on a mission?"

Her words surprised him, especially coming from someone not much older than some of the victims of the particular mission that had sown his distrust in Silver. He spun the phone on the table and let it come to a stop before picking it up and placing it in his pocket.

"Did you do something because of Silver?" Ashley asked.

"It was not intentional. And it was not direct." He stood, grasping his cane as his hand tremored, this time with guilt, not nerve damage. *This girl does not deserve to hear this . . . not today.* "But I am responsible. And I assure you, I will do everything I can to make sure it never happens again."

Ashley said nothing in response. She looked at him with a stillness he found unsettling, as he was sure her mind was processing the coldness of his former life and the other unspoken sins he had committed. She stood slowly and then took deliberate, tentative steps over to him and stood chest to chest.

"Ashley—"

She placed one arm around his back, then the other, and pulled him gently into a hug. "'Good can imagine Evil; but Evil cannot imagine Good.'" She squeezed again. "W. H. Auden said that. You're a good person, Aaron Olsen."

# Chapter 23

*Xanadu – The Winery Dogs*

The GPS indicated the van was several miles away from the rendezvous. Dana had been navigating all morning while Ashley drove, as she was more comfortable traveling unmarked roads and driving in the desert. Olsen sat behind Ashley, offering short cryptic bursts of information on the way. His current calm demeanor was a striking contrast to his morning rundown after he had woken the sisters up to prepare for the meeting with Silver.

*Silver.*

The name didn't evoke any emotional reactions for her, juxtaposed by Olsen's facial twists and quiet growls. Until this morning, she had only known that Silver was a man who provided technology to the black ops forces working both behind and against world governments. Olsen, however, painted a different and much deeper portrait.

"Remember, we aren't walking into a happy meet-and-greet." He sipped from his coffee, conserving the lukewarm brew. "I was really surprised at the timing of Penny's initial call to set up this meeting . . . a little too fast."

"Well, you're a special man, Mister Olsen, and you attract some weirdos," Ashley replied, laughing to herself.

"Dammit, I think we're late."

He pointed toward the windshield at the dark blip in the sky slowly approaching. As it drew closer, Dana could make out a twin-engine propeller plane turning slowly into a wide circle. The propellers mounted on the end of each wing pivoted ninety degrees, pointing upward as it hovered in place. "That's an Osprey."

"Nope, that's definitely not a bird," Dana said.

"Not a *bird*. It's a V-22 Osprey, or vertical takeoff and landing craft—VTOL. It's in use by some armed forces as a candidate to replace Blackhawk helicopters. If we're able to use Odemo and Perry again, they can bring in Boo-Boo; he has access to one."

"Boo-Boo?" Dana blurted. "Are you seriously considering using a pilot named Boo-Boo?"

"We'll cross that bridge if we come to it." He tapped Ashley on the shoulder. "Slow down as you approach. No surprises."

The van pulled to a stop as the heliplane's rotors slowed after touchdown.

"Stay frosty. I speak first. No impulsive moves. Just listen and answer questions directly." Olsen placed his phone under the seat. "Phones in the van. *Ashley, repeat everything I just said.*"

"'Stay frosty. I speak first. No impulsive moves. Just listen and answer questions directly.'" She yawned. "'If you have to pee, use a bottle or something. We can't be late.'" Olsen blinked and turned toward her. "You said that about three hours ago."

"Good girl. Everything, and I mean *everything* Silver says, you commit that to your funny little eidetic memory, and we'll run the transcript into your program back at the ranch."

"Technically, it's more like hyperthymestic syndrome, but close enough."

"I am truly the least useful thing in this van," Dana said to no one except herself.

"My left foot begs to differ," Olsen replied with a flat smile and wink. "Come on, mates."

The cargo door on the aircraft opened, and a tall thin woman in a white pantsuit with a white scarf loosely wrapped around her neck stepped out. She opened a white umbrella to shield herself from the midday sun and walked with confident steps across the brush. Standing several feet from the trio massed in front of the van, she flicked her wrist to check her smartwatch and sighed.

"You're late."

"And you're not Silver," Olsen replied. "Hello, Penny."

"There has been a series of incidents that I am afraid have altered his availability."

"Is he coming?"

"He's dead."

"When?"

"Several days before our call."

Dana noticed Olsen's hand moved ever so slightly toward his belt where he usually carried his sidearm. She felt Penny's eyes boring into her.

"Well, hello there, Dana Jefferson." Penny extended a hand, which Dana quickly shook. Penny's palm felt cool and dry yet firm as her grip closed. "And this must be Ashley. You two have both become quite the outliers."

"You came to us, so talk," Dana barked. Olsen bit his lip and leaned forward on his cane.

"What my colleague meant was—"

A woman's voice shouted from the interior of the heliplane.

"What she meant was that she wanted to know how much shit we've all stepped in."

Director Jameson emerged from the fuselage, her short silver hair framing her glasses. She wore hiking boots and brown cargo pants with a tan ribbed long-sleeve shirt, much different from the usual black suits Dana had grown accustomed to from their brief previous in-person meetings.

"Director Jameson—oh, excuse me, *Carmen*," Dana cooed. "Is this the part where you reveal you're in cahoots with the bad guys?"

"Quite the opposite," Carmen retorted. "I've always been the middleman between you all, haven't I? There's an individual from Rhodes's attack crew being kept under lock and key at a military hospital right now. He was captured before media came on-site in Sioux Falls." She glanced at Dana's feet. "Prosthetic legs with what look like your skates bolted to his ankles."

Dana scoffed. "So, why are we here? Why do you need us?"

"Despite all our secrecy, there are some things you can't hide from some people." Carmen nodded to Penny. "She called me last night to verify a few things about the situation, especially regarding Olsen being on the 'good guy' team now. Then our conversation went down the rabbit hole."

"And *she* stepped through the looking glass," Penny said. "Carmen did provide her side of the events, which backed up yours, Mr. Olsen. My apologies. Anyhow, as you probably surmised, the prototypes that Rhodes provided to Silver were indeed Ashley's skates, and I connected them to my neurologically integrated prosthesis components."

"You built those monsters on purpose." Dana's head pounded. A white heat burned in her temples. "So, you directly helped him create those murderers on skates to kill innocent people." She clenched her fists and spit on the ground. "I've a good mind to kick your ass."

"*Dana.*" Olsen's face reddened and his veins began to protrude from his neck. "Please bring the theatrics down a notch."

"No, she makes a good point," Penny said. "It was no trite lapse of judgement. Rhodes has done plenty to ferry my goals, so I failed to realize his recent radical pivot in ideology." Penny twirled the umbrella lithely between her fingers.

Ashley tapped Dana's foot. "Hmm?" Dana met Ashley's gaze. Her eyes narrowed as Ashely mouthed the words: *She's Silver.*

"Speak up, young miss." Penny strode over to Ashley and held the umbrella over them. "Speak *up*."

"Silver isn't dead. *You're* Silver. You used 'we' on the phone the other night, which caught my ear, but today there's no 'we' at all, just 'I.'"

"Observant little girl. I suspected I was on speaker phone with Olsen. Very observant." Penny paused, held up a finger, and opened her phone. After a storm of taps, she smiled curtly and put it back in her pocket. "Apologies. There was a major bank data breach in London—all fixed now. Where was I? Oh, Director Jameson! Care to chime in?"

"'Silver' was a program, or actually the offshoot of a program, that was funded jointly by the government and private wealth, a little side club at the Bilderberg meetings. It was created to work on genetics and neurotechnology."

Dana leaned back against the grill of the van. She raised a finger to pause the conversation, ran into the van to retrieve her coffee, and then resumed her position against the vehicle hood. "I'm sorry, so who exactly are you, Penny? A vampire or something?"

Penny smiled and tilted her umbrella, allowing the sun to fully engulf her. Her wispy shoulder-length blond hair sparkled, but she did not burst into flames, much to Dana's disappointment.

"I am older than I look, but no, I'm not a vampire. I consider myself the current caretaker of a long-term plan to help humanity and society mature across the world. I do what the United Nations—they're practically the PTA—cannot and will not." Penny pointed to her chest. "*I* am the one to steer the ship through waters of inequality and world crisis. This is what I do, what Silver does as an organization. And currently, *I* am Silver.

"Let's look at South Africa, for example. A country with a large physical geographical presence, full of resources both self-sustaining as well as commercially viable—like diamonds, petroleum, and gold—and it has a lower class, workers who can be hired cheaply for labor and manufacturing, but also a technocratic elite. And yet, it was held down by the Afrikaans and the Apartheid regime. While the United States battled through the Civil Rights Movement, the people of France rose up with the riots of 1968, and so on, yet South Africa remained chained to the old guard in Johannesburg."

Ashley stepped forward. "So, are you saying that you ended Apartheid or something like that?"

"Something like that." Penny smiled, an open-mouthed grin of unnaturally white teeth. "Silver was the guiding hand behind the process, organizing the revolutionary violence or, in some cases, preventing it. But then we had the AIDS crisis as Apartheid was entering its final act. Silver frantically sought a cure, or some type of preventive measure in the genomes, but it was a two-front war against the poor: the macroeconomy and politics, and the dual threat of biology and viruses. Quite the challenge." She flashed her teeth. "We were very close. South Africa should be a superpower by now. But India, ah, I did good work there, although there is still more to be done. If I could have—"

"I'm sorry," Dana interrupted, "but it's hot and we don't all have the shade of a parasol that probably cost more than my entire credit line. Can you get to the second act, please?"

Penny flattened her smile, her eyes a frigid blue as she stared hard into Dana's.

"I did hear you had quite the mouth." She turned up the corners of her lips. "I'll do my best. Anyhow, back to Rhodes. He and his team were part of the United States's contributions to the equalizing programs. Every time he turned an election against a dictator, liberated a village from a warlord, or provided the United States with the false flag needed to set foot into another nation-state, he was bringing the world one step closer to peace and harmony.

"Unfortunately, Rhodes lost his way; he was becoming obsolete as a means of *execution* for the plans. At the same time, he found the potential profits too tempting. I've seen some of the deposits, and I know what other parties would pay for some of the items and information he had access to during each job. Then he lost it." Silver's face softened for the first time in the entire exchange. "He experimented on his own daughter before she was born."

Dana felt Ashley's hand tighten around her wrist. They both had fought Nina Rhodes, the failed experiment herself, but Dana knew her sister felt this all the more keenly because of what had been done to her.

"Right now, even as he's working on his little project to start a civil war, it's not about any ideology." Penny paused to brush a dry leaf off her pant leg. "It's about money. Excessive amounts of money that he can make selling secrets to people with very deep pockets who lack any sort of moral compass.

"I didn't realize that his most recent request for specialized technology coincided with him being disavowed by the government. I thought it was a bit clever on his part, working as a fugitive as the ultimate deep cover." She straightened her back and lifted her chin. "I took him at his word that this was something for the greater good. That was my mistake."

Olsen cleared his throat. "So the man that Rhodes has been talking with for the past several years was a stand-in for you, an avatar. Just some hired hand to be the bloody mouthpiece of your grand design for humanity."

Penny retracted her umbrella and slid it under her arm. She cocked her head and frowned.

"*Silver* is an avatar. Having one or two faces other than mine for meet-ups provides a level of protection to our methods. *My* methods." She pivoted to Ashley. "You, little outlier, you're a pleasant surprise. You should know, your father asked *me* to help guide your genetic development. I said I wouldn't because I knew about Rhodes and poor Nina—*and* how his experiments killed his wife—but your father went ahead anyway with his limited resources and did the best he could. And may I say, he did a remarkable job; he was more capable than I thought. You're quite the specimen, you know.

"Your mother, of course, disapproved. I did my best to help, but then it became more prudent for me to stand back and let her disappear on her own, lest I become a liability to her. And to you, Ashley."

Dana leaned forward and put her head between her knees. This was too much to comprehend. Somehow, she had stepped into a science-fiction movie, a story of new world orders and genetically modified babies. But what she was hearing, if true, was indeed threaded through the bits and pieces, the breadcrumbs and fingerprints, of her entire life. This was all real.

"Penny," Dana said, "what do you want us to do with all of this?"

"Simple: I want you to stop Rhodes. He's going to set the world back several decades if he achieves even half his goal of dividing this country. Whatever your opinions are, the United States is still the big dog in the junkyard. And I need a very big dog, not a wounded pup."

"Why can't you do it?"

Penny grinned like the Cheshire Cat, a wide smile bereft of any underlying emotion. "I can't be too close to the actors. That's why I use Silver. It's not about ego; my work *is* that important to the world. But this situation has changed things due to the urgency and Rhodes's new resources— resources I provided."

Penny turned to the aircraft and snapped her fingers at the pilot. He scurried into the cargo hold and then sprinted out to the group, presenting a small black wristlet with a black dial to Olsen.

"Connect this to your phone. It's a tracking signal I put into the skates that I built for Rhodes's roller-skating gentlemen." Penny raised an eyebrow to Dana's quizzical face. "You don't think I would create something and not have a way to monitor it?"

Dana rolled her eyes. "There's no self-destruct mechanism, Dr. Evil?"

Penny smirked. "No, not possible. But it's the same tech that people use to track their luggage, except this version is even more brilliant. It's capable of finding your Louis Vuitton—or, in your case, I'm guessing a JanSport or one of those drawstring bags you get for free for signing up for a new credit card—if it overshoots JFK and ends up next to Amelia Earhart's bones. The beacon is hidden deep in the circuit boards. Director, I've already provided you with one. Use it however you can to prevent an . . . incident."

Carmen held up her hand and addressed the group as a whole. "I understand this is a tremendous amount of information to unpack." She looked at Dana. "You must have some questions."

"Yeah, about seventy. Penny, if you're not a vampire, how does this, *all* of this, work?" Dana flapped her hand at her. "Moisturizing baths in wrought iron tubs full of baby tears?"

Penny flashed a short smile. "Your father and his predecessors were excellent scientists. Before they isolated the circuity of the organic nervous system, they stabilized it. A human's metabolism changes in cycles of approximately seven-year intervals. But if the intervals can be extended," she said, turning her palms upward before placing them lightly on her cheeks, "we can significantly slow the march toward natural death."

Ashley crossed her arms and bit her lips. "So, you're an experiment, too." She turned to Dana, tears welling in her eyes. "Like me."

Penny interjected. "You were not subjected to what I was. Mine was a much cruder and an initially painful form. There were terrible records of the experiments, nothing anyone could replicate. Your father tried, but he could not copy my genetic manipulations." She stepped toward the sisters and took Ashley's hand. "You will probably *not* outlive your kin; I probably will."

Dana walked away from the group to try to gather her thoughts into a coherent stream. Even though she knew Ashley had been the subject of neonatal experiments, the reminder pulled at Dana's heart.

She hated her father now more than ever for being associated with this twisted secret group that attempted to control the march of humanity. And she hated herself just a little for being too curious and headstrong to not walk away from this long ago.

"Okay, Penny," Dana snarled, turning back around, "what if we decide to just go home and let you clean up your own damn mess? How about you take down Rhodes and take back your own damn roller skates?"

"I am a scientist. I am a corporate officer. I am not a military commander. That's how Silver can work in the shadows." Penny gestured toward her heliplane. "This is mine because I am wealthy, not because I have a private army. I do have bodyguards and corporate security staff. I have laboratories and accounting departments, not bunkers full of munitions." She pointed to the tracking wristlet in Olsen's hand. "Follow that, find them, stop them." She started to turn away, then stopped and snapped her fingers. "Oh, right! One more little thing."

Olsen looked down. Dana watched a veil of frustration fall across his face. He spoke softly. "How do we pay you?" Something is his tone implied to Dana that he was asking a question he already knew the answer to.

A man wearing flight gear stepped out of the plane holding a small white metal case. He opened it, releasing a blast of white mist and revealing a small syringe and vial. Penny lifted out the needle.

"Ashley, have you ever been sick?"

The younger sister shook her head.

"Coughing fits? Fever? Gastrointestinal distress? And goodness, you do have such perfect skin. I'm guessing you've never had pimples."

Dana shot Ashley a look. *What is going on?* Olsen stared into the distance.

"No, ma'am, come to think of it. We've been on the run all the time, but I don't recall ever seeing a doctor."

Penny stepped toward Ashley. "I need a sample of your blood, just a small one, to see what exactly your father did to you. Otherwise, I turn off that tracking device I gifted you and you never see me again." Penny nodded at Dana. "I don't need your blood, sweetie."

Ashley looked to Dana, then Olsen. He shook his head. "I'm sorry, Ashley. Please?"

She nodded and curled her lips over her teeth, offering her arm. Penny held it gently. "I know what it's like to be an experiment, I do. But think of this: your blood sample may help hundreds of thousands of people someday." Ashley nodded and rolled up her sleeve, allowing Penny to prick her. The syringe filled halfway with dark-red fluid.

"Are you done?" Ashley asked. Penny nodded.

"Payment has been received. Carmen, you can hitch a ride with them. I must depart from here to deal with a small matter up in Northwest Canada. Someone reported an alleged Sasquatch snooping around one of my biolabs." She shook a clenched fist. "Exciting!"

Penny handed the white case, now closed, and the syringe back to her man, then stepped into the aircraft without a parting glance. The rotors whirled, assailing the group with a burst of sand and dry grass as it rose into the sky and turned abruptly west.

"Well, that was . . . intense," Ashley muttered. Olsen placed a reassuring hand on her back.

"Thank you. I didn't know she would ask for that, specifically."

"Not the first time I've been reminded I was someone's potato-clock experiment, and I'm sure it won't be the last. I'll cry into my pillow when we get home." She brushed his hand away. "I'm fine. Really."

Dana slung her arm around Carmen's shoulder. "So, where can we drop you off, sweetie?"

# Chapter 24

*Strong Enough – Sheryl Crow*

Dammit, PEG!”

Simone heaved her socket wrench across the barn. It bounced across the floor until it met its final resting place in front of Dana's sneaker. Dana bent over and picked up the tool, kissing it lightly before handing it back to her mother.

"I think you hurt its feelings, Mom." She picked up a half-empty bottle of warm beer and held it up. "How many of these have you had today?"

"Not enough, Star," her mother quipped as she snatched it out of her hand. She downed the remaining contents and handed it back to her daughter. PEG hung in the middle of the barn in her harness, two legs and one arm attached. The helmet unit sat on the workbench tethered to a laptop. The black glass of PEG's head blinked to life, blue dots appearing on the reflective surface.

"Mom, is she . . . alive?"

"Hell no. Dana, it's just a suit, a tool. I'm having her track my movements here in the barn to improve the motion-learning process. The sensors for movement are good, but the balance algorithms are still a little off." Simone reached into the body through the open arm hole and, after some grunting and wiggling, pulled her arm back and frowned. "Here we go."

PEG's legs straightened and extended, touching the ground and leaving slack in the harness connected to the pulley above. The head blinked rapidly on the bench as the legs wobbled, then buckled.

"Appears she's a little drunk right now," Dana said dryly, eyeing her mother. Simone had slept in the barn, again, leaving her daughters and their guests to run the nighttime security protocols. Dana was starting to feel comfortable with it, but all it took was one mistake on the wrong night to compromise the entire ranch. She pulled a chair from the workstation and set it in front of PEG, then seated herself on the workstation itself. "Mom, take a break. Sit. Talk."

"Fine," Simone said, acquiescing to her daughter's commands. She looked tired, more than usual, as the dark patches under her eyes sagged. Her face had thinned slowly over the past few weeks. "Obviously, I'm not well, Star. I'm burning the candle at both ends, and there's a hot plate underneath me as well." She cut Dana off from speaking by holding up a long screwdriver like a conductor's baton before the start of a symphony. "Grab that metal first aid box on the shelf. The blue one."

Dana scanned the rows of highly organized containers and spied a red cross on a white background on a faded metal box. She pulled it off the shelf and held it toward Simone, who shook her head.

"Open it, Star."

The stiff latches required some effort, but finally they snapped open in Dana's hands. She immediately recognized a photograph of her father on top of the small stack of prints. She held it up to show her mother and was met with a nod and smile. Dana continued to thumb through the pictures.

"Did you guys take any photos that *weren't* at a government lab or base?" Dana asked, screwing her face as she rotated some of the pictures to the correct orientation. Candid shots of her mother, father, and some of the science team and military brass dragged her mind deep into her own memories. Only a few faces were remotely familiar to her, people she had met at a party back home or a picnic somewhere. She couldn't recall any of the names.

After a few moments of silence, Dana stopped and held up a print. In it, her mother sat on a barstool, her hair long, her mouth caught in mid-laughter as two men, one on each side, kissed her on the cheek. The man on the left, her father; the man on the right, a near spitting image. His jawline, brow, and nose all recreated similar angles. Their haircuts were nearly identical, but then military scientists often scheduled their buzz cuts together.

She flipped back through the photos and stopped at one of her father holding up a tool. At first pass she had missed the man in the background, but there he was again, her father's doppelganger.

"Mom, who's this guy who looks like Dad's twin in this picture here?"

Simone glanced at the photo and allowed herself a bright smile. "That's Nathan. Nathan Casey. Princeton physicist and special project contractor. He was your dad's best friend."

"They really could have been twins."

"Well, they all look the same. Nerds, that is." Simone winked. "Anyway, your father met him at Princeton and got him looped into our mission. Very nice man." She bit her lip. "He got sick working on the program, too. He was a *good* man. It was a shame he never met the right girl."

"Is this the part where you tell me you had an affair with him and he's my real dad?"

"No." Silence spread across the barn. Dana continued to stare at the photo until her mother finally spoke again. "Dana, he's a guy who never got credit for anything. Nathan—*Nate* worked on the Atomic Juggernaut because your father asked him to, and he loved your father like a brother. At times, I thought your father was taking advantage of him, his kindness, his support. And when things went out of control and the project was crashing . . ." Simone paused, fighting back tears. "Well, I wouldn't have been able to escape when I was pregnant without his help." She wiped her cheeks, stained with dirt and oil, creating smudges that reminded Dana of war paint. Simone laughed. "And yes, I did make out with him once before your father and I were officially dating. But that's as far as it got."

Dana's chin quivered as she felt her mother's painful journey pulling again at her own heartstrings, plucking obscure memories of her father back to life. "Is that why you wanted to show me the box of pictures? To force yourself to confess to your pre-Dad fling?"

"Ha. No. I wanted you to know just *one* of the many people who was affected by the program. One of the many nameless people forgotten by time." Simone stood up and leaned on PEG. "Another one of the people Rhodes ultimately killed. Your father was by no means a perfect man, you know that, but he surrounded himself with people who were better. Without people like Nate to reset his moral compass from time to time, he would have been completely lost."

When her mother had played the old recordings of her and her father arguing over Ashley's development as a guinea pig for the program, Dana had assumed he was a doomed cause. Simone had painted a black-and-white picture of a dark, determined father who would propel the project forward at any cost, but now Dana saw a shade of gray filtering over his life. The haze, however, was still prevalent.

"Mom, where would you say Dad ended up? I mean, on the 'bad guy to good guy' scale?"

"One to ten? Probably a seven, more good than bad. There were only a few times he was truly less than a five, I'd say." Simone placed her hand back inside of PEG's torso unit and jiggled her arm until the robotic suit beeped and powered down. "He had a sense of the big picture, but sometimes he tripped up along the way until someone showed him how he had hurt people.

Nate was good at that, course-correcting your father. A spouse can't always point things out without opening a can of worms and leaving someone to sleep on the couch for a night or two."

A set of footsteps approached from the barn's wide doorway. Nick cleared his throat to announce himself. "Hope I'm not interrupting?" He shoved his hands into his back pockets.

"Just reminiscing," Dana answered. "Talking about Dad."

"Ah."

*Shit, I'm so insensitive.* Dana hopped off the bench and closed the space between her and Nick.

"Hey. How are you holding up?"

"I'm okay. I mean, there are a lot of distractions, but sometimes things are just too surreal. Like, I'm waiting for a random song to come on the radio and bring me to some kind of closure as I'm rolled up in a ball, crying." He smiled as he looked into her eyes for a moment. "Thank you. For asking."

"If you want to talk—"

"I know."

Simone entered the space around Nick and Dana. "Nick, can you help me with something after dinner? I have some fuzz in the lines on PEG and it's messing up her balance. Mostly I need an extra pair of hands, but I also need someone who knows the difference between a gyroscopic balancing sequencer and a TV remote."

Dana crossed her arms. "Hey!"

"I love you, baby, but I need Nick's brain. You can go skate with Angela. She needs as much training as she can get on those things."

Nick nodded in agreement as he looked over PEG's harness. "Simone, why don't you take a night off? Rest up. We can tackle it fresh in the morning and work straight through until dinner." He winked at Dana before turning his pleading eyes to Simone.

"Sure, that sounds like a good idea."

Dana looked past Nick toward the house and saw Angela sitting on the back porch cleaning her skates. Again.

"You know what, Mom? I think I'm going to take Angela to skate now. Don't wait for us for dinner."

# *Chapter 25*

*Spy in the House of Love — Steve Winwood*

The clattering of dishes in the sink was followed by a heavy sigh. Olsen leaned over, balancing on his better leg, to pick up an errant tablespoon with a grunt. The hot water barely registered as he continued to wash the rest, automatic and methodical, his gaze fixated on the darkness beyond the horse paddock. Nick and Jennifer were settled on the stools at the kitchen island, hands interlocked.

"Jennifer," Olsen announced, still facing the window, "I think you should leave in the morning. Nothing personal, but we've got a lot to manage, and I don't think you're safer here than at home."

Olsen turned and met Jennifer's narrowed gaze.

"*I* think I should stay with Nick." She released his hand and stood. "His dad just died. I can't leave him now, especially after all of this. And I'm more than capable of handling myself."

"She's right," Nick said. "She's capable. Although, I'm doing okay." He turned to face her. "Jennifer, I'm doing okay. I'm managing. It's fine."

Olsen grunted. His primary concern remained keeping the team cohesive and focused. They had no plan for an offensive maneuver against Rhodes's clan, and their defensive plans were theoretical at best. Simone had provided a few briefings on bug-out drills and continued to divulge the secrets of her fortress ranch in drips and drabs. It was only this morning that she confided in Olsen that she had purchased all-terrain ballistic-proof tires for her van from a retired off-road racer in town and that they would need to pick them up this weekend due to the seller needing to "leave town ASAP."

Her connections were provided by a handful of businessmen and lawyers who had purchased her paintings, mostly to assist with their money laundering, and in return she obtained the contact information for their cleaners and errand boys. Olsen's prior connections had been mostly cauterized by his perceived death months ago, with exceptions like Perry and Odemo, thanks to Rhodes making some calls and eroding his circle of trust. Paranoia ran high through all factions now.

"Nick," Olsen continued, "I'm not one for personal diplomacy, but you understand that Jennifer's presence is . . . difficult for Dana. I need her to have a clear head. She can't chase Rhodes with her heart on her sleeve and a chip on her shoulder."

Jennifer shrugged. "You should talk to Angela, then. She's the one with the obvious love epaulettes."

"Is that your observation?" Olsen asked with a hint of disappointment.

"Yep." She planted herself in front of Olsen. "She's obviously only here because she's carrying a torch for *her* ex. I've seen the little things—the touches, the smiles, the way she watches Dana. And I've heard about her outbursts. Ashley told me about the incident at the bar." She paused. "Listen, I like Dana, and I'm comfortable with her proximity with Nick. I'm confident in my relationship. But I don't think Angela is someone we can rely on doing what's best for the *group* in a dangerous situation."

Nick cleared his throat. Olsen gestured for him to speak. "I think that's a . . . possible . . . assessment."

Olsen turned and placed the dishes from the drying rack into the cabinet. He folded the dish towel into thirds and hung it in on the handle of the dishwasher. He tugged it a half an inch at a time, slowly, until it was perfectly centered. Then he turned around to find Jennifer and Nick motionless, waiting for his reply.

"For now, I retract my recommendation that you leave in the morning. Set your alarm early. You'll start chores with Dick after breakfast."

*By then, that background check Dan is running should be ready,* he said to himself.

Olsen checked his watch in the fluttering orange glow of the firepit on the back patio. Nick and Jennifer had headed to bed, and Angela, Dana, and Simone were finishing the last of their beers while sitting on the back porch behind him. Dana stood, kissed her mom on the forehead, and went inside. Angela followed, racing ahead of Dana to grab the door handle, but they ended up grabbing it at the same time. Olsen noticed Angela's hand lightly resting on Dana's before the two women slipped into the house.

"Simone," he said, "can I ask you something about Dana?"

"Sure, tiger." Simone stood up with a wobble in her legs before settling back down into the chair next to him. "Shoot."

"Has Dana made any comments about Jennifer? Something she might not have told me but would, you know, confide in her mother? I know I'm crossing a parent-child boundary here but, you know, in the interest of security, anything of note?" He ran a finger over the opening of his bottle. "Just, you know, tensions between them."

Simone arched her back, stretched, and shook her head. Floating embers of the fire framed her sunken shoulders.

"She appears to be totally fine with Jennifer. I think—and this is coming from a mother who was AWOL for over a decade—Dana moves on somewhat easily from people that she's had romantic feelings for. But she's loyal to friends. *Very* loyal, Aaron." She lifted her beer to take a sip, but stopped short of her lips. "I think that's why she recruited Angela. There's a still a bond there, a loyalty that remains. Dana can trust her."

He nodded once. "So, nothing strikes you as a problem in the current group dynamic?"

"No problems I can see, and I'm paranoid about everything and everyone. I think the group has gelled into a rather capable crew. Did you know Ashley is helping Jennifer with her college courses? She's proofreading one of her papers." She laughed and swatted at a smoke plume that turned toward her from the pit. "I heard them during one of my breaks, laughing and discussing verb tenses." Simone pointed her beer at Olsen. "She's a good egg, I think."

"And the background check that Dan ran on Jennifer?"

"Got it a half hour ago. He said she's clean. She's an only child, and her parents are on the faculty list at a state college in New Jersey. Her last job was part-time at a very popular coffee chain that some would claim is an urban invasive species."

"Okay. I suppose that's sufficient. And how is your cancer?"

Simone spit out her drink. Olsen knew the power of a well-timed topic jump during an interrogation once the informant had slipped into a comfortable conversation.

"You sure are direct. It's fine," she replied as she wiped her chin. "I still have time. I did a little too much today, got winded, had to sneak a lungful of air from my oxygen tank." She stood and poked the fire. "I have an extra tank hidden behind the welding kit in the barn."

He raised an eyebrow and tilted his head. Simone continued to poke the now dying embers and huffed. Several minutes passed as each of them remained unmoving until she stared at him with a toothy smile, eyebrows arched.

"Olsen, I can play the silent game, too, you know. But I don't have time to keep this going. Fine, yes, I *am* running out of time. Someday, this cancer will kill me, and it will be sooner rather than later." As she stood between him and the firepit, her silhouette was backlit and faintly glowing. "And that is why if I had any inkling about anyone in this house not being trustworthy, I'd have already given them the third degree. If I suspected anyone here wasn't on the level, they'd already be gone. That goes for you as well." She leaned closer and pursed her lips. "Take me to my room. I'm drunk."

"That's not a wise decision."

"I'm not asking you to sleep with me." Olsen blushed, hoping it wasn't obvious in the dying light of the fire. "I'm asking you to help me walk through the house and make sure I don't piss myself."

"Don't lean on me too much. I still need a walking stick, you know." He stood with effort on his cane and offered his free arm. She threaded her tattooed forearm through his elbow and slowly led him through the patio doors.

"You know," Simone said as she tried to silence a belch, "I'm glad I didn't have another beer in me. I might have shown you *all* my tattoos."

# Chapter 26

*Love Will Tear Us Apart – Joy Division*

Dana. Dana. Dana. Dana."

Dana opened one eye and dragged her face across the pillow. A saber of morning sunlight stabbed her from the gap in the bedroom curtains. "Ash, I'm sleeping."

"Get up! Follow me. Come on." Ashley began to pull down the thin coarse sheet. "And put a shirt on, please. I don't need to see that."

Dana scooped up her blue "Chocolate Lover" shirt and slid it over her head with some effort. She cracked her neck, suddenly aware of Ashley's posture, bent over and glancing quickly and intermittently over her shoulder through the open bedroom door. Her usually soft jawline was clenched with an urgency Dana had rarely seen.

"Ok, Ash. I'm up." The words barely left her mouth as her sibling grabbed her wrist and led her on tiptoes into the bedroom next door. "What's with all the cloak-and-dagger?"

"Shush! Close the door."

Dana obliged as Ashley hurried to her desk and lifted the screen on her laptop. A glowing vector image of a snowflake slowly rotated, a handful of points highlighted in red. Dana sat on the edge of the bed next to a plush cat pillow and rubbed her eyes.

"What's going on?"

"Okay, so, I was helping Jennifer with her paper for school, checking some grammar, citation formats, blah blah blah, and I left it open on my laptop last night. But I was also running my text AI in the background, going through the hard drives from Olsen, and *this* popped up." She tapped her finger rapidly on the red dots on the snowflake.

"Which is?"

"Dana, these are hits!"

"Okay, so you got some more leads in the email trails. I don't see what—"

"*It's Jennifer.*"

Ashley ticked on the keys and one of the red dots expanded to reveal the sentences of an email chain. Dana's eyes widened. "Say what now?"

"These are all hits! The program uses speech and grammar patterns to correlate pieces of text to find the same voice and suggest patterns. I didn't close Jen's paper, and the program kept running across all of the docs on my hard drive. *All* of the docs." Ashley exploded the other red dots. "This, this, and this! These are all written by Jennifer!"

"That's a hard sell, sister."

Ashley frowned and scrolled down through one of the correspondence trails. An email in the middle of one thread opened with a single word salutation.

*Jennifer.*

"Ash, it's a really common name. You can't possibly think that this means anything more than a coincidence." She began to read the next sentences. "Oh . . . oh shit, shit, shit." The screen stared ominously back at Dana as she read the next email:

*Jennifer,*

*I understand the depth of the work, but we need solid data now. If there's nothing at the Andrews residence, we'll have to find a way to flush her out. You can't possibly think that this is an indefinite cover assignment for which I pay for college and you can skip around in the Pine Barrens. You have 30 days before I book you a one-way ticket to Tel Aviv.*

*R.*

The hair stood on the back of Dana's neck. She attempted a deep breath but was met with resistance as her lungs constricted.

"Ashley, where's Jennifer?"

"She's in the barn already with Nick and Mom."

"Okay, let me read more."

A series of footsteps down the hallway startled the sisters. The asymmetrical plodding indicated it was Olsen making his way through the kitchen, followed by the dull scrape of the old sliding door out to the back porch. Dana covered her mouth. "Does he know?"

"Olsen? No. I just found out right before I woke you up. Look at this part." Ashley scrolled through a different email. "She's been looking for 'the tech' and 'thumb drives.' When Nick would go to class, it looks like she would stop over, talk to his dad, and then rummage about. And over here." Ashley tapped at the screen. "Look at this."

"Wait, wait, wait—you read faster than me, you stupid genius. Hold on." Dana sighed. "Oh, shit."

The next exchange in the web of red dots relayed a conversation between Jennifer and an unidentified counterpart in which Jennifer expressed frustration that Dana and Nick had had no correspondence. Dana's chest ached for a moment as she realized that even by shutting him out of her life, she had still managed to put him in danger. They were using *him* to find *her*.

"Oh my God, oh my God." Dana leapt off the bed and paced back and forth in the short space between the mattress and the computer desk. "Oh my God, oh my God, Ashley! When I went out for the funeral, I literally walked right into it, and, and, and . . ." Her voice trailed off into a soft but high whisper. "I led them right here."

Ashley grabbed Dana's sweaty palm and laced her fingers through her sister's. "Hey, Mom can take care of herself against some rookie spy. I mean, Jennifer's barely older than you. That's probably why they recruited her to date Nick and—"

"Ash! I'm swatting images out of my head that, frankly, are the least of my issues as of right now."

"Right. So." Ashley gestured for them to lower the volume of their banter. "You can keep reading, but all the other emails and texts I've read so far all contribute to the narrative that Jennifer is working for One Hundred Roads."

"Okay. Shit. Okay. Shit."

"Cursing doesn't—"

"Oh, will you shut the shit up for a second?! I'm thinking. Do you have a gun? Get a gun. I'm going out to the barn and you follow behind me. I'll pull the big reveal and you cover me. That should give Mom enough time to grab her ninja swords or whatever and TCB."

"TCB?"

"Take care of business. Like Elvis? Jesus, you may be a literate nerd, but you have giant gaps in your pop culture references."

"Is *this* what we should be bickering about? Wait, let me text Olsen. He's out there."

"No!" Dana hissed. "What if he's in on it, too?"

"How do we know that? Or how do we *not* know that?" Ashley stared back at the snowflake. "I just answered my own question, I think. You're right . . . we can't assume anyone except you, me, and Mom is cool right now."

Dana sat back down on the bed. Her leg bounced rapidly as she knotted her fingers behind her head. "And Angela and Nick. I just know they're okay.

I mean, Ash, Nick's dad just died. And Angela . . ." She paused. Now was not the time to unbox secrets only they had shared. She knew that Angela would die for her, and that they were linked by unbreakable bonds at the very core of their friendship. "You gotta trust me. *Trust her.* Angela's clean."

"Fine. Look, we need to do this right now. Put on real clothes, please, in case we need to do anything extreme. You can't walk out there in your pajamas." Dana just now noticed that Ashley was wearing her hiking pants instead of leggings, her tactical boots laced tightly. "I'm going to go stash the laptop in one of my cubby holes here, then I'm texting Carmen and Dan to give them a heads-up. Get dressed and be ready in sixty seconds."

"I really wish I woke up earlier and had breakfast." Dana clawed at her stomach.

"There's a protein shake in the fridge from Mom's morning mix—you can chug it on the way to the barn. Let's go."

# Chapter 27

*Dirty Work – Steely Dan*

Laughter echoed from inside the barn as Dana and Ashley fast-walked toward the open doors. Dana could make out Angela leaning against the frame, waving when she saw the sisters approaching. She shot a confused look at Dana's flat expression.

"Hey, girls," she said. "Looks like the gang's all here."

"Yeah, apparently," Ashley deadpanned, then dropped her voice to a whisper. "Can't explain. Stay close to us."

Dana drew a deep breath as she planted her feet on the dirty interior floor. Her mother was smiling as she tapped on her laptop, connected to PEG through a web of wires. Nick—*Crap, poor Nick!*—kneeled next to PEG, tightening a set of connections under the exposed kneepads of the robotic suit. Olsen rummaged through the tool chest nearby, holding up various sizes of socket wrenches and shaking his head.

"Your tool kit is a mess," he noted. "The complete opposite of your workbench."

"*That,*" Simone objected, "is organized by frequency of use, then size.

Three of those sockets are used ninety-two percent of the time." She shook her hair to shoo a fly away and resumed typing. A figure emerged through the back door of the barn with an empty bucket.

*Jennifer.*

"Hey, everybody," she smiled. "It's nice to have everyone together this morning."

Dana grit her teeth. She had no clever plan in mind; she just had to execute this now while the team was all together. Surprise was her only advantage.

"Jennifer," Dana announced, "is working with Rhodes."

Nick shot up, his jaw tense. "What the heck are you talking about?"

Angela looked at Dana and, without words, asked her what she needed to do. Dana nodded to one side of the barn and Angela quickly glided over, creating a wider circle of adversaries against Jennifer.

"She's been corresponding with Rhodes for months. Ash?"

"We found emails and texts in the hard drives that Olsen brought back from the cabin."

Jennifer shook her head and let out a shallow laugh. "I don't know what you guys are smoking, but you know how ridiculous that sounds, right?" She put her hands on her hips in a defiant pose. "You were there when we ran from New Jersey from a bunch of crazy guys trying to rummage through Nick's house. *He's my boyfriend.* You're all so paranoid. The apple doesn't fall far from the tree." She glowered at Dana, then Simone, and nonchalantly pulled out her phone and began to type.

"Hey," Nick interrupted. "These are my friends here . . . well, except for him." He pointed toward Olsen.

"Noted." Olsen nodded. Dana watched his hand slowly slide to his pocket.

"Hey, dingo, no fast moves." Dana took one step forward. "Were you the one who told her I was going out to New Jersey for Mitch's funeral?"

Olsen's face registered surprise. "Dana, slow down. I didn't tell anyone. I went to the cabin with Angela to retrieve the gear." Olsen looked back and forth between the tense faces: Dana to Nick, Nick to Jennifer, Jennifer to Dana, Dana to Angela.

Nick froze in deep thought. Dana knew that look: His big brain had just drawn a conclusion. His eyes narrowed, his jaw tensing as he glanced upward before turning to face Jennifer. "I mentioned to you that I told Dan Sun about my dad, and how I thought that maybe he would tell Dana." He lowered his head and his voice. "I said that I thought maybe she would even come out for the services."

Jennifer's facial expression mutated. Her soft, gentle cheeks hardened. Her eyes narrowed, creases folding into her forehead. "Simone, stop right now."

The entire assembly pivoted to see Simone inching toward the worktable, a large pipe wrench hanging on a hook immediately in front of her.

"Shit." Simone shrugged in defeat.

Jennifer dipped her hand behind her back into her waistband and brandished a small pistol, leveling it at Simone. "You. Come here, now. Everyone, hands up. *Slowly.*"

Dana's ears buzzed with white noise. She watched her mother walk cautiously over to Jennifer, who quickly grabbed Simone's wrist and twisted her arm behind her back. Dana guessed that if her mom were healthy, she'd have been able to overcome her, but Simone had looked so much thinner, *weaker*, over the past weeks as she fought a war of attrition from her illness. She looked into Dana's eyes with a pleading gaze—no, an apologetic one. Jennifer pressed the pistol to Simone's temple.

"Jennifer, put down the gun. We've got you outnumbered." Dana glanced at Nick; he only stared at Jennifer, his mouth slightly open. She thought she could almost hear his heart—his loyal and wonderful heart— breaking inside of him.

"I don't need to kill my way out here, Dana. All I need are your parents' files. That's all I was meant to retrieve. We thought that Nick had them at first, kept for safekeeping. Why else would you have sent him away to New Jersey without you?" Dana's heart sank as Jennifer continued. "But they weren't there. Then Rhodes realized Simone was alive, *again*. So, when you finally made it out to New Jersey, I just had to follow you back to wherever your mom was living." She waved the gun toward PEG, hanging limp in the harness. "And let me just say this is a nice little bonus for me to bring to Rhodes. That will fit nicely into his portfolio."

Olsen stepped forward, leaning on his cane. "Excellent work, Jennifer!" he exclaimed. "Rhodes will be pleased."

Dana stomped at the dirt. "You traitor—I knew it! You son of a bitch! You bastard!"

Olsen looked back at her with a blank expression. He pulled out his sidearm concealed in his coat pocket and held it out in front of him. Jennifer, mouth agape, turned her gun toward him. He met her surprise with a simple smile.

"Jennifer, it's alright. Rhodes needed another layer of insurance. I didn't have the time to talk to you in private with all the people here muddling about."

Dana's blood boiled. "You scumbag! I'm glad I broke your back. You're not even a man, you're a rat. You're . . . you're . . . you're pathetic!" She spit in his direction. "I *trusted* you. And now I hope you die, you crippled sack of shit! *I hope you die!*"

Her voice broke as she shouted the last words. Her eyes welled, overwhelmed with anger at Olsen, the impact of the humiliation of trusting him and Jennifer countered by the deflation that this woman had lied to Nick and used him to find Simone. Dana couldn't understand how she could have been so stupid to not see any of this herself. If she had just talked to Nick during all this time, if she had *acted* like his friend, maybe she could have prevented this, or at least seen it coming their way. She felt shame boiling underneath the vortex of her emotions. She hadn't pushed Nick away for his safety; she had pushed him into the fire.

"Simone," Olsen said, "do you have any weapons on you?"

"A utility knife in my front pocket with a dull blade," Simone replied.

"Okay. Jennifer, slowly pull it out. And Angela? You can stop right there." He pointed his gun across his body, past Jennifer, at Angela's crouched form just a few feet away, next to the stack of tires that Simone had just purchased for the van. Jennifer's head whipped back and forth from target to target as Olsen moved closer to her side.

"Jennifer, how are we getting to Nevada?"

"Nevada? I thought Rhodes said California."

He glanced back at Dana and locked eyes with her.

He winked.

"Thank you. Simone . . . duck!"

Simone dropped, pulling Jennifer off balance as she yanked her arm out of her grip. Angela leapt from her crouching posture and yanked Simone toward her.

Olsen fired a round at point-blank range into Jennifer's torso. Jennifer fell to her knees, groaning, but had enough strength to lift her pistol toward him. Before she could shoot, he fired two more shots into her chest.

She fell back onto the floor, dead.

Dana's heart pounded, hot blood rushing into her head. Her ears crackled with static. She stood still, frozen. She saw Nick collapse to his knees and sob.

*Move. Breathe.*

Olsen stooped over the body and pointed to Ashley. Dana couldn't make out the words with the noise in her ears, but her sister nodded and reached into Jennifer's front pants pocket, pulling out a phone.

Dana saw Simone massaging her wrist, Angela pulling a tarp out from under PEG's rack and draping it over Jennifer, Ashley frantically thumbing through the cell phone.

The white noise roared in Dana's ears.

Simone ran toward her laptop and typed feverishly, shouting out commands that Angela and Ashley responded to by sprinting to various points in the barn. Dana's eyes filled with gold flecks.

Olsen, leaning over Nick, patted him on the shoulder. Nick nodded slowly.

*Dana, snap out of it. You need to be present. Dana, move. Dana . . .*

"Dana!" A different voice broke through. "Dana! Are you having an episode? Are you okay?" Olsen now stood in front of her.

Her ears popped. She could hear at last. She wiped her cheeks.

"Olsen, I'm sorry . . . the things I said—"

"Apologies later. I need you to function. We're evacuating." He held up Jennifer's phone. A text message sent by her just minutes ago had just one word:

*RAID*

# Chapter 28

*Dare – Stan Bush*

Olsen tossed the van keys to Nick. "I need you to drive. You need to focus, or we all die. Can you do it? Say you can do it."

Nick nodded. "Yeah, I can. I can do it."

"Good." Olsen paused and placed his hand on Nick's shoulder. "Focus on the objective. Just a little longer, mate. You got this."

Simone turned to Olsen. "Follow me to the front porch and grab a gun on the way from the living room."

He nodded and shuffled as quickly as he could out of the barn. He marveled at her command skills, her ability to stay task-oriented in crisis; she had the tools and guts to survive. *This must be how she was able to stay off-the-grid for so long and keep Ashley safe.*

"Who's got the tracking watch from Silver?!" Ashley yelled.

Olsen dove his hands into his pockets and pulled out the device. With a few quick taps, Ashley opened the laptop and pulled up the synced broadcast. A map of the ranch showed a collection of red dots pulsing toward the road that led to the driveway.

"Oh, you've got to be shitting me," he muttered. "Everyone," he bellowed back to the barn, "headphones, earpieces! Confirm with me when you're live!" He jammed in his earpiece and tapped the power button. Ashley had caught up and passed him as he entered the house through the back door.

"Ashley is live," she said, tapping her ear. "Mom, I have the go bags from the barn in the van. I'm grabbing the laptop from my room and I'll start the uploads."

"Good girl," Simone shouted back. "We've only got a couple of minutes. Hustle! Hustle!" She had already pulled open the false bottom to the couch and loaded her assault rifle. Olsen grabbed a matching one and loaded a clip into the magazine.

"Angela here, online," his earpiece buzzed.

"Nick online."

*Dana? Where are you, girl?*

Ashley bolted out of her room with the laptop and a squid of dangling cables, a hiking bag slung over her shoulder. "I've got the skates, too!" she yelled as she sprinted to the white van now parked in front of the barn.

"Dana, let me know when you're online." *Come on, Dana. We need you.*

"Olsen!" Simone shouted from the front porch. He returned his attention to the task at hand and jammed an extra pair of magazines into his coat pocket. He stumbled onto the porch where Simone had already pushed two benches on their backs and into a *V* shape.

"The seat planks are reinforced steel—"

"—for an impromptu pillbox bunker." He smiled at her.

"Right." She smiled back.

He struggled to get into a crouched position behind the benches, resting the barrel of his gun on the makeshift wall. He pushed his breath into a slow, steady, controlled rhythm and scanned the horizon. A plume of dust snaked up from the road just beyond the driveway. He looked through the rifle scope and counted.

"Four two-seater pickup trucks, so assume eight opponents."

"Eight against two." Simone pushed the stock of her rifle into her shoulder. "I like those odds."

"Your math is suspect."

Simone shrugged and smiled. "Ashley, where we at?"

"Van is almost loaded. Angela is grabbing the last bags from the house. Nick's fiddling with the front tire, low air."

"And Dana?"

"She's in the van."

"Okay," Simone exhaled slowly. "How are those uploads doing, sweetheart?"

"Eighty percent, Mom."

"Copy that. Keep me posted. We're about to engage."

The four pickup trucks fanned out as they pulled around the last bend and closed in. Simone nodded to Olsen and opened fire. Her gun's barrel rattled against the steel bench as she fought to keep it on-target. Olsen fired short bursts to follow hers as the operatives leapt out of their trucks into firing positions behind the vehicle doors.

"Eighty-five percent, Mom."

"Copy."

Simone fired another volley, felling two men immediately. Olsen continued his slower methodical shots. *Inhale, then exhale.*

One. Two. Three.

Three shots, three kills. Three men who would not be going home to anyone tonight. He felt the gravitas of the situation more than ever before. His job had always come with such necessary evils, sins for him to own and repent for before his own death. Simone seemed to show little remorse as she continued to level the playing field, dropping two more assailants. He saw her as a lioness, killing by instinct to protect her family, which now included him.

"Simone, we've got more company!" Olsen shouted. He pointed farther out along the road where another larger cloud of dust moved toward the house. He swung his gun to get a better view through the scope. "Six more trucks. *Six.* And two have extended cabs."

"Shit. Ashley, where are we at, baby?"

"Ninety-six percent. There's a large file hanging things up."

"Shit." Simone popped up and fired a dedicated burst at the final man from the initial group, dropping him violently to the ground. The next group of trucks pulled in behind the first four, using their bullet-riddled chassis as cover.

"Mom, one hundred percent!"

"Okay." She reloaded her gun. "Olsen, let PEG do the heavy lifting. Focus on the targets."

"PEG? Who's suiting up in PEG?"

The corners of Simone's mouth curled up in a sinister smile. She looked at her smartwatch and tapped it twice. *"No one."*

An explosion of wood and steel startled Olsen as the front doors of the house burst from their hinges, flying over their heads and into the driveway. A flash of carbon fiber leapt over their barricade as PEG landed in the middle of the drive, frozen in place in a sprinter's pose. Olsen was in awe as he admired the technological wonder standing between them and One Hundred Roads.

Simone tapped her watch.

"PEG, *polo grounds!*"

The robotic humanoid suit ran toward one of the disabled pickup trucks and was showered by a cascade of bullets from the men. PEG's arms spread wide before clawing into the sides of the hood, lifting it overhead, and tossing it into one of the new arrivals.

"Attagirl." Simone laughed as she popped up again to get off another round of shots. Olsen allowed himself a moment of distraction to watch the robot yank a front wheel cleanly off one of the vehicles and toss it like a

Frisbee into the windshield of another. PEG then turned around and rolled behind a truck for cover, revealing a hastily spray-painted pink cat face on the chest plate. Olsen smiled at what he assumed was Ashley's handiwork and resumed his firing.

"Simone, we need to get back to the van and exit over the fire road!" he shouted. "Ashley, status?"

"Nick reinflated the tire!" Ashley shouted into the earpiece. "We'll pull alongside the house and you can fall back to us there."

"Ash," Simone yelled, "left side or right side?"

"Left when facing the house."

"Copy—"

Simone screamed as a red mist burst from her shoulder, then a second by her collarbone.

"Simone!" Olsen ducked and crawled to her. He immediately assessed the two shots had bored straight through her right side—critical wounds he had seen too many times to count. "Hang on!"

"Aaron," she gulped, clutching his collar with her other arm. Her breaths were far too short and fast, a sign of very bad things, by his field diagnosis. "Take care of my girls." She coughed, sputtering through her plea.

"Not without you," he muttered. He grabbed her smartwatch and held it up to his face.

"*PEG, protect Mother.* Is that a thing?"

Simone pulled her arm back and put the watch to her lips.

"*Goalie Madonna.*"

PEG halted mid-throw, a pickup truck rolling out of her hands and onto the driveway. She pivoted and ripped the hood off another wreck, hauling it effortlessly back up the driveway toward the porch. Olsen waited for PEG to stop next to the bench bunker.

"Aaron," Simone gasped, "save my daughters. I'll cover while I can. Go." She adjusted her fingers around her rifle's grip.

*"I'll* cover. You're coming with me. Come on!" He stood behind the truck hood shield held up by PEG and hoisted Simone up by her good arm, slinging it over his shoulder. A tingle surged through his body. He was a soldier again. "No one left behind."

Bullets rattled against PEG and the truck hood. Olsen leaned on his rifle as he stepped, dragging his bad leg. He shuddered as his heart pounded, forcing blood into every working vein in his body. He stomped again and dragged his leg, his arm already cramping with the weight of Simone pulling down on it.

"Come on, Aaron!" he yelled at himself. He glanced at PEG's side, her form slightly larger than his own, an oversized shadow. As he moved, PEG mimicked him, a living suit of armor deflecting and occasionally absorbing bullets. He stomped and dragged his leg; PEG stomped and dragged her leg. Step by step he moved, pausing briefly to rebalance and fire blindly under PEG's armpit into the battlefield. *Step, drag, balance, and fire.* Sweat poured down his face.

*Step. Drag.*

"Come on, boy!"

*Balance. Fire.*

"Stay with me Simone," he barked. *Focus on the objective.* Each breath came harder, his lungs shuddering. His earpiece buzzed.

"Dana online. I'm okay."

*Attagirl.*

*Step.*

*Drag.*

*Balance.*

*Fire.*

The van slid around the corner of the house. Errant shots ricocheted off the bulletproof sides as the back doors swung open and Angela leapt out and reached for his hand.

"No, Simone first," he protested. As Angela lifted Simone's arm off his shoulder, he swung toward the advancing men and unloaded a sweeping spray of bullets. A thick clamp on his shoulder pulled him into the van as it rolled forward. PEG's hand gently released him as Angela yanked the doors closed, and he fell back onto a rough pile of duffel bags.

"That'll do, PEG. That'll do."

# Chapter 29

*Wait for It – Leslie Odom Jr.*

H ang on, we're about to pull off the fire road!"

"How many behind us, Nick?"

"I count four: two pickups, two Jeeps."

"She's losing blood. Ashley, get your tiny fingers in there a little more."

"I'm trying, Aaron!"

"Hang on! Bump!"

"Hold Simone steady!"

Angela pushed her hands against the van's ceiling as Nick swerved off the hard-packed dirt of the fire road onto the highway's pavement. Voices battled back and forth: Olsen shouted commands as Ashley struggled with a bandage and the medical kit supplies on the floor next to the bench seat. Dana rattled off exit numbers and mile markers from her phone to navigate Nick toward the hospital. Simone struggled to keep her eyes open, sprawled across the backseat. PEG gently rattled in the back, clanging against the bulletproof underlay of the van's sidewall, a silent sentinel. The frenzy had an odd intrinsic organization to it, everyone playing a role.

*Except for me*, Angela thought. She was just a body taking up space.

Angela leaned over the front seat to spy out the side-view mirror.

"They're right behind us!" Dana shouted. "Nick, can you—"

"I'm practically standing on the gas pedal, Dee!" Angela saw the look of frustration he shot Dana, but she also saw a concern for her above himself. "I'm doing my best."

"I know," Dana said. "I know."

From the back seat, Olsen braced his bad leg against the wall and stretched his free arm to reach another duffel bag that he unzipped with one hand. Angela reached back and helped him pull out a second medical kit resting on a pile of guns. She looked at the shotgun sitting on top of the pile. Steeling herself, she struck down her helplessness with a hammer of purpose as a hot flame burst into her mind's eye.

She reached for her own backpack and slid out her skates.

"Angela," Olsen shouted, "what are you doing?"

She clicked the first skate onto her left foot, then the second one onto her right. She leaned over the duffel and pulled out the shotgun.

"Angela."

*I'm not useless.*

She dumped a box of shells and began to slide them one by one into the shotgun, quickly but carefully loading them the way Olsen had taught her.

*I am not helpless*, she affirmed to herself. *I am valuable, right here, right now.*

"Ashley, keep pinching right there. Angela? Angela!" Olsen shouted again.

*Everyone here has an important role right now. That's why it has to be me. This is why I'm here.*

She grabbed the handle on the side of the van door.

"ANGELA!" Olsen yelled. She looked up, astonished at the calmness in his face juxtaposed with his ferocious bark. She felt the hardness of the gun's handle in her hand. He nodded to her, his brows lifting for just a moment.

"Quality shots," he deadpanned. "Watch the kickback on the skates."

She nodded back.

The wind lashed at her hair as she flung the door open. Her wheels screamed upon impact with the moving pavement, sparks flying up and beyond her head. She immediately slid backward on the highway, headed past the rear of the van, and focused on the two Jeeps in the lead behind them. She pressed the stock into her shoulder and fired into the rear tire of the closest vehicle. The kickback immediately distorted her balance, pushing her back onto one leg. She barely recovered as the Jeep swerved and then careened over the shoulder into an embankment of dry grass.

For a moment, faces swarmed her memory. Faces of young men she had met as a teenager. Faces that had laughed at her through cruel sneers.

A gunshot redirected her attention. She rebalanced and observed the passenger of one of the trucks attempting to level an AR-15 at her. She pressed the accelerators in her skates and sprinted in his direction, then steadied the shotgun again.

*Yes, Olsen, I can kill.*

She fired, nearly point-blank into the door of the truck. The gunman howled and doubled over in his seat. This time, she had been ready and accelerated as she pulled the trigger, pushing her center of balance forward over her toes and forcing her shoulder forward as she fired.

Those faces were still in her head, one of them now screaming. Slurs filled her ears, temporarily muffling the sound of the churning engines and screeching of tires.

*I am in control.*

Angela dropped back again, rotating her torso to aim at the next target, one of the approaching pickup trucks. She leveled the gun over her shoulder.

*Quality shots.*

She fired at the windshield, washing it in a cascade of spidering glass.

The driver swerved left and right, his vision obliterated. Angela looked back at the van, the engine revving in the highest gear as Nick undoubtedly tried to maintain their speed. A small blue sedan, overtaken by the motley chase, swerved into the shoulder, barely missing Nick's bumper. She tapped her earpiece.

"Olsen, how are we doing?"

"There's a junction that shoots over to the hospital in a couple miles. We're going to hit a hard right, right at the exit ramp, and hope we catch them off guard." A cluster of voices yelled in the background before Olsen replied again. "Angela, you've got company! Look left!"

She snapped her head over her shoulder just in time to see a man in gray fatigues leap out of the bed of one of the pickup trucks. He smacked into the pavement, a burst of sparks announcing the collision, but instead of falling, he charged forward. *On skates! Just like mine!* The grating metal whine of his wheels reached a crescendo as he soared toward her. Under his checkerboard helmet and visor, she could make out an uneven smile.

"Hello there!" the skater snickered, his fist slamming into her back. Her hands locked onto the shotgun, an instinct from years of team sports, but her weight moved too far over her skates. She stutter-stepped, almost falling onto her face before stretching out her front leg to reset her footing.

She let the gun slide in her grip until the barrel rested in her palms, then swung it back and up at him, nearly connecting the butt of her gun with his neck. He caught the stock and pushed her against the side of the speeding pickup.

*That was not a quality shot.*

Her skates scraped at the pavement; she was pinned against the speeding truck, held captive by a stronger body intent on killing her.

Her mind continued to flash through faces.

Laughter. Jeers. Hands holding her down.

Nick broke through her thoughts through her earpiece. "Angela, you're in our blind spot!"

"I'm in control!" she growled, twisting her legs to form a heel-toe pose. She spun, the gun still pressed against her, and reset the leverage, reversing their positions and pinning the mad skater against the truck's fender. He gritted his teeth, spittle racing out of the corners of his mouth.

"You're a dead girl," he snarled.

*I can kill.*

His face blended into the faces of her past. The same smile, same sneer, same ugliness.

Angela jerked the gun and pulled the trigger the moment the barrel overlapped part of his body. She closed her eyes as the gunshot rang in her ears.

*I can fight. I have to survive.*

She opened her eyes, the corners of her vision catching a wall of red on the side of the truck. *Don't look at it.* Her skates whinnied like a pair of stallions with the rapid speed changes, her focus diverted now to the Jeep closest to the van and an exit sign approaching rapidly on the side of the road.

"Olsen, give me a countdown when you're going to turn on the side road!"

"It's here in ten, nine, eight—"

The blast of a deep truck horn behind the group startled her. She turned just in time to see a white flat-front semitruck surging forward, rear-ending the Jeep.

"—two, one!"

The Sprinter van cut a hard right onto the exit ramp, the tractor trailer continuing to push the Jeep along the main highway. Angela slowed for a moment to steady her shot, the barrel pointed at the front tire of the Jeep. The passenger rummaged in the cabin, finally retrieving another assault rifle, but wasn't fast enough.

Her shotgun blast was perfect. The front tire of the Jeep exploded, the vehicle twisting to the side and, with the assistance of the tractor trailer's push, spinning and rolling over onto the side of the road. Angela and the truck slowed in unison. She glanced back at the side road and saw the diminishing image of TIARA's white van racing off, free and clear. Her eyes welled up. Her friends still had a chance.

She reached up to grab the semitruck's side mirror and hung limp, letting her skates roll to a stop alongside her anonymous benefactor. Her earpiece buzzed again; Dana's voice had never sounded so good.

"Angela, we're on a straight shot now to the hospital. Mom's stabilizing. Are you okay? Angela-la-la?"

"I'm good," she replied, gasping and dropping to a seated position on the faded white paint of the lane lines. "I'm good." She smiled. "Dana-na-na-na."

Angela panted and glanced at the white passenger door to the semi, lightly coated in black road dust that almost obscured a light-blue stripe running across it. The door slowly opened. The driver, an older woman in a floral-print top, slid over to the passenger seat with a large revolver held in front of her, but not pointed directly at Angela.

"You alright, miss?" she asked with a sweetness in her voice.

"Yeah," Angela answered. "I'm okay. Thank you for . . . you know . . . all of that." She waved her hand at the smoking overturned Jeep.

"Big Joe here just has a mind of his own sometimes. The airbrakes felt like they hiccupped and, wham, he took those turkeys right out." She hopped down to the pavement and pointed her gun at the wreck. "Let's just check for survivors before we skedaddle. I have a hunch you don't want to talk to cops about all of this. And frankly, neither do I."

The two women made their way over to the Jeep where both the driver and passenger lay on the ground, dead. Angela knelt and quickly pulled out their wallets, just like she had observed Olsen and his crew do at the cabin. Driver's licenses, debit cards, cash, and two keycards—one for each attacker, both from the same motel.

She turned the keycards over again and noted the address. Back along the highway, Angela could make out the twisted body of a skater, his leg sticking straight up in an unnatural position, shining as the sun glinted on the metallic prosthetic leg. A small explosion burst from the skate dangling at a right angle. She shuddered and handed the keycard to the truck driver.

"Ma'am, any chance you're heading this way?"

The woman gently took out a pair of frameless glasses from her shirt pocket and studied the address.

"Yeah, I can give you a ride there. It'll take a couple of hours. Can you kill some time with light conversation?"

Angela checked her shotgun and the now empty chamber. She handed the gun to the truck driver.

"I can kill."

# Chapter 30

*Why – Annie Lennox*

If there was one thing Dana hated about hospitals—besides the ridiculous circumstances of her life that repeatedly placed her inside of them—it was the coffee. She stared down at the bottom of her now empty paper cup, marveling at how in such a short time, her drink had already stained the inside surface. It was bland and flavorless, and the temperature plummeted quickly from scalding to freezing by the time she had finished it. Only the slightly burnt scent remained as she shoved her nose deep into the wax paper vessel. She placed it on the armrest of her chair in the surgical waiting area and settled back into the rough upholstery.

Dana slowly opened the spigot of her short-term memory to retrace her steps. After a bombastic rush into the emergency room, the group had stood by helplessly as the doctors quickly took Simone into the operating room. Olsen had assured the sisters that he would locate a motel where they could regroup, hitching himself a ride from a kind nurse in the parking lot as Nick parked the van containing PEG. Dana closed her eyes and shut off the replay.

Ashley slowly paced around the room in the empty space away from the chairs and ancient magazines. Dana had had the unfortunate luck of already losing her mother once, but this was all new for her sister, this unknown outcome looming somewhere in the surgery suite. She could see that Ashley was slowly shutting down, her replies to Dana's questions dwindling to just phrases or single-word answers. She stopped making eye contact. Dana could guess what her sister was going through.

Dana became hyperaware of her own composure, her calmness as she walked over to the coffee machine. Oddly enough, no signs of a panic attack. It felt like uncharted waters. *How am I suddenly handling things better?* She filled the cup with the nearly boiling coffee and took a tiny sip. She saw Nick returning from the restroom, where he evidently had scrubbed off the blood and dirt, a ritual that occurred too frequently when they were together.

"Hey," Nick said, filling a new coffee cup for himself. "What's the word? Anything from the doctors or staff yet?"

"Looks like we're about to find out," Dana replied, pointing to the surgeon making his way down the hall. The doctor wiped his bushy black eyebrows and pinched the bridge of his nose, slow beads of sweat scrolling past the tan lines at his graying temples where his glasses sat. She absorbed the details, mentally preparing to tackle the minutiae of the prognosis.

"So, she's stabilized now after surgery. But, as I'm sure you're aware, we saw cancer is raging in her chest cavity from the x-rays." The doctor turned to Ashley as she finally lifted her head. "Postoperative anemia, infection due to depleted white blood cells, and general cardiac trauma are all dangers. She is fighting a war on several fronts right now." He paused and inhaled deeply, giving Dana a sense of his own exhaustion hidden by his calm demeanor, then folded his hands, placing his fingertips together without letting his palms touch. "Right now, we're doing all we can. Prayers can't hurt. Her body is fighting, but it's been through a lot. Rogue hunting accident, you say?" He raised an eyebrow.

Dana nodded in agreement. Ashley relocated to a seat closest to the doctor. She looked up to Dana first, as if asking for approval, then to the doctor.

"Can I see my mom?"

"Not yet. She's going to need constant observation overnight since a cardiac event is my main concern." He placed a hand on Ashley's shoulder. "We will be watching her very closely so we can catch anything as it happens, or even before." He turned to face the group slowly. "*If* something happens at all. Hopefully, we will see improvement with time and willpower."

Ashley let out a guttural laugh. "*Willpower?* You seriously don't know my mom, buddy." Dana felt relieved to see a momentary smile on Ashley's face, even if it was slightly sarcastic and meant to repress her emotions. Nick crossed his arms and placed his thumb on his chin. Dana felt another wave of relief, seeing him assume his command pose.

"Doctor, the nurse has our cell phone numbers. What should we do now?"

"Go home, get some rest, and we'll call you if we need do. If you don't hear from us, be here at nine in the morning and you can see her." He shook hands with each of them and headed back through the double doors to the surgery wing. His sandals echoed soft padding sounds as he faded down the hallway.

Dana just now realized she was holding Ashley's right hand and Nick's left. If she had a third hand, it would be empty, waiting for Angela.

"Okay, let's go down to the lobby, text Olsen to see where we're staying, and then Nick, you bring the van around." Dana's phone vibrated with a text. "Hang on."

"Who's that?" Nick said as he peered over her shoulder.

"Olsen, speak of the devil. Here's an address . . . and he says Angela is safe but she's hitching a ride with a trucker to another location for, as he phrased it, 'a recon assignment.'"

"He does not stop doing what he does," Nick noted. "He's always on duty." He pressed the elevator button for the lobby and blew out an exhausted sigh. "It's still daylight, but I feel like I've been up for three days."

Dana sighed. "Same."

Ashley nodded in response.

The elevator doors slid open, revealing the expansive general lobby of the hospital. Floor-to-ceiling windowpanes surrounded them, blocked by mini-blinds tilted to reflect the late afternoon sun back to the tinted glass. Large couches faced each other, flanked by another chair in which a man sat with a newspaper pressed to his face. Two men stood by the entrance doors, each in plain black workpants and matching jackets. Dana noticed they had similar beards and oddly congruent facial features. She thought she knew them but couldn't place how.

"Dana. Jefferson," a familiar voice spoke as they moved through the lobby. The man in the chair lowered his newspaper and stood. His chest was broad, his face etched by time, and his head was topped with hair speckled black and silver. He wore leather gloves, which he used to smooth the buttons on his green dress shirt, worn over a high-necked black compression workout shirt. He extended a hand to the couch to his right. "Have a seat."

"*Rhodes*," Dana whispered. *Colin Rhodes*. Here. Now. The man who was the cause of every trauma in her life was only a dozen feet away. Every time they met, someone she loved was hurt, or worse.

Looking over his shoulder, she now recognized the twin idiot henchmen she had loved to hate, Eugene and Zeke. She froze and turned to Nick for his assessment. "Nick?" His lips parted slowly.

"*Fuck.*"

# Chapter 31

*Can We Still Be Friends? – Robert Palmer*

H ow's your mother?"

Dana's eardrums filled with a slow high-pitched whistling as Rhodes's voice echoed inside the lobby. He was here, just a few feet away from her, in broad daylight. He looked *bigger*, she thought, noting that his biceps and triceps bulged under the sleeves of his open coat. The wrinkles from decades of malice created a lattice of mysteries over his face, but she intended to find out as many as she could, right now. He sneered as he extended his hand again to the couch next to him.

"Rhodes," she hissed, "if you touch my mother, I swear I will rip off your face and feed it to you." She bit her lip as she pondered the procedure to execute her threat. Nick pressed his hand on her shoulder. His voice quivered as he forced himself to stabilize both himself and her.

"Take a breath, Dana. Let's not escalate things any further."

"He's a sharp one," Rhodes replied with a snarky tone, pointing his finger at Nick and cocking his thumb. "Sharpshooter. Nick Andrews, right? Good with a paintball gun, from what I remember."

"You've put on weight," Dana shot back. "Steroids and cake?"

"And you still have quite the mouth, Dana. How about you just give it a rest and listen to what I've got to say?" Rhodes leaned over and retrieved a paper cup, sipping slowly and grimacing. "This hospital cafeteria has the worst coffee I've ever tasted, and I've had some really crappy brews from all over the world. Come, come. Have a seat."

Dana took slow, deliberate steps toward the couch. A quick scan of the lobby revealed a handful of nurses and people sitting and talking in small clusters. The twins casually stepped closer to flank Rhodes. The one closest to her, Zeke—the one without a limp, if she remembered correctly—wore his jacket tied around his waist, covering a bulge on his hip.

"I see you brought the jackass twins," she snarled. "So, are you going to draw this out, or kill me now?"

"Dana, please, I'm asking again. Just sit." He motioned with the cup toward the empty seat. He shifted with a slight groan in tandem with his chair creaking under his weight.

"Jeez. How many burgers have you been eating since you busted out of prison?"

"Again with the mouth! You know, in all the times we've run up against each other, I never thought about just, you know, *talking* to you and working things out." His hand, still outstretched, remained frozen until she sat on the edge of the couch cushion. Nick and Ashley sat down on the opposite couch, his face a dull mask, hers a smoldering war face with a tight jaw. Rhodes acknowledged this and smiled at Ashley.

"I'm not going to hurt your mother. That's kind of the point of why I'm here. I know things, and you know things, so let's put our heads together and come to a resolution."

Dana curled her toes inside her shoes, forgetting momentarily that Laverne and Shirley were in the van, not on her feet. She could lunge and choke him before the twins were able to grab her or shoot her. She could scream for the security guards. But Rhodes was a calculating man; he knew he'd be on the hospital surveillance cameras with his two henchmen, so this had to be a calculated risk he was taking.

She put her hands on her knees and looked him in the eyes. "What resolution could we possibly reach?"

"Dana. This series of skirmishes between us, it's really doing a lot more damage to both of our factions. I've spent a lot of money, and lost a few men—good men, by the way. *Patriots.* What I want, simply, is your mother's secrets. I want her blueprints, her files, her devices, anything you have on her inventions. Anything that your father worked on, too. Things like, I don't know, maybe recordings, papers, notebooks. Photographs with blackboards in the background, anything and everything. I thought we'd hit the mother lode at the ranch, but between dealing with you and a very quick response from the feds, well, I'm locked out by all accounts."

"This is the part where I tell you *I won't give you shit,* and you counter by threatening to kill my mother, correct?" Dana checked Ashley, who was focused on Rhodes's face. Ashley's lips parted slightly as Rhodes continued.

"And then I offer you a bit of a carrot on a stick. But I'd rather cut to the chase and give you the whole enchilada right now."

*Enchilada right now.* Dana's eyes dashed to her sister. Ashley's lips moved slightly, miming Rhodes. *She's recording him, mentally. Good girl.*

"I'm not going to let you burn down the country while you profit."

"You're half right, kiddo. I do want to profit. That really is, and has been, my goal all along. It was never about patriotism or safeguarding the country, or even revenge for the knife in my back when this nation turned on me." He rubbed his fingers together. "And I don't have to *win* a civil war. Frankly, these militias don't stand a chance against even some of the more well-equipped local law enforcement agencies—I just need it to keep going. As long as there is a conflict, my bank account gets filled." His eyebrow arched ever so slightly. "And there are many foreign groups who would love to fund me, *pay me,* if I can give them the tech to keep this up."

"What tech?" Dana bit her lip. *Keep up the poker face.*

"That's the stuff your mommy and daddy made, dear." He uncrossed his legs and leaned closer. "And if I can wound the country that stabbed me in the back in the process, that's fine by me."

"Money. That's all this is, really. You're just a war profiteer, and now you're bringing it to our backyard."

He chuckled. "That's one way to look at it, but you'd be somewhat incorrect." Rhodes leaned closer, his eyes locking on hers from beneath his furrowed brow. "But I don't have time on my side. I am dying slowly from the same causes that afflicted your mother and father, the Atomic Juggernaut program. And it is *very* expensive to prolong my life. My daughter is somewhere, God knows where, lying in a bed, a quadruple amputee. And maybe somewhere in the archives of your brilliant parents, there's something that can help her . . . and me." The corners of his sneer twitched for a moment.

Ashley's lips continued their telegraphic movements. Dana rolled her gaze to Nick, who nodded slightly, and then back to Rhodes.

"Everything's gone," Dana started. "Remember when you wrecked *my* house and everything in it? And you'll get nothing from my mother's house with the feds there. I still can't believe you haven't asked about Jennifer! Sorry about that, but we had to take out the trash." Dana immediately regretted shooting her mouth off as she saw Nick swallow hard. *That may just be the most insensitive thing I've ever done. I hope he understands I'm just playing hardball. Pivot.* "Your daughter can keep rotting in her cell."

Dana didn't pull away from Rhodes's stare. A slight sheen formed on each of his eyes, the physical moment of weakness by a father making a plea for his daughter. Had he ever shown any emotion when he killed Dana's father, his colleagues? Had his lip quivered when his daughter was born deformed after countless injections and experiments on his pregnant wife? Had he even cared when his wife died? Or was this all still a chess game, where Dana was the novice with three pieces left on the board and Rhodes was the grandmaster declaring checkmate?

"Dana, the things I need are not cheap. I'm tired of fighting. I just want the time I have left to be happy, and have that time with my daughter. I want to give her back the life I stole. Walk on the beach, holding her hand, and watch the Pacific Ocean—things like that. There are marvelous machines and medicines out there in the dark corners of the world that could regrow Nina's limbs or make polysynthetic prostheses." His hands tightened their grip on the arms of his chair. He lowered his voice again. "To do that for her, I need whatever you have left of your parents' work, and I need more money—more than I already have."

Rhodes reached into the crevice of his seat and produced a tablet, placing it between them as he brought up a bank website with a few quick swipes. He turned the tablet to face Dana.

"This is *one* bank account. The poor chaps in my makeshift army have been gracious enough to donate their funds, sign over assets and pensions, and, when possible, deposit money from some of the more illicit operations through one of my laundering projects. Every day, money goes in, but money also goes out. I don't have the time to drag this out ad infinitum for years. *You* have a whole life ahead of you to do whatever you want." He reached into his coat pocket and produced a check. "Like, say, using this to give your mom the best care for however long she has left." He folded the check and placed it on Dana's knee, leaving his hand there and pressing the check against her leg. "A short-term expense. For my long-term returns."

"You can't buy me."

"Dana, dear. We don't need any more casualties. Simone, my men, Jennifer, Nick's dad—"

"Nick's *dad*?" Dana blurted out, slapping away his cold hand. She swung her head to look at Nick, who sat unblinking, then Ashley, who gulped even as she continued to silently mimic the conversation. Rhodes pursed his lips.

"Oh, goodness," he purred. "I would have thought Jennifer might have clued you in during your final exchange. You know, it was her idea, really. Very brilliant girl when given a little poke. She guessed that if there was any way to get you and Nick talking, that would be the thing to flush you out. She did a little recon, kept tabs on Mr. Andrews's doctor visits, and figured out just the right time to swap out the refill of his heart medicine."

Dana's heart pounded.

Her head felt light.

Gold sparkles flooded her field of view.

Through the haze, she could see that Nick remained still, motionless. Her own legs felt wobbly, even as she sat. Mr. Andrews, *Mitch*, one of the nicest people she had ever met—now another victim of Rhodes. This was more than she could wrap her head around. What kind of person was she now in Nick's mind? She created more danger for everyone she cared about than she could have imagined in her worst nightmares, and now the prince of nightmares made manifest sat before her sipping a cup of bitter, burnt, room-temperature coffee.

Rhodes smiled. He reached down to pick up the now fallen check.

"Dana, this is only *half* of what I'll give you. And, yes, there are two commas in the number. To get this down payment, just bring me your father's journals." He handed her a blank card with ten digits. "Take this phone number. Call when you're ready to work out the final details." He stood up with a groan, placed the check back inside his jacket, and patted her on the shoulder. She shrugged it off.

"You son of a bitch."

"Sticks and stones, Dana Jefferson."

"Eat. Shit."

"Sticks. And. Stones." Rhodes signaled for Eugene and Zeke to head out before him through the doors. He paused and turned back to the group. "Oh, and Nick, sorry about your dad, and about Jennifer. But that's what you get for hanging around the Jeffersons. Sticks. And. Stones." He walked outside and into the sun.

Ashley leapt out of her seat and ran to the gift shop. "Paper, pen, pencils, *Pacific Ocean*!" she was shouting. The cashier obliged her as Dana lowered her head.

"Nick, I—"

"I'll get the van. Wait out front."

He rose from his seat, ran his fingers through his hair, and plodded out through a side entrance to the lobby. Ashley returned from her shopping spree and frantically began to transcribe the conversation with Rhodes.

Dana put her head between her knees.

And she wept.

Dana didn't know how long she had been sitting there, but at some point she felt a hand under her arm, lifting her up. Her legs moved independent of her thoughts, taking her outside and up to the van, still caked in dirt and marked by a smattering of bullet holes. A hand hooked under her armpit and pulled her into the passenger seat. She felt the belt fasten around her waist and saw the door close.

The world passed outside the windshield, the silent hum and chug of the van interrupted only by a dull rapid thudding that indicated one of the run-flat tires was finally losing the war against a bullet hole. Nick's phone sat in the cradle attached to the dashboard, occasionally lighting up as Olsen texted directions to their hideaway. The Sprinter van pulled into a parking spot on the side of the motel's outer parking ring. Dana remained buckled in after Ashley and Nick left. She watched them talk to Olsen and receive their room keys. She remained in the passenger seat alone for several minutes. A knock at the window. Olsen. He brought her back to the reality she had created.

"Come on, Dana. Let's unpack some things."

# Chapter 32

*You're Not Good Enough – Blood Orange*

Nick, can we just talk for a second?"

Dana dropped a duffel bag at her feet, only to have it snatched by Olsen. Nick kept his head low and matched his voice to his posture.

"I don't think I'm in the *right* mind to *speak* my mind without saying some things I can't take back." His throat tightened. "I have a lot to do right now."

Nick rifled through a rucksack in the back of the van until he found a ratchet set and a pair of mechanic's gloves. He was shutting her out, and she felt a rock in the pit of her stomach. *He hates me.* The uncertainty of her mother's condition, Dana's indirect role in Mitch's death, all of it clouded her head. She felt like she was drowning in a sea of anguish, sadness, and fear, gasping for air and holding on to the dire hope that Nick would throw her a life vest.

"Please, let's just talk," she pleaded, clutching his forearm. He pulled his sleeve out of her grasp and crossed his arms.

"Right now, you need to be there for your sister. That's where you should focus your energy." It was rare to see Nick's jaw this tense, his brow this crooked. "I'm really sorry about your mom. She's a fighter. She'll make it." He looked over at a black SUV pulling into the motel entrance drive. "Frank's here with Dan. I gotta go."

He jogged to the end of the parking lot and leapt into the waiting truck. Dana saw Frank Iron's black-and-gray hair poking out from under a bucket hat as he waved to Dana with a familiar smile. Dan Sun emerged from the passenger side to embrace Nick briefly before leading him into the back seat. The vehicle roared from Frank's lead foot as it cut a wide U-turn across four lanes of traffic. Dana looked back inside the white van, the piles of bags and backpacks, and PEG's slumped body half covered by a blue wool blanket.

*Useless* was one word that kept repeating in Dana's head, the incessant thought that she was too useless to do anything for anyone. *Shame* was another as her memory listed all the names of the people whose lives she had wrecked just by being close to them. Here she stood, alone in a parking lot in God knows where, without a friend in the world to lean on.

Olsen's voice behind her startled her. He pointed his cane at the rear wheels of the van. "We're down two tires, but hopefully Nick can grab four new ones so we've still got two spares. I called Jameson. She's trying to get jurisdiction over the crime scene at the ranch so she can make sure things are left as intact as possible. If she's at the site, Nick might be able to grab the tires from the barn, but I gave him a stack of cash just in case. I used the rest I had in my money belt to secure the rooms here."

He tapped his cane on the large rectangular canvas bag full of cash at his feet. "I didn't want to open up one of these at the front desk, and we can't afford to give ourselves away using electronic payments." He shrugged. "Rhodes is too close to our location, and we can be sure he's watching the hospital."

Olsen handed her a room key and nodded back to the complex. The old motel, a nondescript C-shaped two-story concrete building, encircled an outdoor pool behind a chest-high plastic fence. Save for their van and a handful of cars, the parking lot sat mostly empty. Ashley emerged from a room on the second floor and waved at Dana.

"Free Wi-Fi, and a whole mess of cable channels!" she shouted. Dana marveled at her resilience and mask of optimism despite their mother lying at death's door. She needed a cheerleader like Ashley right now.

"Great." Dana turned back to the bags, waiting for Olsen's instructions with outstretched hands.

"That one," he indicated. She picked it up, immediately feeling the heaviness of its bulk. "That's the last one full of cash and goes to my room, first floor on the end. I'll carry the guns." He slung a longer, lighter bag over his shoulder and closed the doors, then tapped on the window. "PEG stays here. I'll move the van alongside my room when that little Subaru at the end moves."

She swallowed hard before setting her jaw. "Are we safe here?"

"As safe as we can make ourselves. Ninety minutes to the hospital isn't ideal, but at least we're halfway between us and Angela, more or less."

"And where is she, exactly? And don't say 'on a mission.'"

"She's on a mission." He smiled. It was rare to see him smile, or make jokes, during a crisis. Dana knew his standard operating procedure as ambivalence sprinkled with a pinch of sourness and dire consequences, but this change in tone was out of his range. She had even heard him laugh when Nick arranged for Frank to pick him up: Olsen just couldn't believe he was on the same side as Frank now when Olsen had previously helped One Hundred Roads attempt to swindle the reservation out of palladium mining rights.

"Olsen, you can't keep me in the dark here. *Where's Angela?*"

"She's *on recon.* She's a smart girl, clever even. She checked the wallets of those militia boys that she took out—"

"You mean *killed*."

"Okay, *killed,* and found a handful of room keys for a motel north of here. We've got a short window to go see if there's anything useful in their rooms, assuming they haven't already been cleaned out by the other operatives. We need breadcrumbs to keep following the trail."

"What about Silver? Or Penny, I mean. Or your guys, like Odemo?"

"I'm working on it. Not everyone is available at the drop of a hat. We have to work with what we have in the short term, like Angela."

Dana walked ahead and waited for him to shuffle to his room. She proceeded to throw the duffel on the floor at his feet as he entered. Her eyes followed a pattern of blood spatters across the dark canvas of the bag. Blood spilled because of her, either directly or indirectly. She glowered at Olsen.

"Angela's not a special agent, you know. She doesn't have training like you or the militia bros we've been able to stay ahead of so far. If she gets into trouble, the only thing she can count on is losing her cool and getting angry."

"I'm aware of that," he said with a nod. He gently sat the gun bag on the bed and unloaded several pistols. "Can you close the door?"

She slammed it shut.

"Thank you." He counted out boxes of bullets and paired different guns with different ammunition sizes. "Angela only took a handful of shotgun shells."

"Hey, hey!" Dana snapped her fingers at him. "Stop talking around it. Where is Angela right now?"

"She texted me that she's in Alamosa, making her way on foot to the Armadillo Inn. I told her not to get dropped off any closer in case someone recognizes the eighteen-wheeler that plowed into the Jeep. She'll text me in about an hour once she gets out of the motel on foot."

"Why hasn't she texted *me*?"

"I told her not to." He placed the guns, except for one handgun, back into the bag in an organized stack. "You've been through a lot of trauma and I need her, and you, focused. And for now, I'm cutting down the static and chatter."

"Yeah, well, that's not gonna fly with me." She poked him in the shoulder and snorted. "That's my friend, not your errand girl. And if she gets into a jam—"

"She'll get angry, I know. And I've been meaning to talk to you about that, about what happened to make her like that."

"That's information you're not privileged to know. You're not her friend. You don't know."

He opened his phone. "I got an email here. I asked Odemo to run an additional background check. I needed to know a little more about who I'm dealing with here. I know about Angela, why she left high school, the court case—"

"Hey!" Dana pushed him. He steadied himself but held his ground. "You *don't* know. She's loyal to me, not you, and I'm loyal to her, not you. You have no idea what she's been through, and I don't think she'd appreciate you snooping around. Those files are supposed to be sealed, you know. She was a minor." *Careful, Dana, you're playing poker against a pro, and you don't want to show any cards.*

"Dana, I'm not the bad guy anymore." He sat on the edge of the bed and held his cane in his open palms. "Angela is out there breaking into the motel rooms of *actual* bad guys. You're wasting energy and time, and anger." He sighed. "Right now, I'm not worth your attention."

She couldn't help but feel sad for him, just for a moment, as he sat slumped and weary, the lines and bags under his eyes more prominent from the lack of sleep and overexertion during their escape. But she also remembered that this broken man in front of her was a bastard capable of unemotional destructive acts when he felt they were necessary.

"You're a shitty leader, you know that?"

He looked down at his cane. "One of the reasons for protocol in the military is for discipline. Keeping a cool head, keeping focus on the mission, letting capable people do capable things to keep moving the ball forward. Angela's good at that: moving the ball forward."

"I think you lean on her too much. I think you're projecting your lost masculinity on her and taking advantage of her eagerness to seek approval." *Did I just say that out loud? Where did that come from?*

"You're probably correct, even if that's not my conscious intention. Like it's not your conscious intention to use her friendship, her broken heart, to keep her here with you." She winced at his matter-of-fact inflection and tone. "I can't help but notice several people in our camp have a chip on their shoulder or their heart on their sleeve, or both. Including you."

His earnestness and insight pierced through one of the layers of anger wrapped around Dana's heart. She knew he had no reason to be here, to help, except for revenge and a blindly noble cause to stop Rhodes. Olsen was the one who had stayed up late with Ashley to work on the computer, woke up early to help Simone prepare breakfast, worked through lunch to show Angela new self-defense moves. If anyone was giving to the group and receiving nothing in return, it was Olsen. And despite all his planning and preparation, he still had to improvise when the situation spiraled from one crisis to the next. *Not at all the portrait of a shitty leader.* She sat down next to him on the bed and took a breath. *I'm not giving him a hug.*

"I said some shitty things to you, in the barn when we were with Jennifer. I apologize."

"Not necessary, but appreciated."

"And nice move you did back there, getting Jennifer to admit California was a viable location."

He curled his lips over his teeth and looked up, not quite at her but just off-center, not making eye contact. "An interrogation trick. Nothing special."

"It was good, in the moment. So, big guy, when does Angela come back?"

"Assuming that she's traveling by foot across town, anywhere from two hours onward." He smirked. "Unless she steals a car. Has she done that?"

"No, she has not," Dana replied, almost smiling in return. "So, we sit tight, hope she doesn't get into trouble. We wait for Nick to get back with the tires. And tomorrow, we go to the hospital to visit Mom."

Olsen stood. He shook out his left leg. "Dana, your mother is tough. The wounds were bad, but your sister did good helping me slow the bleeding and keep her stable. Just remember it's the doctor's job to prepare the family with the worst-case scenario."

"On that note, I'm going to grab my bag from the van and head to my room." Dana stopped in the doorway and examined the well-worn doorknob. An idea flickered. "How far away is Angela, about an hour?"

"Give or take."

"I won't wait up, then."

"Dana," he said with a tenderness in his voice she rarely heard, "are *you* alright?"

"I'm fine." *Liar.*

Dana closed the door gently and walked back to the van. She slid her backpack over her shoulder and listened to the dull clanks of Laverne and Shirley as she plodded up the stairs.

# Chapter 33

*Physical – Dua Lipa*

The sky bled orange and red behind the last visible clouds. The Armadillo Inn's sign flickered to life, but the parking lot lamps remained dark. Angela sat crouched next to a dumpster. She pulled her hair back into a ponytail and wrapped a scrunchie around it before putting the bag with her motorized skates under a wooden pallet leaning up against the bin's rear. *Go time, girl.*

In socked feet, Angela jogged around the corner and up the stairs to the motel's outer balcony. She slid the key card for room 209 out of her rear pocket as she leaned against the door and placed an ear against it. Nothing. Through the window, there was only darkness; no lights on inside, no television on in the background. She slid the card into the reader quickly and waited for what felt like an eon for the green light to indicate the door was now unlocked.

She closed the door quickly and quietly before turning on the light. A basic room: two queen-sized beds separated by a weathered nightstand, and a long dresser adorned with a flat-screen television from a discount store.

She headed first to the closet alcove and opened a small suitcase. Inside, under a layer of unfolded shirts and jeans, she unearthed a laptop bag.

A small outburst of laughter outside the room startled her.

Angela froze, listening to the rise and fall of the voices, fixing the corner of her vision on the door as she fingered the assortment of papers in the bag with the laptop. A pink flash caught her eye as she paused on a page from a shipping manifest. She folded it and slipped it into her back pocket with the room key, then thought twice and grabbed the entire handful of papers.

Suddenly, a click followed by a beep broke the silence. The door opened.

"Well, well, well, you're a pretty little maid," snorted the first entrant, a bulky man in jeans and a camouflage thermal shirt. He stroked his thick brown moustache, which contrasted with his pale face. "Deebo, you see this lady here? That is some grade A talent."

The second man, Deebo, smiled. He was larger in height, slimmer in build but with similarly pale skin, and wore a tan work shirt and matching cargo pants. "You got that right, Gordo. Hey, missy, did the boys order you up here for a little party time? I know they were with some strippers a couple nights ago." He cracked his knuckles. "They've been MIA for a few hours, but we can start without them, if you know what I mean."

Angela turned slowly, pushing the laptop bag to the side with her foot. Her stomach gurgled as she looked them over, letting their words sink in. Gordo sucked in his gut.

"We won't bite. Our mamas raised us to treat ladies right. Even the hookers."

She bit her lip and smiled, walking slowly toward them.

"Take off your shirt, Gordo," Angela said in a slithering voice. "Let me see what I'm about to manhandle."

Gordo laughed and began to pull off his shirt. When his arms and head were locked in his sleeves, Angela spun and kicked him square in the chest, then planted her feet and swung an uppercut into Deebo's stunned face.

"You dumb bitch!" screamed Gordo as he threw his shirt to the ground and punched her between the shoulder blades. "Deebo! Get your belt off so we can give this girl a real ass whooping!"

Angela spun around and kneed Gordo in the groin. She caught the glimmer of a belt buckle in her periphery and dodged it as it swung her way. She delivered a high kick to Deebo's scrawny chest, followed by another punch to Gordo.

She waited for the next attack. Her breath slowed as she focused.

*Wait.*

She stood in place as Deebo threw his next punch.

*Block.*

Her arms flexed as she moved her wrists in front of her face.

*Catch.*

Angela grabbed his hand and leaned back with the impact.

*Throw.*

With her knees bent, she flipped Deebo over her head and onto the bed.

Angela snapped back to an upright pose. Gordo stood next to the door, curtain rod in hand, and was suddenly accompanied by two new adversaries, one in a gray fatigue shirt and jeans, the other in a red sweat suit. Gordo sneered and licked his lips.

"Girl, there's no easy way to put this." He playfully tossed the curtain rod back and forth between his hands. "We are going to make you *beg* for us to kill you."

A sweaty arm slithered over her shoulder and around her neck. Deebo laughed from behind her and yanked her arm against her back. "You ready to party now?"

In the distance, beyond the open door, a faint whirring and grinding echoed through the parking lot. It grew louder, separating into distinct tones and notes, like an out-of-tune guitar screeching through a chord. Angela smiled and shifted her weight to her heels.

"Let's party."

A scream of metal announced Dana as she flew up to the balcony with a soaring leap and Laverne and Shirley met the skulls of the two additional men. Angela dipped into a crouch and flung Deebo overhead into a stunned Gordo, then turned and stomped on Deebo's ankle.

"Dude!" Dana yelled.

"Dude!" Angela replied, pointing to Deebo as he rose once again, almost unfazed.

"Got it!" Dana spun and heel-kicked Deebo into the wall.

"Bitches!" The man in the sweat suit stood slowly and rubbed the back of his head, his face as red as his shirt as he grabbed Dana and threw her against the wall. Angela leapt forward, scooping up the curtain rod, and swung it upward into the man's chin. He stumbled backward through the door out to the balcony.

"Enough!" Angela yelled as she swung again. Her blood felt hot as it rushed under her skin, her cheeks burning with rage. She pressed the rod against his throat and pushed him back to the wrought iron railing.

"Enough!" she yelled again, her voice filled with hate, her iron fists crushing the rod against his throat. His back arched slowly over the rail. Her thighs turned to stone as she pressed him further, inching him closer to the tipping point.

"Angela!" Dana screamed from behind her. "No!"

The man's eyes bulged. Strands of her loose hair fell onto his cheeks, sweaty and red, speckled with blood. Her muscles tightened as she continued to boil every drop of adrenaline.

"ANGELA!" Dana grabbed her shoulder. "NO!"

Her body relaxed at Dana's touch. The man's eyes fluttered as she released the pressure of the rod on his throat. He slid down, flopping to his knees before landing face-first on the balcony between her feet.

"Angela-la-la." Dana's hand touched Angela's cheek. "Enough," she whispered.

The rod felt heavy in her hands. She dropped it with a clang and turned to examine the room. All the men appeared to be unconscious. Looking back at Dana's face, Angela saw fear reflected in her eyes.

"Dana-na-na-na."

Dana's dark sweaty curls enveloped her face. Angela hugged her tightly as tears stormed down her cheeks. She was there again in her mind, back at the day that still haunted her, the day that had trapped her on the darkest rocky shores until Dana became her lighthouse.

"It's okay, sweetie," Dana cooed. "It's okay. Listen. We have to go. We have to go right now. It's okay. Let's go."

"My skates," Angela said as she broke their embrace. "My skates are behind the dumpster."

"Then get going—I'll catch up. I was able to jump up to the balcony with a little help from that Corolla down there," Dana said, nodding to a dented car roof below, "but going down a staircase in skates will take me a minute."

"Got it."

Angela jogged halfway down the stairs and paused. Again, in the distance was another faint droning of metal, the sound of skates. She turned back to Dana.

"Is Ashley on the way?"

Dana paused before clumsily lurching down the stairs two steps at a time. "No, she's not. Get your skates! Go!"

# Chapter 34

*Thunderstruck – AC/DC*

Olsen counted again: two duffel bags, each holding about $400,000 in US currency, and a smaller bag of mixed euros, yen, and pound sterling worth another $100,000. He grabbed a couple handfuls of the US money worth about $40,000 and placed it on the dresser next to his phone as it started to vibrate. He clicked his earpiece.

"Olsen here, go ahead."

"It's Dana. I'm with Angela and we're on 285 heading south to the motel."

"Wait, hang on." He pulled the drapery aside to confirm the lights were off in Dana's room. "You're not here at the motel? What's going on?"

"I went to back up Angela, and we're in a mess. Look out!" A truck horn blared through his earpiece. "We found a nest of Rhodes's idiots and we've got two of them skating on our heels!"

"How far are you?" He slipped his pistol into his shoulder harness and zipped up his coat.

"Half hour? Forty minutes? We're faster than these guys, but Angela's exhausted and fighting muscle cramps. And—hang on, whoops! I just had to swerve around a Beetle. We could use some backup, or an extraction, or whatever you call it."

Olsen peeked around the curtain and spied the blue Subaru in the parking lot that had been there since he arrived. The owner was unloading a suitcase from the back seat.

"Stay on the highway. I'll come get you." He reached back inside the duffel bag. *Satellite phone*. He shot a text to Odemo. *Cash*. He grabbed the stack from the dresser. *Gun*. Already in his holster. *Wheels*. In progress.

Olsen headed out of the room and straight for the Subaru. He dialed his accent to New Yorker and enthusiastically waved. "Hey, guy, is that your WRX? That's a beauty!"

A young man with bronze skin in a tank top smiled and closed the car door. "Sure is. GT model, too."

Olsen rubbed his chin, leaning in to spy on the steering column. "You got those paddle shifters in the GT package, right? That's included? I'm a bit of a gearhead, you know what I'm saying?" He tapped his left foot. "I used to have a Hemi. I was a muscle car guy, and I need steering wheel paddles now. Bad foot means I can't do a clutch pedal anymore."

"That's a shame, bro."

Olsen's earpiece buzzed with Dana's voice.

"Olsen? Buddy? Are you about to steal a car? Olsen?"

He reached into his pocket and pulled out the bundle of cash. Trust earned, he pivoted back to his native accent, a tactic he had learned when he needed to switch from lion to lamb for maximum effect.

"So, mate, I gave you this, you give me the keys. I'll be back in an hour."

"Yo, man, look—"

"This is not a negotiation!" He tossed the money toward the man and pulled his gun from his holster. "It's an emergency! Keys! Now!" The man held out his shivering hand holding a plastic fob attached to a tiny plush fox keychain. Olsen grabbed the key. "I'll double your money if you keep your mouth shut. I'll be right back." The man remained frozen as Olsen tucked his gun away. "I promise. You have my word."

Olsen ripped open the door and jumped into the driver's seat. Shining black leather, chrome accents, and a fully digital display screen lit up as he started the car. His hands slid over the leather wrapping as the engine vibrated, his fingertips lithely touching the tips of the paddle shifters behind the steering wheel.

"This . . . is . . . lovely."

He shot a quick reply to Odemo and shared his location via the satellite phone. "I hope you're around, buddy." The Subaru roared with the open throttling of the gas. He glanced at his hand clutching the wheel at 12 o'clock, the black wristlet from Penny peering out from under his cuff.

"Shit." He pulled off the wristlet and wrapped it around the steering wheel. A pair of red dots blipped on the screen as well as a distance meter. *Good, I can see how close the skaters are.*

Biting his lip over a smile, he threw the car into reverse, skidding briefly as he slammed the gearshift back into drive. His right foot slammed on the metal pedal as his fingers readied for the shifts with the ascending RPM gauge. He cut the wheel and fishtailed onto the highway.

"Oh, I do miss *driving*!" He laughed as he passed the first car in his lane. The high whine of the rotary engine almost drowned out Dana's shouts into his ear.

"You *did* steal a car, oh my God."

"I'm still waiting on the van's tires. Stay on the highway." *Location. Distance. Time.* "Where are you girls now? Got a mile marker?"

"I saw something with a seven on it."

"That's not helpful," he responded as he twisted the steering wheel and passed a motorcycle in the left lane. "Here's the plan: I'm in a blue Subaru WRX. I should be able to see you when you're a mile away from me on the straightaway section. Try to bring them to *your left* and I'll cross the median to take them out."

"Does that Subaru have stilts? How are you getting over the concrete barrier?"

"What concrete? It's just a grassy median." He glanced ahead at an upcoming gentle bend in the highway. The grass narrowed between the north- and southbound lanes before a rising fin of white concrete bisected them. "Oh, shit."

Olsen gripped the wheel and downshifted, throttling the car into the dry grass between the directional lanes. He was now driving on the wrong side of the road as the concrete barrier rose on his right.

"New plan, Dana. I'm in your lane heading right to you." A pair of semitrailer trucks, side by side, barreled toward him. His adrenaline surged, seasoned with a pinch of fear.

The trucks bleated their horns at Olsen in his blue rocket. He juked to the left, rumbling and bouncing in the shoulder as the trailers barreled past him. He swerved again onto the road, dodging an oncoming station wagon followed by a heavy-duty pickup truck.

"Everything's fine!" he shouted. "Woo!"

"Olsen, you cannot have a 'woo' moment right now! Where are you? These brutes are right on top of us!"

"I don't see you yet, but I'm swimming upstream. Hang on a little longer." He shifted again and the car surged, the racing suspension punishing his tailbone with every bump. "I see you!"

Ahead, he spotted four silhouettes in a sea of headlights. He glanced down at the emergency brake handle, then at the tracking watch.

"Dana, do exactly as I say, you hear? Stay as true to the dotted white line as you can. Come right at me and jump over or to the side at the last second. I'll stay right on the dotted line. Clear?"

"Copy that."

*Good soldier.*

He held his right hand over the brake handle. The forms of Dana and Angela were now more distinct in how they differed from the taller, wider stances of the militant skaters behind them. The women closed in on the lane markers, almost shoulder to shoulder, while Rhodes's skaters remained in their wake. Olsen drew a slow, calm breath. On the tracker, the distance steadily decreased between him and the red dots.

"Dana, counting down from three. Three. Two. One. *Jump!*"

Olsen yanked the handbrake as hard as possible as he cut the wheel hard left. The car began a violent spin, whipping his head from side to side. He caught a brief shower of sparks spreading over the hood as the car slid perpendicular to the lane. He tightened his forearms and fists to hold steady, his jaw locked. Two loud thuds impacted the side of the car, followed by shattering window glass as the Subaru continued to spin. He jerked the wheel back, releasing the emergency brake as he sputtered to a standstill. He was breathing heavily but steady as he focused on the next objective.

"Holy shit," Dana whispered over his earpiece.

Olsen opened the car door with a heavy nudge of his shoulder and held his gun at the ready, pointing at the two bodies of the male skaters in the road. He approached slowly, looking for any indications of life, but found none unless he counted the wheels on the skates whining slowly to a stop. One of the skater's helmets, painted green with yellow and white stripes down the center, had rolled to the side of the road. Olsen stooped and stared into the unblinking eyes of the fallen man, barely an adult. *This is on you, Rhodes.*

"I think they're dead, bro," Angela coughed as she rolled closer, holding her side. "Shit."

"Are you hurt?" Olsen extended his hand to touch her, the same spot where he had once stabbed her, appreciating for a moment the irony. He let his hand drift back.

"Just side stitches. Did you know skating is a lot of work for your core?

I should wake up with six-pack abs in the morning." Her face soured as she looked at the helmetless skater. No words needed to be said; Olsen could see Angela's empathy wash over her face. "Shit."

"I'm glad you're safe. Both of you. Come on, off the road. Into the field." Olsen hobbled back to the Subaru, grabbed the tracking watch and the contents of the glovebox, and then hurried back over to the shoulder of the road. He felt Dana's arm around his waist helping him.

"Left your cane at home?"

"I did," he huffed. "Keep going. Straight line out into the prairie, or whatever this is." Behind them, a boxy sedan slowed and stopped at the wreck. The driver and passenger leaned over the bodies and gesticulated wildly at the damaged Subaru, one of them holding up a phone.

"How are we getting back to the motel?" Angela asked, her pace slowing. She winced with each step as they navigated the dry weeds and rocks in the darkness on their skates.

"I already called a ride."

"Out here? Did you hit your head?" Dana mocked him with a smug smile.

Olsen held up his phone and checked the signal. "I know a guy." He clicked through his texts. "Bingo."

He led them further into the darkness, the smattering of lights from the highway growing fainter. After several minutes, a small open area emerged from the brush, surrounded by a cluster of dead bushes. "We can wait here. Angela, how did the recon go?"

"I got some stuff," she said, grimacing as she reached into her back pocket and pulled out a folded pink paper. "Some kind of shipping record. Seemed important. I've got some other papers rolled up inside my sleeve."

"Alright, good."

Angela flexed her arm. "We had to fight through about four jerkholes before the skate club showed up." She brushed a sweaty strand of hair away from her forehead. "What do we do about the car?"

"I'll have Dan tidy up the report with the local police, and I'll drop off some additional hush money back at the hotel with the car's prior owner. And get a rental for him." He sighed, glancing at the registration and manuals in his hand from the glovebox. "Something like that."

Olsen checked the time again. "Everyone sit tight." A low humming above the huddle was followed by an increasingly strong blast of air. A large shadow crossed over the group as the heliplane touched down several yards away. Dana yawned.

"Let me guess: the Boo-Boo crew?"

"Yes, Odemo and the gang." Olsen stood on his own power and brushed the dirt off his pants. "Dana, call your sister when you get a signal and tell her we're on our way." He looked at the incoming message on his satellite phone.

"Good news?" Dana asked. "I'll take bad news, too. Any news."

Olsen tucked the phone into his coat. "Nick's back at the motel now."

# Chapter 35

*Everything – Lifehouse*

Dana could see light peeking out from around the edges of the curtains of Nick's motel room, leaking thin golden beams onto the balcony. Dana leaned her ear onto the door and listened to the quiet mumbling of the television inside. His pickup, obviously retrieved from her mother's house, rested silently in the parking lot, the four van tires in the bed.

She was so tired. The heliplane had dropped them off a half mile from the hotel, and the walk back was exhausting. But sleep wasn't in the cards tonight. Her head was swimming with too many emotions, but one raised its hand and asked to go first.

She held her hand up to knock at the door, paused, and then tapped it lightly with her knuckles.

"Nick? It's Dana."

Silence.

"Nick? I can see your light is on. I know you're in there. I need to talk. You don't have to say anything, but I need to say some stuff."

She leaned her forehead against the door and closed her eyes. She was exhausted in body, mind, and heart, but a wave of nerves in the pit of her stomach buoyed her. Losing Nick again was unimaginable, *inconceivable.* No matter what had happened before, she had always expected that he would somehow be there. She understood now that it was selfish to take him for granted, crazy that she thought she could control the circumstances. She braced her hands on the doorframe, head still pointed down, and exhaled.

"Just . . . listen. I am sorry, I am so sorry. It's my fault your dad was killed. Oh God, I loved your dad. He was such a good man. He made you into an even better one. I got him killed, and I have to live with that. I can't ever get him back for you. I can't fix this. And it's crushing my heart to know that your heart is shattered.

"And I know Jennifer turned out to be, you know, an evil bitch, but before that, she made you feel special. I know all you wanted was to fall in love like in some 1980s romantic-comedy movie. I feel like I took that away from you, too.

"Oh God, Nick, I am so sorry. I ruined everything. And I was so scared I would put you in danger if you stayed around, and somehow I ended up putting you in danger anyway.

"Anyway, I don't expect anything from you. I don't need you to say you forgive me, or that you understand, or even that you hate me. I just need to tell you this, all of this. Because I'm selfish. I only care about me, and right now I'm dying inside without you. *Without my friend.*

"I miss you. I just wish I could go back, that *we* could go back. Sitting in the back of your truck and eating junk food, or washing dishes in the rancher." She broke into a weak laugh. "Remember when you would have to clean up the counter after I was done because I got soap suds everywhere? Every little thing like that . . . I want it all back."

Dana tapped her head against the door. Tears rolled off her chin, forming tiny puddles on the ground beneath her. She tried to imagine her mother's hand on her back like when she was a child, soothing her while she cried. Everything hurt. She shut her eyes.

"I'm sorry. I just needed you to know. All of this."

Her knees began to buckle. She gripped the doorframe for dear life. There was nothing left to say except the final truth. Her lips quivered as she forced thoughts into words.

"Nick, I love you. I love you so much. And it's not that I need you to know that I love you, it's that I need you to know *how* I love you. I can't be a better person, ever, without you. I'm going to spend the rest of my life trying to be half the person you are. Because you're a part of me, and I never realized that until I tried to tear you out and leave you behind. I love you, Nick. You're *everything*."

A cough behind her back startled her. A voice, soft but slightly hoarse, floated over her shoulder.

"I went down to my truck to get something."

She turned around. Nick was leaning against the railing holding a plastic bag. Dana shuddered, embarrassed suddenly at her soul-bearing speech to an empty room.

"How much did you hear?"

"*Everything*." He reached into the plastic bag and pulled out a pair of roller skates. "Jameson snuck me into your mom's house, and I thought I should grab Lenny and Squiggy for you." A tear rolled out of the corner of each of his eyes.

"Nick."

"Dana."

She lunged forward and grabbed Nick by the shirt collar, pulling him toward her. Dana pressed her lips against his, desperate, frantic, a silent prayer for forgiveness. She slid her arm around his back and squeezed, inhaling his pain and exhaling her own in return. The salty taste of their combined tears and his arms holding her made her feel safe. She shook with a mix of relief and joy, as well as shame for all the pain she had caused him. Slowly, she pulled back and frowned.

"I'm sorry. Was that okay?"

Nick nodded and held up his motel card. "We should put these skates inside—"

Dana grabbed the card, slid it through the reader, and pulled Nick into the room. Dana grabbed Nick's collar again and kissed him, harder than before, but with a rising well of happiness. He dropped the bag and grabbed her gently by the shoulders, gasping as he removed his lips from hers.

"Dana, wait, wait, wait. *Wait.*" His eyes darted back and forth, weary but still shining blue. "I'm really not in the most logical state of mind right now. I'm hanging on by a thread here." She nodded. His hands still gripped her shoulders. "We're *both* not in our best minds right now."

"You are such a grown-up. Dammit," she said with a short laugh. "This is one of those moments where it's better to regret something we didn't do rather than something we did, right?"

"I think I understood that. Yes." He slid his calloused but gentle hands down to hold hers. "But I don't want to be alone."

"Me neither."

In silent agreement, they each sat on the edge of the bed, shoulder to shoulder, and took off their shoes. Dana slid off her jacket, as did Nick, followed by the simultaneous emptying of their pockets and removal of belts. Nick reached over and pulled back the bed sheet. Dana slid in first, facing away from the window. Nick turned off the light, then rolled in behind her, his chest against her back. He reached his arm around her waist.

"Wait. Nick, will you take off your shirt?"

He obliged and laid back down, facing the window this time. Dana sat up, her back to him, and slid her shirt over her head. She laid down, her chest against his back now, and felt the warmth of his skin against hers.

"Uh, Dana—"

"I just need to feel you." She stared out the window through the threadbare, almost sheer curtains, surprised how she could still make out the stars. "I don't know what's going to happen tomorrow, or for the rest of our lives." She placed his hand on her bare sternum. "But tonight, it's just us. I love you, Nick Andrews."

"I love you, too, Dana Jefferson."

"I still owe you a motorcycle."

"I didn't forget about that."

She laughed and nestled her head into his neck, kissing him softly next to his ear. His body shivered, then began to slowly heave. He whimpered, crying slowly at first, and then he sobbed harder than she had ever seen him. It was finally his turn to break down.

"I'm here, Nicky," she whispered. "It's okay. Just let it out."

"I miss my dad."

"I know. Me, too." She ran her hand through his hair, her fingers digging tiny troughs across his scalp. "I know." Dana let her own tears run silently down her cheeks. "Just let it out. I'm not going anywhere. Ever again."

In that moment, she understood, finally, the bond and love between them—as friends. She wanted him to find love, love she couldn't give in return to him fairly, because he deserved so much more than she could ever be. But their type of love, the unconditional way they cared for each other, was real and forever.

Dana pulled her arms tighter around him as he cried, until their breathing slowed together. She placed her hand on his chest, warm and soft, and felt his heart beating. She wanted to stay together like this for a little while longer.

A light snore told her when Nick was finally asleep. His thumb on her arm twitched lightly; she hoped he was already dreaming. She stayed up a little longer, long enough to watch a single star move from one side of the window to the other. One single star coming into view, blazing bright, and then finally sliding behind the curtain.

# Chapter 36

*Kings and Queens — Aerosmith*

From her balcony on the other side of the pool, Angela had been relaxing with a beer when she saw Dana kiss Nick right after he presented her with a pair of roller skates. She understood that reconciliation had finally occurred. After they entered Nick's room together, she swigged the rest of her bottle and tossed it underhand into the trash can at the top of the stairs just as Olsen reached the top step. He flinched as the bottle hit with a crash.

"I'm guessing they're okay now," he stated flatly, coming to stand next to Angela. In his free hand, he held a half-empty six-pack. "I had a beer with the Subaru's owner and handed over another pile of bills for his silence." He lightly rattled the bottles. "Need another one?"

"Yeah. You could say that." She opened a bottle. "Nothing a good sleep can't fix."

"You sure?" he asked, nodding toward the closed door across the way as the lights turned off.

She leaned over the railing, eyeing the pool glowing unevenly blue from whatever underwater lights weren't burnt out. "I'm good."

"Are you sure?"

"I accept that Dana and I just weren't meant to be. We're not a love connection." She drew a long drink from her bottle.

"But you still love her."

She looked at her feet. "Of course I do." She hesitated to say more at first, but then chose to give Olsen a little more of herself. "That doesn't go away. It just changes. She's like my . . . sister now."

"Your only sister. You were raised in a family of boys, right?"

Angela smiled weakly. Olsen was always paying attention, and she had a hunch she knew where he would eventually steer the conversation, even with a light beer buzz. She grabbed the wheel.

"Come with me. We're going swimming." She bounded down the first half of the stairs and turned to see if he was following. "It'll be good for your leg, old man." She skipped to the gate and held up the open padlock before entering the pool area.

"Great security here," Olsen grumbled as he made his way into the courtyard.

"Off with your threads!" Angela announced, flinging her shirt at a lounge chair, followed by her jeans. Still wearing her underwear and bra, she stepped into the shallow end, which was still warm from the day's baking sun. She pinched her nose and submerged herself, listening to the sounds of the water, a dull arrhythmic humming and sloshing from the filtration system and her small wake. She counted a few more seconds before shooting up and flailing her hair, white droplets spraying into the sky.

"You coming in?"

Olsen nodded and slid off his boots and fatigue pants. He sat on the first step in his boxers and pulled his sports shirt over his head. Angela subtly checked out his tattoos and scars as they rippled over his tired muscles, more defined than she had expected for a man she assumed was in decline physically from his curbed mobility. She wanted to keep her hands on the conversation's wheel.

"You still look good for a man of your age."

"I'm immune to flattery." He slid down the steps until only his shoulders broke the plane of the pool's surface. The illumination from below highlighted the deep wrinkles at the corners of his eyes and the tiny imperfections on his chin and cheeks, remnants of scars from long ago.

"So." Angela spread her arms and rested her elbows behind her on the concrete ledge. "You can't stop being a mercenary. So, I'm guessing right now, you're on a recon mission to find out more about me."

He ran a handful of water over his head. "You went to public high school. After junior year, you dropped out; you didn't return for senior year, but you got your GED in parallel with your intended graduating class. You went to community college. You could have been a softball player at a higher level, but your academic handicap left you the blazing star on your junior college team." He rinsed his head again. "That garnered enough attention to earn a tryout for the local Minor League Baseball team, even if it was more of a publicity stunt than a real offer."

"Ding. Winner." She mimed firing guns with her index fingers and thumbs. "You got me. Could never quite finish anything. So, I'm overcompensating for my lack of achievement."

"You know what I found interesting," he said with an exaggerated inquisitive tone, "was a small local news piece that I came across. During your junior year, it seems there was a girl in your town who was assaulted by a group of boys. Big upper-class suburban house. Parents were out of town, so the perfect time for a big party, right? The girl, according to the press and the limited information made available, was in an altercation. She fought for her life. And in the melee, one of the boys fell off the bedroom balcony."

Angela grit her teeth. She realized she was outwitted.

"That boy," he continued, "slipped into a coma and died a few days later." He swam over, mirroring her pose on the concrete next to her. He stared straight ahead, not meeting her gaze.

"Go on."

"My interest was piqued, so Perry and Odemo dug deeper. It seems that there were charges brought up against the girl, because she wasn't the assault victim that night. The *real* victim was taken to the hospital . . . police, attorneys, her parents were all there. But then Dan Sun uncovered the hospital records for *another* person who had been admitted on the same night."

"Me."

"Yes. Apparently, you only had a broken wrist, but they did a full examination." She caught his eyes darting over to her and then returning forward. "They performed . . . well, they assumed you had been assaulted, too."

Angela felt a small fire in her stomach as she listened to her life being narrated by an outside observer. She didn't like it, but she knew he was almost at the end.

"I know this makes you uncomfortable, but I needed to know exactly who is on my team." He finally turned to face her. "At that party, *you* witnessed a crime. It was an absolutely heinous act, what those boys were doing. You saved that girl, and you threw one of those teenaged monsters over the balcony. And that's the first time you killed someone." He dipped his hands into the water. "I don't have any fond memories over my first kill, either."

"It wasn't a 'first kill,'" she finally snapped. She confronted him face-to-face. "It was survival. Do you know what those boys said to me and my girlfriend? That we were 'a waste of two hot chicks.' They said they were going to 'screw us straight' so we'd 'know what it felt like to be normal.'" She fumed, her breaths fast and deep. The fire she could never fully extinguish burned hot. "They grabbed her. They *forced me to watch*. And so when the chance came, I fought for both our lives." Olsen remained still as Angela leaned closer. "And I threw that human piece of shit over the balcony. And at the time, I was *glad* I did it."

Her nostrils flared. Olsen finally yielded, leaning back against the wall of the pool. The quiet lapping of the water and a distant car on the highway were the only sounds.

"I am truly sorry you went through that. I know the family tried to get you on manslaughter."

"Yeah, that's the funny thing," she scoffed. "Since I wasn't the 'primary victim,' I was the instigator. The escalator. Can you believe that?" Her voice broke, but she knew she just needed to plow ahead. "I had to relive all the details *over and over*, while the boys' attorneys called me a murderer. They accused me and my girlfriend of vicious lies. And when the dust settled, my name was clear, but not my head."

She relaxed her aggressive posture and splashed her face with water. "I couldn't hide from it. People whispered, they stared. It didn't go away. I kept reliving it." Her anger swelled, but then a calmness crossed her face. "And then I found roller derby, my new family. No one judged me. I was home."

"And you met Dana."

"Yes."

"And here we are now."

Angela's shoulders slumped, exhausted from reliving it all. She stared at the surface of the water as it fluttered when the edge of a ripple caught the reflection of the underwater lights. It was time for her to finish her story.

"Aaron, there was one night, shortly after I joined the derby team in Asbury . . . I wasn't doing well. I was in my apartment, alone. I was thinking about the *incident* . . . how it drove a wedge between me and my girlfriend. She was afraid of me, emotionally and physically. And I remembered that boy's face, looking up from the driveway at me, frozen." Her lip quivered. "And he *was* a boy, when all was said and done. He didn't even have his learner's permit."

She pursed her lips to breathe. "I put a bottle of pills on the bathroom counter and filled a glass of water. I was going to do it. My phone rang, and for some unknown reason, I answered it. This goofy, stupid, pretty girl named Dana that I met at derby said that she knew it was late, but she really wanted to know if I wanted to grab a burger at the local diner and talk derby. Because she loved the way I skated." She looked up at Olsen, his mouth hanging in sadness. "She called me 'Angela-la-la.' She saved my life. And I can never, ever repay that debt. And so, here we are now."

Angela's face crumbled. Olsen rested a hand on her shoulder as she wept. She leaned forward into him, her body convulsing.

"Angela, you saved *all* our lives when we escaped from the ranch. You are no longer indebted to anyone."

The two embraced in the shallow end until Angela could compose herself. She had been lucky to have a supportive family, a ferocious army of brothers, and loving parents, but she had never truly shared her pain, trying to protect them. Only Dana knew her deepest sadness—and now Olsen.

"Aaron," she whispered, "I would die for Dana."

"I promise to never put you in that position." He gently separated from her and stared into her eyes. "You know, I've been using you all wrong. You're not a warrior. You're not a fighter. You're a protector." She nodded. "You're a *guardian angel*. That's your nature—it's what you've always been. That's why you're here on this earth." He headed toward the pool steps and climbed out to collect his clothes from the chaise lounge, then looked back at her. "I'm sorry that I stabbed you the first time we met."

"Forgiven." Angela smiled. She followed his lead and left the pool, her mind now calm. She removed her wet undergarments in the middle of the patio and let the light breeze blow across her bare skin to dry it. Olsen ducked his head and turned his back.

"Modesty, Angela, if you don't mind."

"I have nothing left to hide. I am proud of who I am."

# Chapter 37

*Tom's Diner – Suzanne Vega*

The aroma of burnt waffles seared Dana's nostrils. The continental breakfast was spread over a long counter in the motel lobby, just across from six tables with two chairs each. Olsen sat at the one facing the entrance door. Dana was beginning to pick up his little habits: what he carried, his awareness of access to exits and views from windows, always on guard. Angela sat across from him, picking at the remains of a pile of toast crusts. She pointed a plastic fork at Dana.

"The eggs are actually pretty okay."

"You know my weird fondness for cafeteria-style eggs," Dana said as she picked up a paper plate adorned with teal and purple graphics. "Is the waffle maker beyond recovery?" She pried the lid open and turned up her nose at the charred fragments in the iron grid.

"Aye, my fault," Olsen said. He sipped his coffee and pulled out his phone. "I've got a few emails to check. Excuse me."

Angela nodded as he stood up, then twisted over her chair to face Dana.

"So, did you and Nick seal the deal?"

Dana felt a rush of blood to her cheeks as her eyes widened. She looked around to see who might have heard but only saw the motel clerk, a middle-aged woman in a bright-green blouse, at the reception desk computer.

"No, *Angela*, we did not!" She slapped a spoonful of eggs onto her plate and stomped over to the table. Angela kicked out the seat across from her in an assist. "We talked, we kissed, we cried, we spooned, we fell asleep!" She paused to gauge how Angela was taking it.

"It's cool." Angela leaned over the table. "I'm not heartbroken. We're way past that. Really, I'm fine."

"Anyhow, I came to the realization that Nick and I work the best as friends."

Dana looked past Angela as Olsen tried to look busy at a spinner rack filled with brochures for local attractions. He held up one for an entertainment complex emblazoned with graphics of laser tag guns and roller skates.

Dana smiled. "We can take you roller skating after we check in on my mom." He responded with a smirk. "Speaking of, has anyone seen Ashley? We should head over to the hospital." She checked her phone. *Dammit, I forgot to charge it last night*. "Hey, Ang, you got a—"

"Yep." Angela pulled a small cord from her back pocket and plugged it into the wall.

Dana's phone chirped to life as she plugged it in. A blizzard of notifications filled the screen: multiple missed calls and messages from the hospital. She scanned the text of the voice mails, recoiling at her own stupidity to let her phone battery die overnight.

"Oh my God, I have to go. We need to get Ashley."

Dana sprinted out the door and into the parking lot, followed by Angela, where they found Nick kneeling next to the van and a pile of tires. He bolted upright as Dana nearly knocked him over.

"Keys, Nick! Give me the keys to the truck!"

"What is it? Your mom?" He pressed them into her hand, holding it for a moment.

Dana spotted her sister walking back from the vending machines. "Ash! It's Mom! We have to go right now!"

"What?! Now?"

"Yes!" Dana flung open the driver's side door to the pickup. "Angela, you help Nick get those tires on the van! Olsen, do Olsen things!"

She paused as she started the truck and Ashley jumped in the passenger's side. Dana's head was a stew of emotions and images, real and imaginary. It was one thing to lose her mother as a child, another thing entirely to lose her as an adult, and a truly unique thing to possibly lose her *twice*.

But the worst thought in all the mess was Ashley facing this loss for the first time.

Angela knelt next to Nick, his eyes locked on the swerving tail of his pickup cutting across two lanes of traffic. Olsen stood next to them and flipped through his phone.

"Poor Ashley," Angela said. "I mean, poor Dana *and* Ashley. But I can't imagine what Ashley's feeling. Her mom has been her entire world."

"I can't imagine, either," Nick offered. "I mean, obviously losing a parent, yeah, I'm kind of an expert now . . . but that's the only parent she's ever known."

Angela placed a reassuring hand on his shoulder. "Hey, if you need anything, just, you know."

"I will. Thank you." He placed his hand over hers for a moment, then let go. "For Ashley, Simone was her mother *and* father. She literally protected her every day from harm. I don't think Ashley even has friends."

Nick looked up at Olsen to get his thoughts, but he wasn't listening; rather, he was scrambling through his pockets. "The tracker . . . where's that blasted tracker?" He yanked the wristlet out of his coat pocket. "This is really bad timing."

He held it up to show Nick and Angela. A series of dots moved in unison from east to west. He zoomed out as best he could on the tiny display. "They're converging and heading west. Something big is going down."

# Chapter 38

*I've Never Been to Me – Charlene*

Words. A tsunami of words. All Dana could do was sort through the infinite options of things to say to her mother as she stood helplessly in the hospital elevator. The doors opened, and she faintly felt Ashley's hand wrap around hers, pulling her down the hall until they lurched into Simone's room.

"Hey." A single raspy word greeted Dana's ears. Simone attempted to lift the brittle, crusted corners of her mouth. Dark-brown bags hung under her eyes, just above the tube that ran into her nose. Dana still saw her mother's beautiful features trying to break through the wear of the past couple of days.

"Mom," Dana said as she gently hugged her. Simone did not reciprocate, her arms lying slack on top of the sheets. "How are you?"

"I'm not going to sugarcoat it, Star. We're at the end." Simone turned her head slightly toward the window as a single tear slid down her face. "Everything is failing internally. It's just too much stress on my body." She turned back to Dana. "It's okay. I'm okay. I'm okay with it all. I'm just happy you're both here to see me off."

Tears welled in Ashley's eyes. "Mom, don't say that. You're tougher than anyone."

Dana joined in on the assurances. "Just, you know, hang on." She didn't believe the words herself, so she didn't expect her mother to buy her hopeful mantra either. "You're going to make it."

"No, girls, it's time." Simone coughed, followed by a long dry wheeze. "I'm ready. I think I did enough. It's now up to you to finish the job."

"Mom, I can't."

"All I've done is run from things. Dana, you run *toward* things." Simone smiled with significant effort. "Dana, show Ashley how to keep running in the right direction."

"Mom, I don't know how . . ." She stopped and took a breath, then looked at her mom who had taken on so much in her life. "But I'll figure it out."

"You both need to run toward your dreams. Run toward hope. Run toward love. Get your heart broken a few more times."

Ashley knelt by the bedside, her head on the faded blue sheets next to her mother's lap, her hand on her mom's leg. Dana pulled a chair next to the bed and sat down, slumping over the side and carefully picking up Simone's hand. She stroked it gently, feeling the mighty tendons and dry skin.

"What are the doctors doing for you?"

"I'm on a morphine escalator. It's as low as possible to start, but they said we're going to cross the event horizon soon. The pain, the strain on my system, it's all coming to a head. I'll soon lose my cognition to the drugs, so I need you to take good notes, okay?" She attempted to laugh, but her breath mutated into a coughing fit. "Because there are things you need to know."

"Mom, you have to make it," Ashley pleaded. Dana leaned over and gripped her shoulder. She saw the finality in her mother's eyes juxtaposed with the clouds of denial in Ashley's.

"Ash, beautiful Ash," Simone said, almost whispering. "Your father was a complicated man. But he was capable of love: loving you, and me, and this country. Underneath it all, he was a good man who made some terrible choices, headed down a dark path for a while, but then worked as hard as he could to fix things. And I still love him, and I miss him. And he loved you both *so much*."

Dana blinked away a new set of tears. Her mother's postulation of her father's love for her as well as the unborn child whom he would never meet swelled inside her. She wanted to add this to the traces of memories she had of him.

"Dana. Star. I need you to do something for me. Take my ashes to Alaska when I'm gone. There's a special place in the wilderness. I had the coordinates etched into the handle of my lucky revolver." Simone smiled again, then winced. Her face suddenly contorted. Her hand shot up to her chest. "Get the nurse."

Dana hit the call button next to the bed as Ashley ran out of the room to find help.

"Dana, you protect her," Simone whispered. "She's your sister, but now you need to be her mother, too."

"I promise."

"Dana, I'm sorry I lied to you."

"Mom, it's okay."

Ashley ran back into the room, followed by a doctor and two nurses.

"It's okay."

"No, Dana. I lied to you about . . ."

Simone's pupils dilated as she spoke those words, her eyes boring into Dana. The monitor next to the bed erupted in a symphony of synthesized beeps and bleats. Simone's eyes bulged before rolling back, her hand releasing Dana's.

Dana felt the firm hands of a nurse pull her to the side as the scrum swarmed the bed.

Her heart beat.

Simone's did not.

Dana's ears filled with a humming white noise, interspersed with shouts and the continuous drone of the heart monitor, a long single note stretching forward in time.

Gold flecks filled her field of vision. Heat ran down her forearms. Bursts of tingly pinpricks shot through her fingertips. Dana's lungs contracted, but air did not flow. Suddenly, Ashley's arms were wrapped around her, her hair filling Dana's nose with a mixed bouquet of wildflowers.

*Ashley.*

The white noise stopped. A cool rush swarmed Dana's limbs as she gripped her sister.

*We have each other.*

The realization she had her sibling with her to face the world calmed her panic. Dana glanced at the bed. The doctor hung her head low as the monitor droned. She turned to Dana and Ashley and whispered, "I'm sorry."

Ashley heaved, sobbing into Dana's chest, clutching the lapels of the old leather jacket. Dana wrapped her arms around her shoulders and squeezed. The guiding hand of one of the nurses led them into the hallway.

The sisters sat silently in a pair of chairs in an alcove. Dana took off her mother's jacket and laid it on her lap, and Ashley put her head down. Dana looked down at her wrist, at the tattoo of the red pickup truck, still vibrant. She thought a shooting star might look good next to it. Someday.

# Chapter 39

*Hackensack – Fountains of Wayne*

The brakes on the red pickup squeaked gently as the tires hit the parking berm next to the van. From the chair in front of his room, Olsen looked up from his pocket Bible and raised his hand to wave before retracting his greeting. He could tell from Dana's and Ashley's faces that the news was grim—the worst outcome. He slipped the book into his inside chest pocket and stood, leaning both hands on his cane.

Ashley approached first, wiping her nose with her sleeve. She forced a smile, shook her head, and walked past him to the stairs and up to her room. He marveled at her resilience; she was just a teenager, but she had more world experience and introspective reason than grown men he had known who had toppled dictators and seen teammates die, all for the cause of alleged freedom.

He decided then and there that Ashley should be given the option, when she was ready, to just leave the group and run. He could carry on the mission without her. He wouldn't allow Rhodes to hurt one more person, he affirmed, especially Ashley.

Shuffling feet interrupted his thoughts. Dana wandered slowly in his direction, dragging her feet, lightly kicking a small stone ahead of her. She looked up, her face emotionless, and pivoted toward her room. She paused.

"Mom died."

"I'm sorry."

Dana stood with her back to Olsen. He knew that the power of silence could draw out information during an interrogation, but this was not that type of situation. He parted his lips to speak, but no words came out. Dana shrugged her shoulders.

"I want to go."

"Okay. Where?"

"I'm done with this," she said in a low growl, turning partially toward him. He could see her profile now, the sheen of dried tears on her cheeks. "Nothing good has come from anything I've touched. Anything I've done." She turned completely to look at him, face-to-face. "It's all for nothing. People just keep *dying*." She held up a finger to stop him from interrupting. "And don't tell me it's for some—some 'greater good' or whatever high-and-mighty phrase you want to pull from your little book there." She swung her foot at the stone, punting it into the parking lot.

"Dana, I don't care if you listen to me or not, but I'm still going to speak. To you. As an adult. As a teammate. As a—"

"Don't say 'friend.'"

"—as someone who has gotten to know you and thinks you are an extraordinary person put into even more extraordinary circumstances. Do you know how you win at the game of life? You play the long game while at the same recognizing you only have right now, *right now*. You plan for the future, but you fight for the moment you're in. That's a mentality not too many people have." He stepped closer and lowered his voice. "And you don't have it—yet. But I can *see it* in you. You're right on the verge of it."

"What the hell am I supposed to do with that?" She threw up her hands in frustration and began her retreat to her room.

"Dana, you're starting to really see it now: The consequences of your actions. The responsibilities you have. And that it's easier to walk away from something than to run toward it."

She halted her steps. "Then for the first time, I'll take the easy way. I'm going to call Rhodes, take his offer, and go buy a cabin in the woods."

"You know you can't do that—*won't* do that." He cleared his throat. "Everything Nick's suffered will have been in vain. And Angela—she believes in you."

Dana sucked her teeth. "And let me guess, you'll be denied your redemption arc. Your whole 'I'm a better man now' since I crippled you story."

"That would be true, but this isn't about me. This is about *you*. And Ashley, your *sister*. And your mother? I'm pretty sure she felt more joy over the past few months with you than in her entire time without you. Having both her girls with her gave her joy. *You* gave her joy. Just by existing."

"You don't know shit about my mom."

"I know enough." He extended his hand, hovering over her shoulder and then finally placing it when she showed no signs of resistance. "Do you know what she said to me in the middle of the gunfight at the ranch? She told me to take care of her daughters." His features softened. "I don't know how to do that, but I know *you* can take care of your sister. And Angela. And Nick. They're your family."

"What do you know about family?"

"My father literally went out for cigarettes and never came home," he said with a short laugh. "My mother has dementia back in Australia, if she's even still alive. *Don't* walk away from these people. You may feel like you've lost everything, but you have so much still to live for. And that includes thousands of strangers who may die if we don't stop Rhodes." He waited for her to respond, but she remained silent. "Dana, I'm fighting for the people I may never know. You're fighting for the people you love. That is so much harder, but so much more important."

Dana's eyes darted between his face and the ground.

"I'm going to my room. Your little motivational speech didn't work."

He stomped his cane against the ground, his frustration erupting into words he immediately wished he could take back. "Fine! Be selfish! I'll figure this out myself and stop Rhodes. Go get a shitty vending machine burrito, a knock-off cola, and hey, while you're at it, there's a coupon on the back of the roller rink brochure for a free game of laser tag. Have a good time!"

Dana flipped him off as she pulled out the key to her room and stomped inside.

Olsen contemplated his outburst, unbefitting and out of character for a team leader. *Some team I'm leading.* He reached back into his pocket for his Bible but thought twice. He looked up to see Angela heading his way from the van.

"Olsen, should I follow her?"

"Couldn't hurt," he sighed. "I'll go tell Nick the news about Simone."

"Dana already texted him while she was driving back," she said. "She doesn't make good decisions when she's in a bad headspace."

"You would know."

"Ha. Listen, you know she's not quitting, right? Maybe the old Dana I knew would have just packed her bags. No speech—she'd just move on and run. This Dana? She's got a chip on her shoulder, and she's flaunting it until someone knocks it off."

"You think so?"

"She's not done with this yet." Angela looked at the closed door of Dana's room. "She's just a mess. She's a volcano that needs to erupt or just vent out some steam."

"I think that's where you come in, Angela. Help her. You too, lad."

Nick had just stepped up behind Angela, clearly hearing every word.

Olsen placed his hand on Nick's chest as he attempted to walk past him.

"What?"

"Hey. You've got a lot on your plate, too. If you want to leave, you can. You weren't part of the original team here."

Nick placed his hand on top of Olsen's own. "Actually, Dana and I, we *were* the original team. I'm not going anywhere."

*Good lad. Good soldier.*

# Chapter 40

*Find Your Way Back – Jefferson Starship*

Dana slumped into the rough upholstery of the desk chair, releasing a cloud of stale motel dust. The others in the room didn't acknowledge the same dull stank that irritated her nostrils. The single blade of sunlight from between the curtains stung her eyes. Everything was just irritating. *Uncomfortable.* Olsen and Angela sat opposite each other on the stiff comforters of the twin beds while Nick and Ashley stood casually against the dresser. Dana picked at a lingering piece of dirt stuck under her thumbnail.

"So, what do we know?" she said with little intonation. Dana had agreed reluctantly to attend this planning session, knowing she was not fully done with the cloak-and-dagger adventures, but nowhere near excited or even interested. She just wanted things to be over.

"PEG is mostly dead," Ashley announced. "I mean, dead as an autonomous entity. Nick and I looked over the damage, and the connections from the helmet to the torso are just shredded from a few lucky bullets."

"I wouldn't even know where to begin figuring out what connects to where," Nick added.

"From what I could gather, the batteries have just been bleeding power. The charging ports are toast. Zero ideas how to fix those. Whatever we have in PEG for juice is all we have left." Ashley pointed two thumbs down.

"Good news, as always," Dana chimed in.

"Sis, we can't rebuild anything that Mom made without her original notes and schematics. We're kind of screwed in the short term."

"It's okay," Olsen said. "I'll call back the boys for another favor if I can. We still have money, but not very much time." Dana saw him kick at a bag tucked under the edge of the bed. He flicked at the pink piece of paper in hands. "According to this shipping manifest, there are four trucks headed to Monterey, California, for some sort of scheduled swap and then continuing onward to the ports in San Francisco. Conclusion? Monterey is where Rhodes is getting arms for his aggregated militias. Per Director Jameson, one will be carrying small arms and the other three larger payloads. That's probably things like light attack vehicles, or worse. Maybe some bigger ammo."

He picked up a short stack behind him. Dana sighed. *More papers.*

"Does anyone else find it funny that we're printing this all out in the office center of this shitty motel right next to the soda machine and tourism display?" Dana asked, her voice dripping with sarcasm. Olsen cleared his throat and continued.

"These printouts are photos of the trailers from older customs records as well as security footage my associates were able to obtain by cross-referencing the trailer registrations. Two maroon trailers, then one white one, and the last one is blue. One of the maroons will haul the small arms, so that's the priority, I believe."

Angela spoke next. Dana was glad that someone else would be asking questions about this impossible mission. "What do we do, exactly, when we find the trailers?"

"Current plan? We mark them, a yellow *X* on top each trailer. That will give Carmen's team a visual for targeting."

"Jesus!" Dana blurted, standing up from her chair. "I need to get there before Rhodes does, find the trailers, spray-paint the tops, and get the hell out before they do an air strike? How am I going to do all of that?"

"I'm going, too," Angela interrupted. "I have been training, you know."

"And me too," said Ashley, puffing her chest and crossing her arms.

"No. Absolutely not." Dana stood between her sister and the rest of the group. Her neck felt hot as she recalled the failures at the airport in New Mexico. Under no circumstance would she allow herself to put Ashley in jeopardy of being kidnapped—again—or killed. "You are *off* the mission."

"It's my choice, *Photograph*. You're not the martyr here. We all have a stake in this."

Olsen held up his hands. "Ladies, I know you are both under tremendous emotional strain right now. I want to reiterate that the moment Director Jameson tells her squads to move, Rhodes will know. By mole or by hacker, he's going to get the heads-up. That's why we need to drop in as fast as possible and find the trailers in the depot." He flipped through his papers and held up another printout. "This is the most recent satellite map that I could grab online. We can't rely on the specific number of trailers in this picture, but we can see the layout of the facility. Five paths radiating out of the center, fenced in on the perimeter, so it's a pentagon with five spokes."

Dana sat back down and stared at the folds of the thick curtains. She noted the single cobweb floating upward in the sunbeam, another neglected piece of housekeeping. Flickers of gold sparkled in the light, worrying her at first, until she realized they were specks of dust—relics of the dead skin of prior guests, desert dust, or dirt imported from other parts of the country on boots and suitcases. Pieces of the past, adrift, waiting for heat or a breeze to displace them. She looked at the fleck of dirt still under her nail.

"Dana?" Nick interrupted her spiraling thoughts.

"Hmm?"

"Do you have any input?"

"Sorry, on what?"

Olsen snapped his fingers. "Do we split you and Angela into two flanks or keep you together once you enter the trucking yard?"

She sat forward, over her knees. "Whatever I say, you'll come up with some reason to justify the alternative, so why don't you just tell us what to do?"

"Dee, that's not fair. You have some agency here, you know," Nick replied.

"Do I? Do I really have agency? I barely know what that even means sometimes."

Ashley raised her hand. "It means that you have the ability to make decisions that—"

"I know what it *means,* Ashley!" she snapped. "But what are we even doing?"

"We're getting payback," Angela replied. "And we're stopping a maniac from getting a lot of people killed."

"I'm not convinced any of this is really worthwhile." Dana stood and examined the group. Each face held a similar expression: a mixture of surprise and tension, waiting for her to explode. She reached for the doorknob.

"Just tell me when I have to do something and what I have to do."

She slammed the door shut as she walked out into the sun.

The clapper on the bell clattered with a dull uneven rattle as Dana shoved open the hotel lobby door. She needed a can of cola from the vending machine, and a minute of silence. The motel clerk on duty was another middle-aged woman, this one with deep dark lines surrounding her features and oily black hair.

"Looking for something to do?" she asked in a soft voice.

Dana turned to the spinner rack of local brochures. Caverns and horse rides, wilderness excursions, a rafting trip, and a village of esoteric footnotes of history and geography. She snorted at one for something called the International Museum of Horse Bridles.

"Is this for real?"

"It's really just a series of shelves in someone's living room. Costs two dollars. They sell T-shirts."

She traced her fingers along the edges of another brochure: pictures of poorly cropped children in birthday hats, frozen in posed moments of manufactured joy. Some of them held gaudy plastic guns and wore oversized colored vests. The brochure designer drew crude lasers firing from the barrel of each weapon.

"That's the Funtertainment Center," chimed in the motel clerk. "It's only a thirty-minute drive from here. Laser tag, arcade games, batting cages, and a roller rink. There's a coupon for a free skate rental on the back of that."

"Yeah, I know." Dana reached into her pocket. She ran her thumb over Nick's keychain. "Don't need it. I've got my own."

# Chapter 41

*Little Red Corvette – Prince*

Dana parked the pickup in front of the Funtertainment Center, which was ironically a large dull warehouse with red and green aluminum skirting around the roofline, making it look more like a Christmas bazaar than a children's birthday party utopia. The parking lot was void of any other cars, it being a weekday. She quickly grabbed her derby skates, Lenny and Squiggy, and walked inside. She hadn't skated—just *skated*—in what felt like forever. She needed to lace up and unplug.

The concourse surrounding the rink was poorly lit and decorated with more green and red piping and star decals. The disco globes on each end of the oval turned slowly, reflecting tiny flecks of white squares of light against the walls. She noted the seemingly required ghastly carpeting in the lobby—always great for hiding vomit stains from children—as she walked to the front desk.

"Morning," said the man behind the counter. He smiled at her as he worked, placing skates onto shelves barely within his reach due to his very short stature. A thin black goatee, almost appearing to have been drawn by a magic marker, framed his large mouth and lips, his hair coiffed tightly in a pompadour. A beauty mark on his cheek and his hazel eyes added to his cartoonish, almost elfish presentation. He was in his early fifties by her estimation. He smoothed the front of his tight black vest, buttoned over a dress shirt, then placed his chin atop his folded hands.

*Is this guy for real?*

"We don't open for another hour, sister." He opened the lid of a fruit cocktail cup and plunged his plastic fork into the top layer.

"Oh, sorry, I didn't mean to disturb your breakfast." Dana sighed deeply. He stared at her, unblinking.

"That's alright." He closed his eyes and waved his fork like a magic wand. "You're in denial that you're a newborn old soul."

"That's a peculiar observation."

"Those are the best ones."

"I'm Dana."

"Neil. Pleasure to meet you."

"Are you a figment of my imagination?"

"Sister, please."

He smiled devilishly and opened the glass doors to a cabinet containing stereo equipment. "Well, since you're here and brought your own wheels, I might as well let you skate out your issues. You don't look like trouble to me."

"Are you seri—never mind. Thank you." She tucked her questions back in. He was already doing her a favor by letting her skate before the rink opened.

"I'm picking a song just for you."

"I was going to ask for a specific song."

"Let the music just happen, girl." He scanned through his digital screens. "This one."

She laced up Lenny and Squiggy and gently folded her jacket, placing it on the end of the counter. As she stepped onto the slick wooden floor, she closed her eyes while the speakers began to ooze a slow wave of synthesizer chords. *Yep, good song. GREAT song.* She glanced back at Neil, still behind the counter, and he gave her a friendly wave and a playful smile.

She pushed off one foot at a time, timing her thrusts with each measure of the song. *Push two three four, push two three four.* The song's vocals echoed throughout the empty hall, aided by the reverb of the original recording. Dana's legs moved without conscious thought, twisting her into a reverse skate around the curved end of the rink. There had never been this much room to move in her grandfather's house. She could only ever skate like this when she had been at boarding school on some forced group outings, made more difficult for her as a girl with few real friends but many imaginary girlfriends.

She turned back around and pumped her legs for speed. Rounding the next turn of the rink, she closed her eyes and slalomed around imaginary cones, her legs rushing with the rising chorus. She loved this—skating, moving by her own will and power, reloading her speed with a pump of her skates. She extended her rear leg and held a graceful arabesque into the corner, then kicked her leg around and stomped the wood in time with the music. *Stomp, stomp, stomp.* She remembered showing Angela how to do an axel jump on roller skates. *I wonder . . .*

The guitar solo filled her ears, followed by a rush of blood. Her heart beat faster as she built up speed, accelerating into the next turn. She was on fire, she *was* fire, and she shot onto the straightaway with an impish smile.

Dana leapt into the air, violent but beautiful, churning like the eye of a hurricane. After two revolutions, she landed with a thunderous clank, still upright.

A double axel.

Neil whistled and clapped from across the hall. She allowed herself a quick bow before swinging her hips with the next rising chorus. She felt alive, she felt beautiful, she felt free from her life. This was a snapshot of how she wanted to feel.

A photograph of who she wanted to be.

Dana closed her eyes, her chest rising and falling as her breathing synced to the rhythm pounding out of the speakers. In this moment, she knew she was the person her mother had wanted her to grow into: a happy young woman without a care in the world. The journey had led her through so much pain, but also through so much love. She now had a sister, a brilliant and optimistic girl with her own road ahead of her. She had not one, but *two* best friends who she had the privilege of loving and in return was loved as herself, despite her own shortcomings. That was something few people achieved even once during a lifetime.

Dana kicked out her leg and slid down to one knee, spinning across the floor planks, then shooting upright. Her fingers traced the wall of the turn as she sped by. Her mind turned to Olsen, the jaded and damaged adversary who saw hope in her, the possibility of redemption. She had given that gift to him without even realizing it. He was almost a mentor, providing stability to her and others when he could barely stand on both of his legs—something that was her own fault but that he had forgiven her for.

And yes, Dana had lost her mom—again—but only after finding her, staying by her side, and cherishing every new memory.

She was blessed. Her world was filled with chaos and anger and sadness, but it was also filled with beauty, love, and inspiration. She wanted a better world for the people she loved. Even for Olsen, she admitted to herself.

As she rounded the next turn, she looked to her left for the rink manager but saw only an empty counter in front of the racks of skates.

"On your right," Neil's baritone voice announced, startling her. She felt his hand grab hers, firmly guiding her toward the center of the rink. She noticed his plain black leather skates with gold wheels, glittering as they spun and reflected the threads of lights speckling the rink. "You got any of that hand jive in you, girl?"

"I got a little." She beamed.

They skated side by side, extending their right knees and improvising a patty-cake pattern over and under their thighs. She laughed as she tried to follow his choreography. He was silky and syncopated at the same time, smoothly transitioning from move to move. A tiny ember of jealousy sparked in her.

"Cha-cha?" she asked.

"Of course," Neil said, immediately shuffling his feet. She mirrored him, skates rocking and stepping with the music. Another rising wave of synthesizer crushed the crescendo.

"Is this the extended mix?"

"Yes, ma'am. It's how it was intended to be heard." He slowed his dancing, and the duo swayed side to side into the next lap. "You know what this song is really about?"

"It's a typical eighties song about a guy trying to get with a girl for a one-night stand. Right?"

Neil smiled coyly. "Listen to it. It's really a song about the loss of innocence, how that drives desire. Our protagonist starts out shy; he tries to imagine what happens if he actually *does* get the girl. By the end, he's confident. He knows what he wants, and he's comfortable in being himself. Desire is pushing toward a goal," he explained, pausing to survey the twinkling lights of the rink. "There's always a loss of innocence. It's a one-way trip; you can never go back. But, if you embrace it, you can have anything your heart desires." He winked. "If it's done right, that is."

Dana smirked. "That's pretty deep for a pop song."

"Most songs have a deeper meaning. It's not their fault they become pop." He pivoted and skated backward in front of her. "We can't help becoming something we don't intend to be. But we *can* help what we do about it."

He spun and sailed across the center of the rink, skipping onto the carpet back toward the stereo. Dana couldn't help but laugh at this tiny muse of a man in the middle of no-man's-land. "Thank you, Neil. You're a prince!"

A flash of white light shot across the rink as the front door flew open, and a large silhouette moved toward the edge of the rink. She shielded her eyes and skated over to the shape.

*Olsen.*

"I thought you might end up here," he announced. In his hands, he held a brochure for the Funtertainment Center with the coupon torn out. Ashley wandered in behind him, followed by Angela, then Nick. "We took the van, since you stole the truck."

"Sorry about that." Dana was suddenly glad to see everyone, together, united to find her. She also felt a pinch of shame that she had likely caused them to worry. "I'm okay, guys. I'm alright."

Nick crossed his arms playfully. "Breaking and entering into a roller rink doesn't make it seem like you're okay."

"The doors were unlocked. And Neil over there said it was cool!" She pointed to the skate rental desk. An empty fruit cocktail cup sat with a plastic fork across the lip. "He must have ducked in the back."

"Sis, are you feeling okay?" Ashley pointed back to the doors. "You were the only car in the parking lot until we pulled in."

"Huh." Dana twisted her head back and forth, no signs of Neil to be found. "Anyone remember passing a food place on the way here?"

She stepped onto the carpet, removed her skates, and went back to the counter where her jacket remained folded. As she slipped it over her arms, an index card fell from the sleeve to the ground. She picked it up and examined it closely. Olsen looked on with a perplexed face.

"What's that, mate?"

"It's a punch card. Nine more skates, and the tenth one is free." Dana smiled broadly. "Alright, gang, let's get something to eat. And then there's something else I want to do before we go get Rhodes."

# Chapter 42

*(It's Hard) Letting You Go – Bon Jovi*

Are you ready, Ashley?"

"I'm going to need a minute, Dana."

Ashley stood at the edge of the hotel pool fiddling with the folded paper boat in her hands. Between the edges, Dana could see the distorted logo of the hotel stationery letterhead. She sat next to her sister on the concrete, Nick on her other side.

Dana felt a different affection now for him, as well as *from* him, and she felt a new, stronger confidence in their friendship. She turned to Angela, who stood several feet behind the group.

"Did you make one, too?" Angela asked Nick.

He shook his head.

"I made one for you," Ashley said, handing him an identical paper boat. "For your dad."

He smiled to himself. Dana patted him on the shoulder as she stood up. "I don't think the hotel management is going to really care, given the overwhelming number of guests here," she said with a giggle. "Lighters?"

Angela stepped forward with a book of matches and handed it to Dana as Ashley and Nick placed their boats in the water. Dana flicked the match, allowing the sulfur stink to bleed into her nostrils, drowning out the chlorine before she knelt and lit the top of each boat. Angela hugged each sister and then Nick.

"I'll let the orphans have their moment together." She bit her lip and looked down. "Sorry. Was that inappropriate?"

"Mom would have appreciated the dark humor," Ashley replied.

Angela receded into the interior of the hotel. The quiet lapping of the pool water on the concrete slowed as the burning boats quickly floated a few feet before disintegrating into an ashy slick on the water.

"I kind of expected a little more, you know, time," Dana said.

"That's a good way to put it," replied Nick. He wiped his eyes. "Can I go first? Do either of you mind?"

"No, that's fine." Ashley wiped her own eyes.

"I'm . . . phew . . . I'm grateful to have met your mother. In another universe, I can see her and my dad talking over a couple of grilled cheese sandwiches about how . . ." Nick paused and took a shaky breath. "They'd be talking about how we turned out better than they ever hoped." He pointed to Ashley, who shook her head.

"I'm not ready. Dana, you go next."

"Okay." She knelt again next to the edge of the pool. "I wish I had time to just, you know, remember more details. From the first time, that is. The first time that Mom 'died,' I could barely understand it all. I had to piece together memories as I found little scraps of her." She felt Ashley's hand on her shoulder and grabbed her wrist. "Ash, you had so much time with her. But now that I have you, you can fill in all those details." Dana's chest heaved. "Oh God, Mom, I love you so much. I'm going to take care of this little brat here." She let go of her sister's arm. "She's my brat, now."

Nick rubbed her back. The floating memorials slowly drifted under the surface.

"Nick, your dad was just amazing. He was my family when I had no one. You and him were my family."

Nick knelt next to her, followed by Ashley. The younger sister leaned close to the surface of the water and blew a kiss into the depths of the pool.

"Mom, thank you for keeping me safe, and leaving enough clues for Dana to find us. You gave me a sister, and I never thanked you for that." A low wail slipped out. "Mommy, I love you."

As Ashley sobbed, Dana pulled her back to stabilize her. Ashley's crying ascended into almost a howl that echoed across the courtyard. A woman stepped out from a room on the upper level, but Dana waved her off and flashed an OK sign. Nick slid over and put his arm around the younger sister, leaning close to her ear.

"I know, it's going to hurt for a while. And it's okay to feel that. When my mom died, I wasn't there." More silent tears rolled down Nick's cheeks. "I used to regret that. I don't anymore, because I just remember the good things, the good times. Your memories will heal you."

"My brain's wired a little different than most people," Ashley said with a smile. She snorted and wiped her nose. "But I'll take your word on that."

"Ash, I don't know if Dana told you, but my dad, he was an alcoholic. We lost a lot of time together during those years. Sometimes I'd want to talk to him about something I did, something I was proud of, but he wasn't present for me to share those things with him. But those times that he *was* there, I loved those memories, even before he died. Those were the good things, the good stuff. And that's really what remains when all is said and done. That's what I'm clinging to right now, and it's what I can pull out of my pocket and hold every day. Good memories."

Dana shifted her weight and leaned into his shoulder. She was once again impressed by what a kind man Nick was, by his empathy, his resilience. She wondered who he would end up with someday, and what an extraordinary person they would have to be. And she felt excited and happy to see him find that person.

"I love you guys," Dana announced. "I'm going to see things through to the end. For Mitch. For Simone." She exhaled unevenly as her chest swelled with a mix of pride and determination. "For us."

Olsen watched from afar as the trio held each other next to the pool. He recognized that they were a unique dynamic, these lost children, this orphan club, and they needed their moment of shared grief. From a tactical standpoint, he needed their heads to be clear, yes, but he also understood the importance of their humanity and the invisible bonds of family, and the pain when those bonds were severed.

"Let me know when to get them," Angela said, interrupting his thoughts.

"They can come when they're ready. I won't break this up." His thoughts wandered back to Australia, to his mother, left alone with her tiny pension and slowly decaying capabilities. "They needed this."

"You got it, boss." Angela checked her phone. "We're still going to be okay on the timetable?"

He checked his watch. "We're fine as long as we leave tonight."

"How much did this cost?" she asked sheepishly.

"Most of what we took from the cabin. The labor is free, but the supplies always have a price tag. Odemo needed to get the fuel via Dan from a few different contacts." He watched the trio at the pool slowly rise, together, and walk toward Nick's room. Ashley broke off from the group for a moment to pick up a stray bottle and throw it into the recycle bin.

"Angela, when we're done with all of this, if something should happen, there's a small tan purse in one of my duffel bags. Give that to Dana."

"What's in there?"

"Just some money. She'll figure out the best thing to do with it."

"That's a bit fatalistic, you know."

"Prepare for the worst, hope for the best." He spun on his good heel and headed for their van. "And it's prep time."

# Chapter 43

*We Run This – Missy Elliott*

Dana dabbed her donut into her to-go coffee cup.

*I am so tired of coffee. Why can't we run into an energy drink machine, or an iced latte stand?*

Even after eating breakfast, she felt the space in her stomach expanding as they parked the van. It had been half a day's drive to the rendezvous point, a desert road miles away from the interstate winding through the Mojave. In the clearing, Odemo and Perry were already waiting in the cargo bay of the massive heliplane, running various checks and tasks. A tall thin man in flight overalls with short brown hair trying to curl over his scalp sat in a camping chair at the bottom of the loading ramp. He was making small talk with Angela, Nick, and Ashley, then saw Dana. He tipped his aviator sunglasses at her and craned his neck. *Boo-Boo, we meet again.*

"Talk to me, Ozzy," Boo-Boo yelled to Olsen. "One more review of the details." He tapped his finger on his temple. "Even though I've got it memorized."

Olsen pulled off his shirt, a thin black moisture-wicking sports top and a matching set of compression sleeves covering his forearms from wrist to elbow. "Two drop points."

"Two." Boo-Boo held up two fingers. "First drop is our skater team. They're our hit-and-run recon. They'll pull any guards or defense toward *their* drop point."

Dana held up her coffee cup. "We can use the tracker from Penny to see where the skaters are, unless Olsen had a silver moment and forgot it." She winked as she smiled at him. "I'm just messing with you."

"You're rather chipper." He didn't smile back, his game face already in place. "As Boo-Boo was saying, first drop is the skaters. As we fly over, we'll do a real-time visual for the trailer colors, see if we can give the girls a final location estimate. We then touch down on the opposite side of the depot. By then, their forces should be aware of us, and they'll divert resources to the second drop. Perry, Odemo, and I will hit the ground running and take those men."

"Excuse me," Nick interjected. Dana knew by the sound of his voice and his thoughtful pose that he had an idea.

"Go ahead, Nick." Olsen ceded the floor. Dana caught a whiff of admiration for Nick's insight in Olsen's tone.

"What about a third drop? A decoy?" He traced a circle in the dirt with his foot. "The skaters appear here, then they'll see we're heading to the second point. That's where you guys all get out, guns blazing, covering fire, whatever you call it." He drew two marks on opposite sides of the circle and then a third one, creating a triangle. "Boo-Boo, you touch down here, pretend you're letting out a third force. They'll be forced to pull men to cover that, too." Nick erased the drawing. "Do you think that's a valid idea?"

Olsen nodded. "I like it. Good job, Nick. Boo-Boo, you make that third drop, wherever you eye up a dead spot. Call in with whoever they have at that point. And if it's too hot, you go just outside the perimeter of the location—anything to make them think there's one more team. Either way, only once you make the second drop, call Director Jameson and tell her to move her people in. Any moles or hackers will have lost any advantage by then."

"They'll be on to the fake-out pretty quickly," Odemo said. "So, we have to be engaged before the decoy drop." His dark eyes glanced at Dana. "Best case is, you'll have identified the trailers by then."

"You got it." Dana saluted, then realized she had no idea if that was the correct form. "Ash, we're ready to load."

Ashley opened her tablet and tapped vigorously at the screen. "From what I can figure out, we have about twenty to thirty minutes of juice left in PEG. She's only useful as a very heavy bulletproof suit at that point. I'd have to manually route power if you need a boost."

Nick reached out to ask for the tablet. "Ashley will be running this from inside our ride. We're going to also have access to all communications."

Boo-Boo stood and folded up his chair. "Glad to have all your eyeballs. Every one of you is critical. Perry, you got anything to add?"

Perry lifted one corner of his mouth as he rechecked his assorted pockets and packs on his belt. "Just that I wish I got to pick the teams. I'd take the tall blonde on mine if I could."

Angela smirked. "Really? You're going there?"

Perry smirked back. "Apparently I'm not. But in all fairness, you're good with a gun, as I recall."

Olsen shook his head. "Angela's on defense. It's where she's best suited." He winked at her, and she winked back with a smile. Olsen held up one hand. "Okay, team, contingency planning. What can go wrong?"

"They shoot me down at any step. But that's not going to happen," Boo-Boo answered confidently.

"There's a larger force than anticipated," Odemo said. "In that case, we fall back and call Jameson."

"Assets are not centralized," Angela chimed in. "The trailers are not all located in the same spot. So, we split up and find what we can. One is better than none."

Dana felt it was her turn to voice her undesired scenario. "Rhodes isn't there."

"Possible," Olsen replied. "But I think I can say with almost full certainty that he'll be there."

"And how do you know that?"

"It's how he works. He always supervises the final stages of his operations in person, especially when it involves high-dollar investments."

"But do you know that for sure?"

"Dana, as sure as I'm standing here, I'm certain of it. Just like he did back in New Jersey when we were transporting the Atomic Juggernaut. And for something as big as this seems to be, I wouldn't be surprised if he drove one of the trucks himself."

Boo-Boo handed each person a helmet equipped with a radio earpiece and microphone. "Hey, Photograph, you ever hit top speed in one of these things before?"

"Nope. Literally my second ride in one, ever."

"You're in for a treat, sugar." He slapped the side of her helmet and almost skipped to the cockpit. A short buzz flickered in her ears, not from the earpiece, but from her nerves. Boo-Boo turned back to her, and his happy-go-lucky tone muted into that of a cautious teammate. "You alright?"

"Yeah. Just . . . thinking about everything coming to a head. And what's on my shoulders."

"Listen," he said, reaching into his pocket, "I know something about that." He produced a small photo of himself and a smiling toddler on his lap. The baby's cherubic face, wide eyes, and relaxed tongue peeking through his lips told her all she needed to know, but she let Boo-Boo speak. "This is my boy. Everything I do, I think about him, because I do it for him." He tucked the photo away. "When someone means the world to you, you want to change the world for them."

"He's adorable. When do you get to see him again?"

"I don't." Boo-Boo smiled. "He's with the angels. So, it's my job to give everyone on the team the opportunity to go home and see the ones *they* love after every mission." He slapped her again on the side of the helmet. "Hey. Kid. Doing the right thing is never easy. And what we're going to do on this op is about as hard as it gets."

She nodded. "Let's do this."

# Chapter 44

*Volcano Girls – Veruca Salt*

I'm not sick, it's just nerves."

Dana tightly gripped the overhead handle in the heliplane cargo bay with one gloved hand as she held her stomach with the other. The volume, the motion, the constantly changing temperature—all of it played with her senses, taunting her with motion sickness. Angela sat comfortably across from her strapped into a jump seat, her bomber-style jacket zipped tightly over her bulletproof vest. Dana moved her hand higher on her stomach and pressed against the stiff Kevlar material under her own jacket, her mother's jacket.

*Mom.*

She let go of the handle and checked the sling bag tight against her back. Three cans of spray paint. A tiny soft-pack medical kit. Emergency radio. Extra socks. One pair of underpants. *Because you never know where you'll end up.*

"Hey, Olsen!" Dana yelled to the front of the cargo bay. "I hate to be that person, but are we there yet?"

Olsen glanced at his smartwatch and the tracker jutting out from the carbon fiber cuff of PEG's arm. He ran his hand over his chest, the pink cat face painted on PEG's torso plate staring back at Dana. "We're just about there."

The heliplane began to drop as the rotors pivoted, maintaining a level orientation. Dana's stomach lurched with the fall like she was in a high-speed elevator. A blast of cold wind mixed with exhaust fumes barreled into the bay as the cargo door opened with a chugging whine.

Dana could make out the California mountains far in the distance along with the ocean, just a thin line beyond. She could almost imagine the salty smell of the Pacific if it weren't for the fuel-filled aromas clogging her nostrils. A hand suddenly wrapped around her waist. *Angela.*

"Helmet on, *Photograph.*"

"Helmet on, *Meatball.*"

Angela gave her a smirk.

"Mamma mia, here we go!"

Dana clipped the chinstrap, put in her derby mouth guard, and flicked down the clear visor. Her earpiece sizzled with Boo-Boo's voice.

"Close your mouths, ladies. Don't want to bite off your tongues. I'll be as gentle as I can." Dana gnashed her teeth into the plastic guard. "Touch-and-go in three, two, one."

Dana barely felt the recoil of the landing gear as she sprinted down the ramp, skates roaring, shoulder to shoulder with Angela. They were two football fields away from an entry gate, propped open for daytime deliveries and defended by a single sentry, a civilian in a yellow vest and matching helmet.

"I think his workday is about to get worse," Dana said as they roared toward the dumbfounded man. Angela shoulder-checked him, sending his body into a pile of wooden pallets behind the gate.

"That wasn't necessary!" Dana barked.

"He could have had a gun." Angela grit her teeth to flash her baby-blue mouth guard. "Spotted a stack of trailers. We're heading left!" she hissed into her helmet microphone.

A labyrinth of cargo containers, stacked one to three boxes high, unfolded ahead of them. The truck trailers that were their targets sat somewhere in the middle of the depot. The two friends swerved together to the right down a larger path, four car lanes wide.

"Wait, wait, wait." Dana held up a finger and slowed her pace. A high grinding noise reverberated from the other side of the trailers, a dissonant set of notes that failed to merge with the sounds of her and Angela's skates. "Boo-Boo? What do you see?"

"Nick here," came the reply voice. "Dana, there are three of Rhodes's skaters moving parallel on the other side of your aisle. You're going to come up to an intersection. Bear left and you'll run right into them."

"Got it. Angela, dig in!"

In unison, Dana and Angela stomped their feet and pushed the accelerators in their skates. Their combined derby instincts and skills merged effortlessly into an unspoken synchronized dance. Angela took the left side to become the blocker as they wound around the turn while Dana stayed in her blind spot. The roaring of the other skaters told them they were just around the corner. Angela leveled her shoulder into the leader, and Dana marveled at her brute strength whenever she used leverage to her advantage. The first skater launched backward into the second, and the third skipped over them before landing and falling.

"Easy breezy. These guys have no finesse," Angela joked. "They've got size and straightaway speed, but that's about it. No skills."

A gunshot rang out against the metal trailers next to Dana.

"But they're armed, of course!" She whirled her hand in the air and pointed forward, a hurry-up cue from their derby days. "Hustle!"

They sped along further into the maze, cutting right and left with quick decisions as single shots rang off. Olsen buzzed into their headsets.

"They've got handguns, but they're clearly untrained in firing and skating at the same time. Just don't get complacent. They're taking bad shots, but those can still kill."

Angela placed her palm over her helmet's ear bump to hear better. "Any sign of the trailers? Colors?"

"Nothing yet, but we're about to touch down. They're taking some random shots at us from the ground, so we're going to have to move our landing spot a hundred yards."

Dana pointed toward a wall of trailers that suddenly dropped in height. "I bet they're behind there." She led Angela around another bend and into the open center of the complex. Four trucks idled side by side at the other end of the clearing: two maroon trailers, one white, and one blue. A pair of white SUVs were parked on one side.

"Olsen, we've got visual. There are two welcome wagons, but I don't see anyone, except—oh shit, shit, shit!"

Dana and Angela slowed as they approached the side of the first trailer. The driver of one SUV stepped out. He wore tactical boots and fatigues and propped his hand on a holster on his hip as he glowered at the girls. Dana would know that broad jaw, that poorly dyed black hair, and those stupid thin glasses anywhere.

This man, this monster, Colin Rhodes stood before her. She knew today was the last time she'd see him, because one of them—or maybe both of them—was going to die.

"*Dana Goddamn Jefferson,*" Rhodes roared. He unholstered his weapon and aimed.

Angela shoved Dana between the trailers as a bullet sailed by. "Okay, we are *clearly* here before the cavalry. Rhodes is alone!" she shouted. "What was our contingency plan for 'arriving early'?"

"We stay in motion and stay on mission," Dana huffed, frustrated at their lack of hiding places. "And we avoid getting shot. I know, it sounds stupidly simplistic."

A bullet rang off the suspension of the truck next to their hiding spot. Angela took the lead to sneak behind the truck's cab. "How about you check the trailers, and I'll run interference with the old man?"

"No, stay together!" chided Olsen over the headset.

"Copy that, Moses." Angela ducked at the sound of another bullet's ricochet. "Where are you guys?"

"We're touching down. Nick spotted the clearing, and we're about to head over to you."

Dana examined the side of the truck cab and the ladder attached to the sleeper cabin. "We go up. We mark the trailers." She reached behind her back and shook her bag, hearing the reassuring rattling of the spray cans in her sling. "We stay on mission." She kissed Angela on the cheek.

*For good luck. And just in case.*

# Chapter 45

*Fortunate Son – Clutch*

Boo-Boo, next drop point!"

Nick pressed his hand against the cockpit glass as the heliplane banked sharply, tossing his stomach briefly. He craned his neck to watch Dana scamper across the top of one of the trailers, spraying a long yellow line, then another, to mark the target. He glanced back at Olsen, who was holding firm to one of the overhead supports as he untwisted the strap of his rifle from his shoulder. "Are you ready?"

"Ready as I can be," Olsen replied. Odemo and Perry nodded as well and clutched their rappelling lines. Ashley stood behind Olsen, tapping into her tablet before spanking the back of PEG's carbon fiber buttocks.

"If you start to feel sluggish, that means the power is gone!" she yelled.

The wind rushed through the cargo bay door as it opened, blasting fresh mountain air back through the hold and into the cockpit. Nick swallowed as he pulled down the clear helmet visor. He looked out over Dana and Angela, still working on the trailers.

"Olsen," Nick yelled, "do good work!"

"I always do," he replied, leaping with a whizzing and whirring sound out of the cargo bay. Olsen landed cleanly but with a loud thud as he sank into the top of a trailer, thanks to PEG's added weight and support. Perry and Odemo followed, hitting the ground and rolling into firing stances. Nick could see their shrinking figures leap from one truck to the next, guns blasting at targets just beyond Nick's view. He turned his attention back to the trailers.

"Dana, how are you doing?"

"I'm good, Nick. We got the trailers marked. I'm going to bust the doors open and take a peek inside."

"And how are you going to do that?"

He watched her smash her skate into one of the trailer latches, followed by a flurry of sparks. She pulled open the door and waved up to him. "I've got buzz saws on my feet, remember?"

"Keep your eyes open. Stay out of trouble." From the corner of his eye, Nick spotted a trio of Rhodes's skaters entering the depot. "And more trouble just arrived."

As the heliplane banked again to circle wide around the trailers, Nick felt helpless in his role. Being the eyes above the playing field was a big responsibility, but he felt like a passive participant in the action below. He knew, of course, that he was of little use on the ground, untrained in firearms or even skating. He had to contribute whatever he could from the air.

"Nick!" Ashley yelled. "Take a look at that!" She leaned over his seat and pointed to a white SUV and a fleet of box trucks rolling into the open area. The vehicles stopped as Odemo and Perry laid down a wall of gunfire, prompting the driver of the SUV to leap out. Nick recognized his stature even from the air.

"Rhodes is back! Perry, Odemo, turn around!"

He watched their primary adversary stride toward Perry and Odemo as they fired, but the bullets ricocheted off his chest and legs. Was he wearing some kind of body armor? With a stone of panic sinking in his stomach, Nick grabbed a pair of binoculars to take a closer look.

"Dana, there's something very odd going on with Rhodes."

"Keep an eye on him," she replied. "The first trailer was all guns and ammo. I'm going to open the second trailer now."

Nick watched Dana destroy the second truck's latch with her skate. As she opened the door, she immediately fell backward onto the pavement.

"Dana, what's wrong? Dana?" There was no reply. "Boo-Boo! Swing by those trucks so I can see what's inside."

The heliplane swooped lower. Angela had been opening the third and fourth trailer doors, but now she seemed to spot Dana on the ground. She ran over as the heliplane blasted over their heads. Nick's jaw tensed. The trailer doors in front of Dana hung open, rattling with the downdraft from the propeller blades.

"I'm calling Jameson now!" Nick yelled into the headset.

Behind him, Ashley had pulled on her skates and her helmet. "Set me down over there, Boo-Boo!"

"What are you doing?" Nick grabbed her by the arm, surprised at his aggressiveness in trying to stop her, but keeping Dana's sister safe was still in his realm of control. "You can't go down there!"

"Nick, I'm going." Ashley gently rolled her arm out of his grasp. "Look, I can help. We need you up here." She lifted her visor and locked on to his eyes. "Dana needs you up here, watching over her. Over *all* of us."

He nodded. "Make smart choices."

"I'm a genius, that's what I do." She winked, then used the overhead handles to pull herself to the cargo bay door.

Dana sat on the ground, frozen, staring into the depths of the trailer. The dark shape was familiar, a hulking marionette looming from floor to ceiling. She recognized the bathysphere central body attached to the thick armored limbs and elephant-footed legs. The front of the torso looked flatter, as if a section of the rotund body had been sliced off like the end of a loaf of bread. She peered further into the trailer only to see another robotic mass, and then another, and another, and another.

*Five. Atomic. Juggernauts.*

"No, no, no, no, no!" She tried to stand, but her body went limp. Her heart pounded madly in her ears, the blood in her chest boiling while her arms trembled with an icy cold. Here was the machine her family had created, mass-produced, waiting to be activated by Rhodes. With each exhale, less air replaced the lost air in her lungs, a panic attack coming faster than any she had ever felt before.

"I got you, baby."

Angela's voice.

Dana peered through the gold flecks in her vision and gasped for air.

"I got you, baby."

Angela placed her hands on each side of Dana's face, her blue eyes calm and focused, fixed on her own.

"Breathe with me, Dana."

Her blond hair floated lightly, tracing small lines across Dana's cheeks. She smelled flowers.

"Breathe."

Dana inhaled the scent, familiar from having shared her pillow at her mom's house. She stared into Angela's eyes—eyes she had seen through the full range of joy and sadness, anger and madness, fixated only on her in the middle of a firefight. Dana slid her hands over Angela's and forced out a breath.

*Just breathe.*

"That's it, Dana. One at a time."

Dana slowly turned her head, just a little, and saw Olsen on his knee next to Angela. He jumped up, his gun erupting in a blast of covering fire, but he turned quickly back to her.

"Come on, Dana. Come back to us."

Dana reached her hand out and placed it on Olsen's chest, on PEG, her mother's creation. Her hand slid down slowly to the remnants of the cat face painted by Ashley. She fought for air. Another voice floated into her ears, breaking through the din. The voice repeated itself through her headset.

"Dee, just breathe. Just breathe."

*Nick.*

Dana filled her lungs.

She pushed out the air.

She filled her lungs again.

"I got this." She exhaled. "Juggernauts. So many."

Olsen rose slowly. "Can you stand up?"

"I think so."

She waved off Angela, standing on her own. Single shots occasionally rang in the background, which she surmised were Odemo and Perry holding the line.

"We can't wait for Jameson. We've got to destroy them. Now."

"Over my dead body!" shouted a voice.

Dana, Olsen, and Angela turned and then froze, aghast in surprise. Before them stood Rhodes, hands on hips with a deep frown. His tattered boots and shredded fatigues barely covered him, revealing an abomination of mechanical arms and legs, a chest replaced with metal, muscles made of motors and wires. He began to walk toward them, each metallic limb creaking and groaning, chittering as his robotic prosthetics flexed. Rhodes curled his metal fingers into fists.

"Did you know that it's easier to just cut out the cancer if you replace the parts of your body one piece at a time?" His pace quickened. "And now, I'm going to tear you all apart, one piece at a time."

# Chapter 46

*Paranoid – Black Sabbath*

Dana remained frozen as she watched Olsen charge at Rhodes, both of their mouths foaming with rage. Simultaneous thunderous punches of clanking metal clashing with carbon fiber launched the two combatants into a pile. The former teammates, commander and solider, exchanged blow after blow, beating each other with punches that would have been lethal against any normal man or woman. She understood that for Olsen, this was a fight for his own soul, redemption for the sins of his past. For Rhodes, this was vengeance for the betrayal of a former ally who now stood between him and his own egocentric goals.

Their anger fed her. These two men loathed each other, but her hate for Rhodes was greater, and it seethed in her blood.

*The mission.* Dana whipped her focus back to the trailers.

"Angela. I'm going to open the cockpits on each juggernaut. I want to make sure that whether Jameson shows up or not, everything is destroyed, inside and out." Her face tightened with her resolve. "Everything ends. Today."

Dana shielded her eyes and searched for the heliplane. A loud *whup-whup-whup* of the rotors echoed over the trailer paddock. The heliplane descended, ramp open. Ashley stood in the bay, skates and flight helmet on, as she clung to the overhead handle.

"This is my fight, too, sis."

"Ashley! Dammit! Get back on the plane!" Dana jabbed a stern finger into the air.

"That's impractical at this point!" She leapt from the open ramp onto the trailer's roof and scampered down the side. Her skates whizzed as she stopped between Angela and Dana, who fumed as Ashley began to bark commands.

"Meatball," she said, pointing at Angela, "go help the Australian. Photograph, I'm with you."

"On it." Angela skated to the lip of the trailer and grabbed a crowbar. Dana looked her sister up and down, this part-child, part-woman tech genius now literally in the middle of a battlefield. Maybe it was time to let her complete her own journey.

"Okay, Phoenix, you gotta work with me, alright? Anything I say is to keep you alive." She curled her lips over her teeth. "Got it?"

"Yes."

"It's demolition time for these juggernauts."

The sisters scampered into the open trailer full of juggernaut payload and studied the chest cavity of the first. It was similar to the one Dana had fought back in New Jersey, as well as the one she had seen partially dismantled on the old Hardy family farm, gutted of its nuclear-powered engine. These, however, were noticeably modified in their chest dimensions: leaner, more svelte, arms ending in terrifying hands that resembled claws.

"Is this what Mom and Dad built?"

Ashley traced the panels until she found the first latch, then the second to open the front cavity. Watching Ashley's eyes widen as she ran her fingers over the hard lines and tight seams of the metal plates, Dana realized that

Ashley had never seen a juggernaut in person, never knew this part of their father. For a moment, Dana recalled the sight of her father's mummified body dropping out of the cockpit onto the floor of the bunker in New Jersey—a horror from which Ashley had been spared. She shook the memory off.

The well-oiled door on the husk swung open gently when Ashley pulled. The interior was small, thankfully retrofitted with the omission of an atomic reactor. A dark cylinder, about the size of a soda can, rested centrally wired to the web of connectors. Another similarly shaped cylinder was attached to the first by a round disc. Dana knew them instantly. These were her mother's inventions: The batteries of near-perpetual energy, the same magical technology that powered her, Angela, and Ashley's skates as well as PEG. Her mother's inventions, the same designs the sisters had attempted to recover from the train in New Mexico, had been usurped by evildoers and now sat exposed, taunting her with another panic attack.

*Not now. Not again. Not ever again.*

Dana ripped out the battery and hurled it to the ground. The sisters ran to the next juggernaut and repeated the process, leaving each one open and devoid of the ability to power on. Dana didn't even notice the stream of tears pouring down her cheeks until she reached the deepest interior of the trailer and finished disabling the first payload. She held the battery, the smooth lines contrasting with the ragged scuffs on the palms of her gloves. Something about it reminded her of her mother's tangled, dirty braids, tied up with silver barrettes and clips.

"Ash, go to the next trailers and destroy every single one of these goddamn batteries. Smash them, grind them under your skates, leave *nothing* for anyone to recover." Her sister met her anger with a determined look. "No one is taking anything from our family ever again." Ashley nodded and leapt to the next trailer.

Dana slid past the juggernauts to the open trailer doors to survey the melee. Rhodes held Olsen by his neck against the ground. Angela menaced behind Rhodes, heaving the crowbar down on their adversary's back. Rhodes tossed Olsen to the side, pieces of PEG's arm and leg armor scattering across the ground. He turned to face Angela.

"You want some of this?" she shouted, pointing the bar at him. "Come on, you little shit!" she cried, chopping downward with the crowbar into his chest. He intercepted the bar and shook it, her grip loosening as she whipped backward and tumbled across the concrete. Rhodes dismissed her with a wave and turned back to Olsen, crowbar in hand.

"*Aaron!*" Dana screamed. "Behind you!"

Olsen rolled away from the impact, the crowbar smashing pavement into dust and bending in Rhodes's hands. More pieces of PEG fell away and scattered. Olsen, exhausted and desperate, looked frail to Dana as he lifted his bare arms to defend himself. Too far to make it over in time, she covered her eyes, ashamed of herself for failing him, this former enemy who had stood by her side and fought for her with no promised reward, just a sense of right and wrong and doing what he could.

A staccato burst of bullets pulled her out from her cowering mask as a flurry of firearms plastered Rhodes. Odemo and Perry approached, firing into his robotic appendages. Angela swooped across the field of fire and scooped up Olsen, bringing him back to Dana.

"Thank you." He tapped his earpiece, his face returning to his stern commanding facade. "Director Jameson? Where is your team?"

Her voice buzzed in reply, "Almost there. We ran into a lone helicopter over the PCH that took aggressive maneuvers against us. It looks like Rhodes had another escape plan, but we removed it." They could hear a note of pleasure in her voice.

"Excellent." Olsen tried to stand, but his leg wobbled without PEG's support. "I'm sorry, team, I'm done." He smacked his left thigh and grunted. "Dammit."

They all turned back to Rhodes as he threw a fist at Odemo and punched him into Perry. Suddenly Rhodes stopped, his chest heaving rapidly, and looked skyward.

He glared back at Dana. "Dammit, Jefferson."

A chorus of helicopter rotors reverberated over the depot. Backlit by the sun, a squad of Blackhawks began their descent to the perimeter of the clearing. Dana surmised by the logos she could make out that these were the good guys, Director Jameson's crew.

"We did it," Dana whispered. She pointed a defiant finger at Rhodes. "We won."

Immediately, freshly deployed soldiers swarmed the grounds and engaged in small skirmishes, each quickly won as Rhodes's fighters surrendered, looking to him for unreturned support. He slowly spun, surveying the closing ranks. Angela stepped between him and a break in the outer circle, fists raised. Dana felt a tiny flutter of pride as she watched Angela standing her ground against a larger-than-life enemy.

"Come on," Angela shouted at him, a small splatter of blood flecking onto her chin. "Come on, you piece of shit!" Her eyes flared red hot with anger.

Rhodes crossed his arms and stared at her quizzically. He arched his back and stood at his full height.

"Against *me*? Are you serious?" he roared.

Slowly, Rhodes rose where he stood, his height creeping up inch by inch. A single line of wheels burst through the soles of each artificial foot, birthing a set of inline skates. It was all becoming clear to Dana now: The procurement of limbs from Silver, the theft of Ashley's skates, the accrued funds—it had all been for his own survival. The instigation of civil war, attacks on infrastructure, none of it mattered—just him. He truly had become a monster, a Frankenstein product created out of her family's legacy. Dana watched in horror as he began to roll forward, directly at Angela.

"No!"

But it was too late. Rhodes barreled straight into her accompanied by an explosion of fiery embers from his wheels, sending Angela airborne until she landed in a heap like a rag doll. His trail of sparks faded through the break in the trailers, down the lanes toward the exit of the depot. Dana skidded to a stop next to Angela.

"Don't talk, just lay still." Dana wiped the strands of hair off Angela's face, stuck to her skin in the thin sheen of sweat. "Just lie still. You've done enough today."

"Just give me a second. I can take a hit . . . I'm just winded." She wheezed and winced. "Or I've cracked several ribs. But my money is on winded." She forced a smile. "I'm okay."

Over her shoulder, Dana could see Ashley supporting Olsen as they distanced themselves from the trailers. He turned, pointed a stiff finger at Dana, then his watch, and finally at Rhodes's trail. She understood. It was time.

"Photograph!" he shouted. "Go!"

Dana's fists burned with rage. She zipped her mom's jacket up to her neck and looked skyward at Boo-Boo's heliplane sauntering in a slow hover, creeping away from the trailer depot.

"Nick? What are you doing?"

"We're tailing him. He's weaving out to the PCH. Can you see us?"

"Yes, I can."

"Then hurry up and follow us!"

Dana dug her toe into her lead skate, drawing in a slow breath that filled the deepest parts of her lungs. *This is it,* she thought. *I'm ending this now.* Her toes flexed, sending power into her skates as she pushed off. "Let's go!"

# Chapter 47

*I Can't Hold Back – Survivor*

The concussive explosions faded into the background, the salty scent of the sea rising in the air. The weathered gray asphalt of the road bent southward into Route 1, the Pacific Coast Highway. Dana looked up to her North Star, the heliplane carrying Nick and Boo-Boo.

"How far?" she yelled into her headset over the roar of the wind blowing in from the west. "I don't have any visual!"

She glanced to her right for a moment, her first view of the Pacific Ocean. Were it not for the urgency and agency of her mission, she would have stopped to enjoy the blue-on-blue of sky and water.

"Nick? Can you hear me?"

"He's moving fast, Dana. We're holding out over the water to keep him and you in our view. You gotta catch up." Nick's voice wavered at the end of his sentence. She rarely heard this level of doubt from him.

"Working on it." The fire inside her legs burned with anger and desperation and she used it as fuel, pumping and skating harder, faster. She wove around a car ahead of her on the two-lane stretch of unfolding faded pavement and focused on staying close to the center markings as the sands from each shoulder encroached on the white lines. The guardrails remained absent on the current stretch of road, a fearful characteristic of the straightaway with the looming cliff below. Boo-Boo broke her sightseeing with his upbeat voice.

"Dana, we can swing down at him and see if we can use a downdraft to slow him down, knock him on his ass for you."

"Negative. We are taking zero chances on any bystanders or cars getting involved." She wiped a dead bug off her cheek. "No one dies." *Except him.*

"Nick here. Dee, you're not going to catch him at your current speed."

"You think I don't know that?" Frustration came through in her voice. She ignored the taunting cramp creeping into her side as best as she could. "It's not as easy as you'd think to just go faster! I've got to lean into some of the rolling downhills to grab every extra MPH possible."

Another winding curve came into view. She shouldered into the turn and let her leading leg whip her through the bend.

"Dee, I'm watching him. He's fast, but he's—well, he's not good on his skates. He's really slowing down through the turns, especially the S-curves. There's a winding stretch coming up. You can make up a lot of ground on him there."

"Dammit, Nick, tell me something I don't know!"

"Listen, have you ever seen motorcycle racers?"

"Well, yeah, I think so." She pumped her legs into another slight downhill.

"When they take a turn, they lean all the way into it. And I mean *all the way* into it—their knees almost touch the pavement. In an S-curve, they whip all the way back and forth, like a pendulum."

"Okay?"

"You're not doing that. You're holding back. Can you go full pendulum? Can you do that?"

"I'll try?"

"Dana." His voice shifted back to a confident tone. "You have to do this. Trust the physics here. Lean all the way in. *All the way*. Then, as soon as the turn starts to bend the opposite way, swing that pendulum." She felt his confidence clawing into her ears. "Bend left, swing left, inside the turn. Then rebound. There's a section coming up in a mile."

"Got it."

"You trust me?"

"No," she cackled, "but I trust the physics."

Dana glanced ahead. The road shifted downward again, a sweeping turn to the left, then whipped back to the right to navigate around a rocky inlet.

"Nick! More physics! What else do I do?"

"Keep your skates shoulder-width apart, knees bent, side by side. When you lean in, fully bend your inside leg and put your butt on your heel. Keep the outside leg straight. Then push that bent leg up to rock the pendulum swing. Does that make sense?"

She had no time to process his instructions, just react. She swooped to her left, letting the centripetal force blast her through the turn. Her hair whipped at the pavement as she leaned fully into it, then snapped back to the opposite side as the road switched back to her right.

*Just breathe, Dana.*

She shot out of the turns onto the next straightaway. A whooping blasted her headset.

"Attagirl!" cheered Boo-Boo. "Photograph is on fire!"

She shot a quick glance at the heliplane and gave a thumbs-up, unsure if they could see the terrified grin on her face.

A small silhouette on the road ahead grabbed her focus. *Rhodes.*

"I see him!"

"Dana," Nick said, "there's another set of turns. And traffic. He's going to have to slow down—there's a pack of cars in both directions. That's the window to catch up to him. It's your big shot."

A gust of wind from the ocean side blanketed her. The cool blast brought a sting of sand and mist across her helmet visor.

She wished for this all to end. She wanted to sit on the beach and let the waves lap at her feet. No more skates, no more guns or robot suits, no more fighting. She wished for calm.

Dana relaxed going into the next set of turns. Her legs pushed and pulled her into the sweeping pendulum movement, dancing full speed as she approached her prey. Rhodes was no longer someone she feared; she was Artemis, hunting *him*. Another bend in the road and he was within shouting distance, slowed by his awkward maneuvering around a pair of small vans.

"Nick, I'm going to hit him on the next turn!" she yelled.

Rhodes slowed; she did not. At full speed, she rammed into his shoulder. The impact stunned Dana, knocking her back, her weight unable to overcome the added mass on his frame from his robotic prosthetics.

"Dana," Rhodes yelled, "you stupid child! You've ruined everything! Everything!"

He swung a metallic arm in an aimless arc. Dana ducked and looped to his opposite flank.

"Dee," Nick said, "it's physics again. Force equals mass times acceleration. You can't knock him over at this speed. He's got the mass."

She gritted her teeth. Rhodes glanced back at her, his own teeth bared, sweat pouring down his temples. Dana waited for him to reply with a snarky comment, but he returned his focus to the road ahead.

"Nick, I've got an idea." She reached up and tightened the strap on her helmet and let herself slip a few yards behind Rhodes. "Boo-Boo, come in hard like you're going to land on him. I mean, come *right* at him—swoop in above his head like you're going to sit on him."

"What about the traffic?" Nick asked. "You told us not to."

"I changed mind. This is my shot. Stay just above it."

Dana clenched her fists and felt her legs burn with the continued strain of skating for her life. The stitch in her side stabbed her like a hot, searing blade. She wasn't sure if there were any other ways out of this, but she saw one, and one was all she needed. The heliplane thrust ahead over the ocean and began a curving head-on descent toward Rhodes.

"I'll fly at him right when the road takes that next turn at the cliffs," Boo-Boo chimed in.

"Dee, you see those cliffs, right? Dee?" asked Nick.

Dana didn't reply.

"Dee? Dana? We're coming in fast on top of you. Which way are you going?" Dana could hear the heliplane roar as the propellers sliced through the air. "Dana, which way are you going? Left or right?"

"*Straight.*"

Boo-Boo buzzed just above Rhodes's head with a thunderous roar, creating a hurricane of pelting sand and pebbles. Rhodes ducked, skidding for a moment into the turn, killing his acceleration. Dana crossed her arms and plowed into her adversary, pushing into her skates as she made contact and lifting him up into the air. He grabbed her jacket as she clutched onto his mechanical arm.

In an instant, they were airborne, sailing over the shoulder of the road. A contrail of sparks glittered behind her as the duo arced over the edge of the cliffside, down toward the crashing waters of the bay below.

She closed her eyes.

# Chapter 48

*Stay — Shakespears Sister*

The blast of the impact shocked Dana despite Rhodes's body breaking her fall, the water feeling like concrete. She had the instinct to take in a lungful of air before piercing the surface of the cool ocean water, but the jolt itself knocked some of the precious oxygen from her body. She unbuckled her helmet with her right hand, her left seemingly unable to move. As the helmet floated away from her head, she looked at the hand of Rhodes clutching her left arm. His limbs glittered as if covered in tiny blue sequins, his face frozen in fear.

*He can't move?*

She kicked at his chest, desperately trying to free herself from his grasp. A burst of bubbles spewed from his mouth, traveling up to the surface as he continued his descent. The electronics and circuitry in his arms, legs, and torso continued their light show, his body contorting slowly without any ability to control it. His back arched as a final blast of bubbles engulfed his fear-frozen face. She stomped at him again and he finally released her, one last glittery coat of sparks flaring as his body burned out. His mouth opened in a scream, but only a muffled noise spread throughout the blue.

She pushed her arms upward and began to kick, but the surface seemed to inch further away with each movement she made. She kicked again only to realize that her skates were slowly pulling her back toward the floor of the bay.

*Don't panic. Don't panic.*

Her lungs constricted. She reached down to her side, grabbing Shirley's shin guard. Her gloves fumbled with the latch; she couldn't get a grip with her trembling, tired fingers. She continued to sink.

*Don't panic. You did your best, and that's all you could do.*

She relaxed her arms and let them drift above her head.

A muted splash followed by a spinning cyclone of bubbles startled her. A hand reached out, attached to a flannel shirt. *Nick.* He was scrambling for Shirley's latches. She guided his hand to her right shin.

*Click. Click.*

She looked into his eyes, her lungs on fire. She let out a burst of precious air.

Nick reached over to Laverne. Dana guided his hand again.

*Click.*

The second latch resisted. A blast of bubbles told Dana that Nick was frustrated, starting to panic. They continued to sink.

*Stupid Laverne!*

She drew her leg up closer to his hand.

*Click.*

With that, Laverne and Shirley drifted down, away from Dana, toward the sandy floor of the bay. She clawed at the water, the numbness in her fingers and toes slowly creeping up her limbs. She felt panic, unsure if it was due to the cold water, the fatigue, the lack of air, or the finality of hope leaving her body. She closed her eyes.

She felt Nick's arm close tightly around her chest and then each heaving movement as he jerked her upward. She pushed with him, unable to tell if she was moving her arms or legs, but willing herself to move, to help *him* escape. The seconds stretched further apart as her head swooned.

Another muffled splash.

She opened her eyes. A new underwater tornado of bubbles swirled next to them. She looked up at the surface, only a few feet away. The arm around her loosened its grip, replaced by a tighter one. Golden flakes started to fill her eyes, but this time they were followed by gold strings of light. A second arm around her. The golden strands came from the same direction. Then a head, a face. An angular jaw pointed toward the surface; familiar blue eyes looked back at her, squinting with effort.

*Angela.*

The trio burst through the surface, battered by the lapping waves of the cove and the downward blast of a Blackhawk's rotors directly overhead. Boo-Boo's heliplane hovered at the edge of inlet, moving safely away from the helicopter as the rescue team's line dropped. Nick grabbed it first and feebly attempted to loop it around Dana's arm. Angela swung Nick's free arm over her shoulder with one hand and lunged for the line with the other, lassoing Dana in one fluid move. Dana waved with her free hand and felt the jerk as the winch began to pull her upward.

She looked back at Angela and Nick, holding on to each other, waiting for their turn to ascend.

*I don't have enough love for both of you.*

"Did you honestly think we weren't going to send another chopper or two after you?" Director Jameson rammed her hands into her hips and laughed. "You're not a planner, are you, Dana?"

"No, ma'am," Dana replied.

She pulled the coarse blanket over her shoulders and shivered. Angela and Nick, in matching blankets, sat across from her on the sandy beach just before the flat outcropping covered with high grasses, surrounded by an array of vehicles. Beyond the whirlybirds, the cliffs sloped upward to the Pacific Coast Highway.

"Medics say all three of you may have dodged a bullet as far as bad injuries, but we'll get you to an exam room nonetheless. Especially you, Angela. I heard you took quite a few hits." A low buzzing noise from the surf interrupted her. A small inflatable landing craft with three divers approached. "Any sign of him?"

"Yes, ma'am," said the first diver. "He's just very heavy. We placed a marker, and we'll get a bird to airlift him out."

"Dead?" Dana blurted. "Rhodes is dead?"

"Absolutely. No surprises." The diver adjusted his mask.

"Okay," Dana said. "Okay."

Carmen turned her phone to Dana. "I thought you would want to know this, too."

The picture onscreen showed Eugene and Zeke, their wrists bound in zip ties, being loaded into a personnel carrier, escorted by Special Forces troopers.

"I know you have some history with these two. Thought you'd appreciate it."

"Yeah. A few events. And they wrecked my kitchen once." Dana allowed herself a satisfactory smile. She questioned whether to ask the diver about Laverne and Shirley, but if she was being honest with herself, she didn't care. That part of her life was closed. She had built her skates herself, based on her parents' meticulous plans and months of research and testing, but she would gladly let them rest at the bottom of the ocean if it meant leaving years of pain behind her.

A group of three men emerged from the grass. Olsen was in the center, hobbling on crutches, accompanied by Dan Sun and another agent dressed in standard-issue field attire. Dana shot up and bounded over.

"No hugs," Olsen said with a raised hand. "I just came to say goodbye."

"You're just going to leave? Now?" Dana stammered. Angela and Nick quickly flanked her.

"Director's orders." He curled his lips and gazed out to the divers returning to the raft, then looked back at her. She saw darkness in his gaze. "Dana, you knew that I was only here under extremely special circumstances. I was only a free man while helping you." He broke eye contact, scanning across the horizon. "It's beautiful here. I wish my mum could have seen this."

A long silence followed. Dana couldn't help feeling sad as she watched him absorb his last minutes of freedom, a freedom that had come to such an abrupt end. It was hard for her to wrap her head around this sudden finality, knowing all that Olsen had done to help this country that was now intent on incarcerating him. Dana felt a new pain she couldn't quite describe—a deep, hollow feeling of sadness and anger, and the inability to change the outcome. She let the group step ahead of her as she reflected.

Nick extended his hand. "Thank you, Olsen."

"Good job, mate. You keep that smart head of yours intact, you hear me?" Angela paused before wrapping her arms around him. "Miss Costanza, I said no hugs."

"I hug my friends goodbye," she said, breaking into a quiet sob. "You're a good person. Thank you."

"Sorry I stabbed you," he laughed as she let go. "Stay out of trouble, Barbie."

"I will. And you're forgiven." She extended her hand and they exchanged a final shake.

Dana stepped back, arms crossed. He crossed his arms in reply, as best as he could on his crutches.

"Miss Jefferson, thank you."

"For making you the man you are today and all that crap?" She finally allowed herself a smile. He nodded.

"No hugs."

"No hugs." She felt a sting in her weary eyes and wiped her face. "I'm not crying. That was just some salt water or something."

"Right." Olsen nodded to Dan and the other agent. "Director, I'll speak to you, of course, during the proceedings." He glanced at the group one more time, his eyebrows slightly arching. "Where's Ashley?"

"She's still stuck in her on-site debriefing," Jameson said. "She was up first since she cleared medical back at the truck depot."

"Oh, right." Olsen jutted his chin out. "Dana, when you see Ashley, can you . . . you know—"

Dana rushed forward and threw her arms around Olsen's frame. She squeezed once, then let go. "I'll give her a hug via transitive property."

A slight sheen on the surface of his eyes shimmered above his thin smile. She smiled in return. They had met as adversaries with their own senses of righteousness, his misguided and hers raw, undefined. But she was glad to have been part of his journey toward a clearer path and was grateful for his presence as her own damaged guardian angel. A father for their misshapen family.

"Goodbye, Aaron."

"Goodbye, Photograph."

# *Chapter 49*

*Nautical Disaster – The Tragically Hip*

ana tapped her fingernails on the stainless-steel tabletop. She glanced at the windowless walls painted the most boring shade of white, if that was even possible. She resumed her mental checklist of calls she needed to make: *A real estate agent. A door and window contractor. A painter. A tax accountant.* It was a brutally hard landing into mundane life over the past week, starting with cleaning out the old rancher she and Nick had lived in when they first came to New Mexico so she could sell it. Ashley had pleaded her case to keep Simone's ranch now that they weren't in hiding, and Dana had reluctantly agreed. For now, Dana needed some type of normalcy to busy her mind before she dipped her toe one last time into the world of mercenaries, militias, and mayhem.

At this moment, Dana sat in silence inside a government office outside of Roswell, a nondescript square building filled with further nondescript square windowless rooms. At the behest of Director Jameson, she had agreed to this meeting. She tucked her hair behind her ears and listened to the clicks and clacks of the security door locks before it opened abruptly.

Director Jameson entered, attired in a black pantsuit, followed by Penny in a full-white ensemble: a long-sleeve turtleneck, sport coat, and flared-leg high-waisted pants that clung to her thin frame. Her pointed shoes shone in the stale fluorescent lights; in her delicate hands, a large silver case.

"You two look like you're ready to coach a women's college basketball game," Dana said, leaning back and putting her feet up on the table.

"Nice to see you, too," Carmen said, stuffing herself into a small chair opposite Dana. "Penny, if you don't mind, the case?"

"Getting right to business here." She lofted the case onto the table and unlatched it, keeping the contents concealed. Penny tucked her thumb under her chin and donned a sly smile before turning the case around and opening it. "I did the best I could."

She reached inside and placed a freshly cleaned Laverne and Shirley on the table. The *L* on Laverne even remained, although chipped and faded.

"I thought that might be sentimental, so I instructed my team not to buff it out."

Dana lifted each skate and caressed one of the newly wound wheels, shimmering as copper-colored cables laced through chromed hardware. She stuck her nose inside and inhaled.

"They don't stink anymore."

Penny slid the case across the table. "I thought this was an appropriate gesture of gratitude. And perhaps a nice signing bonus."

"A signing bonus?"

Carmen pulled her phone from her pocket. "TIARA is no more. Besides the goal of apprehending and stopping Rhodes, I lost the funding and authority."

"You got fired?"

Carmen's jaw tensed. "I was relieved of my responsibilities and reassigned. Working with Olsen and his team was not entirely authorized, despite the positive outcome."

"As such," Penny said, "I need a specialized group at Silver to handle our more delicate operations. *Internally*. Some things that were stolen or misappropriated, for instance, and there are of course many other actors out there who will gladly fill the void previously occupied by One Hundred Roads. Carmen here is going to be our liaison with the government to make sure no one is stepping on each other's toes and such."

Dana gently placed Laverne back in the case, followed by Shirley. She ran her palms over the smooth shin guards, then across the tight angles of the ankle joints. She slammed the case shut.

"No."

"No?" Penny splayed her hand across her chest in mock indignation. "Dana, dear, isn't this what you're good at? Don't you want to continue the work of your parents? Building a better a world, but now without the confines of the government's red tape?"

"My parents—" She stopped and shook her head with a laugh. "You know what? You don't know shit about my parents. You don't know what you put people through."

"Dana, this is a chance to really change the world. Do you have any idea what else your father worked on? Somewhere in his journals and notebooks, there could be a cure for cancer, cellular regeneration—many of the things that Rhodes told me about."

"Yeah, about that," Dana said, her eyes firing daggers into Penny. "When were you going to tell us that you provided him with his artificial limbs? *You didn't.*"

Silence filled the room. Dana hoped it would suffocate Penny, but her wish was not granted.

"Silver made some mistakes in our prior dealings."

"But you *are* Silver! That's on you!" She slammed her fist onto the stainless-steel table. "That's on you! You did that! You outfitted his psychotic roller derby team! *You* screwed up, and people died!" She felt her breath leaving her chest, adrenaline piping into her neck. "You screwed up, Penny! And what about the juggernauts? Did you build them, too? *Oopsie?*"

Carmen jutted her hand between the opposing women. "Rhodes used some of his other contacts to build them. And that's one of the loose ends we need you to help with, Dana."

"'Loose ends' is an understatement. That's my family's legacy out there, but this is your fault. You clean it up."

Penny stepped back and crossed her arms, slowly raising her chin. "Dana, when you make the decisions that I have to make—decisions of such gravitas that people do, indeed, live or die—the mistakes in judgement can carry catastrophic consequences. I wear that crown and bear the burden. I'm not perfect. I'm trying to fix things."

"Then fix things without me. Or my family."

"Your family is extraordinary, and so are you. And your sister, well, the treatments she received before birth have created something very unique. If you could ask Ashley—"

Dana leapt to her feet and grabbed the case containing her skates. She lowered her eyes and leaned into Penny. Before the words left her mouth, her vocal cords growled.

"*Stay the fuck away from my sister.*" Carmen attempted to step between them but was met by Dana's outstretched hand. "That goes for you, too, Carmen. The Jefferson family is done with all of you. I want nothing to do with any of you."

"Photograph," Carmen pleaded, "just hear me out. We could use you."

Dana straightened her jacket and zipped it closed.

"Yeah, you could use me, but I won't let you."

Penny walked to the door and opened it, gesturing for Dana to leave. "Go. Be selfish."

"Oh no," Dana replied, bumping her shoulder as she passed her, "I'm not selfish. I'm not doing this for me. I'm doing this to protect everyone I love—

protect them from people like you."

"Dana," Carmen called, "give it a few days!"

"I gave it my entire life, Director Jameson. I just didn't know it."

With a mock salute, she strode out of the room and out to the little red pickup truck waiting for her in the parking lot.

# Chapter 50

*Don't Stop Believin' – Journey*

The small cowbell hanging over the door of Holstein's Chubby Cactus Diner clanged with the new patron's entrance. A hefty middle-aged man, his wife, and two children stopped in the entrance before being greeted by the hostess, a teenaged girl with long dark braids. Dana sat up straight and observed the party as they walked to the booth across from hers.

*Just another family, not a bunch of mercenaries.*

Since returning to Taos, she had been helping Ashley pack for her trip to Princeton where she would take part in a trial research project assignment for a month, the outcome of which would determine her placement with a professor in the English department. Before leaving, she had led Dana through an internship in ranching, complete with a meticulously detailed schedule of Dick's feeding and care. Tonight would be a going-away dinner not just for her sister, but Nick, too. Dana dreaded saying goodbye.

"Dana." Nick snapped his fingers. "Dessert?"

She glanced up to find their waitress rooted at the end of the table, pad in hand. Dana pointed to a cheesecake in the confectionary display across the dining room.

"Cheesecake. No fruit. Just cake and crust."

"Yes, ma'am."

Ashley waved off the waitress and kicked at her backpack under the table. "You're really distracted. I'm going to be fine, idiot."

"I know, idiot," Dana snarked. "Just let me say it all one more time."

They spoke in unison: "Don't drink without a friend. Don't get pregnant. Don't put on your skates."

Nick laughed. Dana admired his resilience after all she had put him through. His smile and hope remained, and she playfully slapped him on the shoulder to acknowledge it. "Thank you for being my friend."

"Same." Nick nodded toward something over Dana's shoulder.

"Did you just nod at someone you don't want me to look at?"

"I just don't want you to be obvious. There's a woman. Red hair. Really pretty." He swallowed. "She keeps looking over at us and then checking her phone."

Dana slung her arm over the back of the booth and craned her neck. A pale redhead with soft features, seated by herself at a table for two, glanced away. The woman looked upward at the slow-moving ceiling fans, back to Dana's booth, and then back to her phone.

The cowbell on the entrance door clanged again.

"I'm not doing this," Dana whispered. She reached over to Ashley's place setting and slid the butter knife into her hand, concealing it blade-first inside her sleeve. "I'm going over."

"Dana, wait, wait, wait!" Nick hissed.

*Too late.*

Dana strode over to the woman's table and pulled out the chair opposite her. She slid into the seat, her arms concealed under the tabletop. The startled woman bolted upright.

"Hey, Red. Hi. My name's Dana."

"Um, hi. I'm Cheryl. My friends call me Cher."

"Okay, *Cheryl.* Here's the deal. I noticed you looking over at me and my friends, and frankly, I'm a little on edge and suspicious of a woman sitting by herself and spying on us. Who are you after?"

Cher's lower lip quivered. Her big blue eyes widened. "David. His name is David."

"Where's David from?"

"This dating app." Cher held up her phone. Dana squinted and leaned over. The screen displayed the profile of a moderately handsome man named David, from Taos, and a profile stating he was into books, hiking, and baseball.

"Ooh-kay."

*Shit. I think I made a boo-boo.*

"I was in town for a job interview, and I didn't get it, and, and, and I figured, 'Hey, why not see if I can get a date and eat with someone instead of by myself?' and I think he stood me up. But that's just par for the course, you know," she said with a forced laugh. "It's always, 'Hey, Cher, you'll meet a nice boy someday, you're not too boring,' but then this happens, again." Her eyes began to stream. "I'm sorry, um, Dana? That's what you said, right? Dana?"

"Dana." She reached over and grabbed Cher's hand. "Okay, Cher. Listen. First of all, *speak more slowly.* Second, I've had a pretty tough couple of weeks recently, so I'm a little on edge." Dana held up her thumb and index finger about an inch apart. "I've got a pretty short fuse right now. Sorry."

"That's okay." Cher picked up her napkin from her lap and blew her nose. "I'm sorry, that's so gross."

"Ah, you haven't shared a room with me. Tell me something, Cher. Why were you staring at us?"

The cowbell on the door clanged. Dana twisted her head, observing a food delivery driver jogging in to pick up a bag from the hostess. She returned her attention to Cher's soliloquy.

"It's just, you know, I just want to be happy. Meet someone. And I thought you two were a couple, and you looked so happy. I'm just daydreaming." She exhaled and looked up at the fan. "He's cute, the guy you're with. I just want to meet a nice, cute guy who's down-to-earth and, you know, nice. Did I already say nice? I just wish I could, you know, meet someone and fall in love like in some eighties movie."

The butter knife slipped out of Dana's sleeve and clanged onto the tile floor. "Do you like cheesecake?" She grabbed Cher by the wrist and yanked her out of her seat. "Come on."

The duo scampered back to the booth, where Nick sat with his chin on his wrist. Ashley held up her phone and stood. "My ride's here!"

"Shit. Okay. Ashley, this is Cher. Cher, Ashley. Ashley, text me when you're done with your errands. Love you."

"Love you, too." They had plenty of time for tears and hugs tonight, and Dana was happy to let the new distraction of this redheaded girl subdue her anxiety over the departures of Ashley and Nick. Dana heaved Ashley's bag out from under the table, then pushed Cher into the booth. "Nick, this is Cher."

"Um, hi. I'm Nick."

"Cheryl. Cheryl Hill."

"Wait. Hold on. I'm sorry, did you say your name is *Cheryl Hill*?"

"I know, it's corny. My parents have a weird sense of humor, so they named me after the town I grew up in."

Nick blinked rapidly. "Come again?"

"Cherry Hill? In New Jersey."

"*No shit.*"

Dana turned her head. This was the second time she recalled Nick ever cursing. "No shit is right."

"You know it?!" Cher waved her hands excitedly. "Anyhow, the story is, this local girl finally leaves town for a job interview in New Mexico, bombs that, and then gets stood up."

The waitress returned with a plate of cheesecake. Dana mouthed, *Two forks, please and thank you.*

Nick puffed his cheeks. "Wow, I'm from Jersey, too, by Hammonton."

"Ah, you're a Piney." Cher smiled.

"Correct." Nick blushed. "I'm a Piney boy. Actually, I'm heading back home the day after tomorrow. I just finished a . . . job . . . out here."

Another clang of the cowbell. Dana looked up and smiled as Frank Irons entered. He tipped his ball cap as he approached the table.

"Hey, guys! Sorry to barge in, but Dana, I got your text and I brought the trailer over."

Nick sat up with a confused smile directed at Cher. "I have no idea what's going on. Which is normal."

Frank reached into his pocket, held up a key, and handed it to Dana. "Here you go. I unloaded it out front. Helmets are strapped to the back. Gotta run. Nice to see you all again! Ma'am." He tipped his cap at Cher. She smiled broadly and waved.

"I have no idea what's going on, either," Cher admitted with a bubbly laugh.

"Nick," Dana announced, handing the key over to him, "I still owed you a motorcycle. Technically, Olsen paid for it. I thought it was the right thing to do."

Nick's jaw dropped as he held the key. Cher leaned over and picked it up.

"I've never been on a motorcycle."

Nick smiled. "Dana, did Frank say 'helmets'?"

"Yep. Two. Since, you know, I figured you'd find a passenger someday. But anyway, sorry I trashed your old bike."

Cher sat back and blushed. Dana couldn't help but notice the matching expression on Nick's face across the table.

"Dana," Nick said, "can I tell her about the bike? The skates? The big, you know, robot thing?"

"Sure." She grabbed the key from Cher and placed it back in Nick's hand. "It's your story."

After a quick dig through her pockets, Dana retrieved a crumpled hundred-dollar bill and placed it on the table. "It's on me." She flashed the keys to the pickup truck. "Taking the truck. I'll give it back at some point."

With a quick wink, she turned away and walked out the front door, the cowbell clanging as it announced her departure.

Dana sat in the driver's seat in the back of the parking lot and waited for Nick and Cher to leave. She'd miss him—more than he'd know, more than she could put into words—but she was happy. They had promised each other to text once a week at a minimum, with Saturday mornings as the agreed upon check-in time. And if she failed to reply in twenty-four hours, Nick had full permission to contact the local authorities and Carmen Jameson. Dana acknowledged it was an odd agreement, but their promise to each other was to never say goodbye completely ever again.

She flipped open her phone. A text from Nick had already lit up her screen. Two words: "Thank you." She smiled and replied with a winking face emoji.

A burst of muffled laughter brought her attention back to the view of the restaurant. Nick and Cher walked out, hands close to touching. He held up the motorcycle key and offered her one of the helmets. Dana watched as he gently helped her place it on her head, brushing her red hair back behind her neck with the back of his hand.

After another bit of muffled talk between them, Cher tucked her skirt and sat on the back of the bike. Nick mounted it and started the ignition, Cher's hands sliding to his back, then over his shoulders. The motorcycle's engine revved as he started slowly, rolling past the restaurant and onto the highway. Dana watched his taillights dissolve into the dark.

*Cher, if you break his heart, I will hunt you down and straight up murder you.*

She twisted the key in the truck's ignition, snapping it off at the shoulder. *Goddamn it.*

# Chapter 51

*What Does It Take – Honeymoon Suite*

Simone's living room still held the scent of freshly cut pine. Dana ran her hand along the new unpainted front doorframe, another thing to add to her growing to-do list. The dark interior of the rancher still revealed a few errant bullet holes when the sun broke the plane of the horizon and shone yellow beams into the house. Dana pulled back the curtains and sighed deeply. Through the back patio door, also new, she could see Dick slowly plodding across his paddock. *He knows she's not coming back*, she thought. But he was an old soul, and she guessed he had seen many people come and go throughout his long life.

Angela waited in the entryway of the hall, her duffel bag slung over her shoulder. She held her motorized skates in her hands.

"I can't take these with me."

"I think I agree with that."

Dana lovingly placed them on the mantel, next to Laverne and Shirley and her mother's skates. The old rifle had been put back in a storage locker under the couch as she waited for paperwork so she could transfer it to Frank

Irons. She thought it was appropriate to give him a token of her gratitude, as well as ensure it was left with a responsible adult—at least one more responsible than herself.

"My ride should be here in a few minutes," Angela said.

"Mm-hmm."

They had barely spoken, unless functionally, over the past week. Dana knew they had to have one final conversation. So, she took the wheel and drove straight into the topic.

"Angela, are you sure this is what you want?"

"I spoke with Director Jameson, and yes, after the interview with Agent Sun—"

"Just call him Dan."

"With *Dan*, I'm going to do it. I'll be going through some kind of special class at Quantico that they set up." Angela leaned her bag against the new front door. "This is my calling. I think I found it, finally."

Dana nodded and reached for her coffee cup to delay her next words. She was happy, proud that Angela had decided to go into this special "fieldwork," yet she also knew that she'd be placing herself in a perpetual cycle of danger and risk. But Angela thrived on conflict and challenge; she was never meant to be tied down to a desk or computer.

"You know you'll have to do a lot of paperwork."

"Jameson and Dan assured me that this particular role will be primarily outside of the office. I can do this."

"I know you can, Angela." Dana smiled and sat at the kitchen island. Now, she decided to swerve into another topic. "Maybe I don't want you to go."

Angela sauntered over and poked Dana lightly in the shoulder. "A part of me wants to stay, too. But you have your things, and I have mine." She placed her hand on Dana's and laced their fingers together. "But we know that we're not in the right place or right time right now to give this another try."

"I know." Dana's heart pushed itself into her throat. "It wouldn't be fair." She watched the last pillars of steam rise from her cup. "Don't wait for me, and I won't wait for you."

"Fair enough."

"You know," Dana started, "I never actually thanked you for coming out here. For helping with, you know, all the ass-kicking and whatnot."

"I wouldn't have changed a thing."

"And I'm sorry I put you through all of this, too. You didn't owe me anything." Dana released Angela's hand. "You *don't* owe me anything. You know what I mean."

Angela curled her lips over her teeth. Dana could see tension and strain in her eyes. "I know what you mean," she said, her voice breaking slightly. "But I'll always be grateful. For you." She checked her phone. "My ride is here."

They hugged, a long embrace filled with deep sighs on both sides, faces buried in each other's hair. A honk outside interrupted them.

"Text me when you get to DC."

Dana watched Angela walk down to the end of the drive where a Prius waited. The small driver appeared taken aback at Angela's height as he placed the duffel into the hatchback. Angela stopped the driver so she could dig into her bag and place her jacket inside.

*Do it. Don't think, just do.*

"Angela!" Dana shouted from the porch. She leapt over the steps and bounded down the driveway. Her heart raced as she ran past the pickup truck and over the scattered remnants of shattered pottery.

Angela caught her with outstretched arms as Dana pressed her lips against hers. They spun in a circle, together, worn and tired but still energized by the bond that could never be severed.

"I love you, Angela-la-la."

"I love you, Dana-na-na-na."

"Be careful out there."

"I will. I promise."

Angela broke their embrace and slid into the back of the car. Dana stood still, watching the Prius drift down the side road, out toward the highway.

Her heart beat.

And then it beat again.

The rest of the day passed quickly. Distractions of paying bills and making phone calls and unraveling her mother's things continued to occupy her mind. Dana had pulled a box out of the closet full of prints and Polaroids from art openings and galleries. Simone beamed in each photo next to her paintings. Dana stopped to examine one in particular: Her mother, smiling, in a loose long-sleeved blue dress, holding Ashley on her hip. In the background, three paintings of tall pine trees that connected to each other, a triptych, being examined by old men in suits. Dana imagined her mother's pulse as the auctioneers announced the bids, knowing that every incremental dollar was another day of survival she could provide for her daughter.

*Daughters.*

She poured one more cup of coffee—the last one, she swore—as she placed the final piles of papers on the kitchen table. All of Ashley's information for Princeton went into an orange folder, all the bills into a green folder. She hesitated to open the last folder, a yellow one.

Dana made a raspberry as she flicked it open. Inside was a printout of an acceptance letter from the psychology department at the state university. She read it again, pausing on the last sentences:

*Also note the attached sheet of pending transfer credits based on your advanced placement high school courses. Pending the outcome of the additional interview, we will be happy to place you as a teaching assistant to Professor Marks in the Addiction and Recovery Counseling program.*

*Welcome to the university, Dana Jefferson!*

She sighed and closed the folder. She had two months—pending the interview, of course—before the start of the semester. *Two months.* Dana looked over at the mantel, at the trio of skates evenly displayed with Laverne and Shirley in the center. Next to Simone's was a tiny cherry-wood box containing her ashes and her revolver, with the GPS coordinates engraved on the side.

Dana opened her laptop and it flickered to life. She typed furiously, looking at maps and regulations for traveling across the Canadian border by car, booking a hotel in Alaska, and checking weather forecasts for the next couple of weeks. She printed each webpage, going on to the next one before each sheet spooled through the printer and fell to the floor.

She blitzed the refrigerator, pouring out soon-to-be-expired liquids and tossing nonperishables from the pantry into a shopping bag. She paused her packing to text Nick, Angela, Ashley, just checking in, and then Frank Irons to ask him to watch Dick. The sun was beginning its final descent, sending long cool shadows along the floor, over her backpack now crammed with fresh socks, underwear, and her shirt from Hershey.

Nick sent an instant reply to her text with just the words "Be safe!" and a picture of him and Cher on the boardwalk in Asbury Park in front of the convention hall. Dana smiled.

With her arms full of her folded printouts, she heaved her backpack over both shoulders and grabbed the keys to the pickup truck. She gently picked up the box of ashes and placed them inside a small tan bag slung across her body. Dana lifted the revolver, felt the textured handle in her palm, and placed it inside the bag as well.

She punched in the alarm code on the pad next to the front door and glanced back at the skates on the mantel. The corners of her mouth curled into a smile.

# *Epilogue 1*

*The Living Years – Mike + The Mechanics*

Olsen sat in peaceful observation and took in the view. Towering pines from the Pacific Northwest crowned the hills, broken up in the foreground by a freshly paved country road. A white fence extended around the expansive lawn of the facility, the grass imprinted with fresh mowing patterns radiating out from the central buildings. The white concrete and copper decorative accents were interspersed with mint awnings over the various entrances to the garden area, dotted with white Adirondack chairs, small tables, and other seats of varying heights for the residents.

He sat on a short-backed chair, cane across his lap, and inhaled the deep woody aroma. *Oregon.* Almost reluctant to break the gentle sounds of birds and breezes, he spoke.

"It's beautiful here, wouldn't you say?"

"Hmph," replied the elderly woman next to him. She folded her hands on a thin white blanket draped over her lap, the edges of her wheelchair peeking out. Her yellowed eyes and freshly washed thinning hair sparkled in the sun. "Are we in Brisbane?" she asked in a thick Australian accent.

"No, we're outside of Portland." An attendant, a young woman in floral scrubs, offered them each a lemonade.

"My son used to love lemonade," said the old woman with a slowly brightening smile. "He was a very smart boy."

"If the fruit doesn't fall far from the tree, I bet he was."

"You're too sweet. He had a bit of a rough streak. He enlisted. Oh! He wrote me a letter last week."

"Did he now?" Olsen sipped from the cool glass. "What is he up to?"

"He said he was going to Indonesia. Or maybe it was Malaysia. It's his first time going overseas. He said he'll be back for Christmas."

"Sounds like a good lad," he said.

At the edge of the grass, Olsen spied Carmen Jameson. She walked slowly around the perimeter of the gardens, looking up occasionally to check on him. He held up his hand and waved with two fingers.

"Is that your mum? She's a pretty lady," said the woman beside him.

"No, she's my friend."

"My son didn't have many friends. Did you know he joined the military? Says he'll be back in time for Christmas."

Olsen looked down at his drink and smiled. In his periphery, Carmen talked to two of the attendants. He spied them looking at him briefly, then turning away when caught by his direct stare. He sat upright and cleared his throat.

"Your son, maybe I know him. What's his name?"

"His name is Aaron. He's a good lad. Bit of a handful at times, but he got straightened out. He joined the army. Or navy?" The woman held her hand over her mouth. "I can't recall."

"I heard your son got into some trouble, but he's all straightened out now."

"Oh! So you did know him?"

"Very well, ma'am. A few people took good care of him. They got him on the right track." Olsen waved again to Carmen, beckoning her to approach.

"Any girlfriends?"

"Never anyone serious. Too busy. But he did meet a very special young woman who . . . helped him find his way. Her name was Dana. He grew very fond of her and her sister, Ashley." He finished his drink. "And her friend Angela, too. She was a very lovely girl, Angela. I think under different circumstances, he would have asked her to dinner." He looked down at the empty glass. "*Very* different circumstances."

"He was a handsome boy. I'm not surprised. One of his coaches used to say all the girls fancied him because he looked like a movie star, like an action movie hero."

"When all was said and done, maybe he was a hero. It just took him a roundabout way to get there."

"That's nice to hear. He was a bright boy." The woman sipped her lemonade and licked her lips. "Delicious. Aaron loved lemonade. Did you know he's coming back for Christmas?"

Carmen stopped short of the two conversationalists and patted Olsen on the shoulder. "Time to go?"

"Time to go." He stood up and placed his empty glass on the chair. He gently kissed the old woman on the forehead. "It's been lovely talking to you, Mrs. Olsen."

"Lovely, yes. Oh! His birthday is soon. He's going to be twenty-two this year."

He pinched the bridge of his nose and turned away. Carmen placed a hand on his shoulder as they crossed the garden. "Thank you," he whispered. He felt the first tear stinging his eyes, followed by several more. He wiped his cheeks. "Thank you."

"The State Department was happy to comply with my request, due to your *unique* circumstances. She'll be well cared for here; it's an impressive collection of people under the best services. We have two former senators here, a Hollywood director, and a few other A-listers. She'll have plenty of people to talk to while she can. This is the best facility in the country." She let go of her grip. "It was the least I could do."

They crossed through an outdoor checkpoint and into the parking lot. He paused to hold out his wrists. "Time for the cuffs?"

"Not yet." She nodded to a white SUV at the end of the lot. The vehicle slowed to a stop at the edge of the walkway. "Like I said, this was the *least* I could do."

The rear passenger door swung open. A thin white pant leg descended first, followed by a white umbrella that sprang open to protect its wielder from the sun. Penny landed on the blacktop with a clickety-clack of her heels.

"This is for you, Mr. Olsen." She extended a large white envelope. "Congratulations, you're dead. If you *choose* to be, that is. Inside is your new passport, a contract, and a copy of the death certificate. If you sign the contract, please use your new passport name. Then I'll have my associates coordinate the placement of your . . . *transport* down a ravine. A nasty accident, so I've imagined. 'Aaron's body was burned beyond recognition,' and so on." She smiled dryly and twirled her umbrella. "Otherwise, I keep all these documents and Aaron Olsen goes back to prison, alive and well."

The driver's side rear door opened now. Angela leapt to the pavement, her usual casual sports attire replaced by a black business jacket and knee-length white skirt slightly askew, a tablet tucked under her arm. She pulled on the hem to straighten it out. "I'd sign the contract."

"What's all this?"

Carmen took the lead. "TIARA is closed since Rhodes is gone. But a private organization can take over the job, if one were to exist, say, under Silver. There are a lot of loose ends and new threads that someone has to pursue."

"You see," Penny continued, "Silver's mission was to guide the hands that needed direction, for the long-term benefit of mankind and, bluntly, civilization. Working in the shadows, someone who can be the overriding authority, setting the stage for the world's greatest play: utopia. We need to be vigilant, prevent war, stop pandemics, and the like. Government bureaucracy is *so* tedious."

He glanced from woman to woman, pausing on Angela. She winked, followed by a broad smile. "It's a good thing, buddy. We need a leader. A veteran."

"This is not a paramilitary organization. As I've said, I'm a technocrat. I'm the elite that the world hates despite my best intentions. If someone has to be a kingmaker for lost nations, I'll take up the cause. And I need knights. Good and righteous knights." Penny eyed him up and down. "Or, at the very least, a ronin with a bad leg from Australia." She looked away. "I have tried to do the right things by myself, and I can't. I know you despise me, which is why I think you're the best person for the job. *You* will hold *me* accountable."

Olsen opened the envelope but did not remove the contents at first. He glanced back over his shoulder at the facility and imagined his mother obliviously sitting next to a billionaire and eating crackers, smiling as she talked about Christmas. He thought about Dana and Ashley, picking up the pieces of their lives, eating burritos and doing chores, admiring the paintings left by their mother—a genius taken too soon from the world she had so much to contribute to, taken from her family and how much she loved them.

"Someone get me a pen."

Angela reached into her coat pocket with a devilish smile.

"Aaron, welcome to CROWN."

# *Epilogue 2*

*Mirrors – Justin Timberlake*

Thin dead leaves crackled under Dana's footfalls. She glanced down at the dry soil, then up above the timberline, hoping to catch a glimpse of Denali fading against the blue sky. With a deep breath, she untied her neckerchief and let it dangle over her leather lapels. Alaska was warmer than she had expected, but it was still late summer, and a recent dry spell had sapped the wetness from the air. The past two hours of nonstop hiking had pushed her farther into the vast wilderness, and she noted to herself that she had earned a break.

Dana unclipped her backpack and let it fall to the forest floor. She slipped her satellite GPS module from her pocket, removing her pink-and-black gloves to tap the screen. She smirked as she rechecked the coordinates from her mother's pistol. She was only a half hour from her destination, but her feet and knees told her rest was needed. Feeling the first signs of exhaustion on the way, she rotated the holster of her mother's revolver and sat cross-legged in the dirt. Her water bottle, half empty, reminded her that she was drinking faster than expected and would need to conserve more or find an oasis if she didn't want to run out on her return hike.

If Nick were here, he would have done something that made her feel dumb, but in a caring way, like marking the side of her bottle for the ideal rate of consumption or just simply bringing more water. She smiled at the imaginary scolding playing out in her mind. In their most recent text volley, he had explained how Cher had recommended new placemats for the kitchen, which Nick obliged. Dana thought about all the times she had dribbled syrup and butter, as well as drips of coffee and bacon grease, onto the old ones.

*Mmm, bacon.*

Still seated, she flexed her arms and leaned back with her palms behind her, enjoying the warmth of the sun on her slightly wind-chapped cheeks. A light yip from the brush ahead startled her. She sat at attention and slid her arm to the pistol on her thigh.

*I've never even used a gun, but there's a first time for everything, right?*

Her thumb flicked at the holster strap, ready to pull the weapon. Another yip followed a light rustling, closer than the last one. A tiny brown-and-gray snout poked out from the bramble, followed by a fuzzy pillow and a matching twin. *Wolf cubs. And where there's children, there has to be a mother,* she recalled. The pups stopped and tilted their heads. Dana cocked her head to the side to mimic their curious demeanor.

*Do not appear to be a threat. Do not appear to be food. Be doglike.*

The tiny drops of sweat on her brow betrayed her calm intentions. A silent paw emerged behind the pups, followed by a gray-and-white wolf. *Mama.* The mother fixed its yellow-green eyes on her own, mouth shut, but sniffed furiously at the short breeze that carried scents between them. Dana's pulse throbbed, and a lightheadedness draped over her. She slid her hand from the pistol back to the forest floor to steady her equilibrium and not fall over.

The first pup yipped and pranced forward, stopping at her feet with a quick growl. It hopped backward and turned to the mother wolf, who still had her eyes locked on Dana. She lowered her snout by half an inch and stepped closer into the clearing, squarely set six feet from Dana.

She watched the wolf raise its head slowly, arching its neck upward.

"Hi." It was all Dana could think to say. The mother wolf stepped closer and nudged the haunches of the closest pup. It turned to look at her and immediately pranced back into the brush, followed by its sibling.

"Are we cool?" Dana relaxed her posture, and the mother wolf turned to follow the pups back on their journey. The occasional twig snap faded in the distance until Dana only heard the white noise of the light breezes through the trees above her. "I guess so."

She stood and heaved her pack onto her shoulders before turning north toward the beacon indicated on her GPS. She glanced back and forth between the screen and her feet once it indicated she was close. Her head down, she saw a root, then the base of a tree as the crown of her head slammed into the trunk.

"Seriously?" Dana stared at the tree sitting on top of the apex of the coordinates. "This can't be it." She placed her hand on the bark at shoulder height, right next to a weathered carving of a star.

*Star.*

This wasn't just a common totem; this was from Simone, for Dana. She flung her backpack to the ground and unzipped her jacket. Searching up and down for another sign, another marker, anything that might connect to Simone, Dana paced around the tree. She glanced back at the star and noticed it was slightly askew, the left shoulder point dramatically longer than the other points.

*Left?*

She dug her toes into the dirt on the left side of the tree, then dropped to her knees and began to dig.

"'Bring a shovel, Dana,'" she muttered in a singsong voice, mocking what she imagined Nick would have told her to do. "'If you're digging for treasure, you need a shovel.'"

She looked to her right and saw a small jagged rock about the size of her hand. "That'll do, Nick."

Dana slashed the rock at the soil and immediately heard a *thonk* just under the surface as stone met metal. She slashed again and started to furrow the top inch of dirt. If her mother had buried something deep, it must have been here for a while, she reasoned, since the weather and years would have worn away the layers of earth. She swiped and dug faster until she fully uncovered a metal ammunition box a few inches wide with a rusty handle on the top.

She pulled at the handle and fell backward with a tumble as she freed the box from its crypt, flinging it several feet away in the effort. It landed with a loud *clank,* and the lid popped open. She crawled to it and gazed inside. A yellowed envelope labeled "Dana," perfectly preserved for years inside the waterproof box, lay on the ground.

A small smile swept across her lips. She felt the contents, a small rectangle, and tore the envelope. *No letter.* She held up a plastic thumb drive and sprinted to her backpack to find her tablet.

"Come on, come on, come on," she pleaded as the screen came to life. She slammed the thumb drive into the port and watched a video open onscreen.

An image of her mother greeted her. She was younger, but gaunt— perhaps from her cancer treatment or the cancer itself—and a familiar tiny baby sat on her lap in a green jumper. Simone wore a flannel shirt with the sleeves torn off, her shoulders lacking the tattoos that she later decorated herself with sometime since then. The audio cracked to life through the tablet speakers.

"Dana, hi. A part of me hopes you never see this. I'm sure if you got to this point, you've found out about everything. Almost everything, or some combination of facts and the truth. Anyway. This," she said, smiling as she propped the baby on her knee, "this is Ashley, and she's your sister.

"When I went into hiding, I was pregnant with her. And I need you to know how hard all of this was. Even if someday in the future you hear it from me in person, I need you to hear it now, while I'm still crying myself to sleep at night." Simone paused. Her lip violently quivered. "You have no idea how hard this was, but they would have killed your sister. She's very special in ways you may eventually understand. But you're special, too. And I have faith. I believe in you." Her voice broke, and she paused her monologue again to sob.

Dana realized she had been crying since the video began. She pulled a glove from her pocket and wiped her cheeks. What she wouldn't have given to have Angela's arm wrapped around her shoulders, or Nick's hand on her back to steady her. She wished someone she loved could have been there to share the moment with her, one of her rocks. The video continued.

"Dana, your grandfather made a deal with a devil, for the sake of all of us. Rhodes was going to blow the whistle on the project, blaming your grandfather unless he turned over his grandchild, Ashley, when she was born. Of course, what your grandfather did working on the program was nothing compared to Rhodes greenlighting the parts that actually killed the engineers and test pilots. Your grandfather loaded your eye scans into the lock programs, even into the hardware chips, and deleted Rhodes's access. He said that as long as you were alive, we would be safe, and Rhodes would never be able to access the juggernaut again. Then he helped all of us plan our escape." Simone wiped her tears with the back of her hand and smiled.

"And you need to know, you need to understand, that the most important thing a parent can do, and the hardest thing we can do, is lie to our children to keep them safe. Parents lie. We do the most dishonest thing we can to our children, *for our children*."

Dana paused the video and shuddered. The stories, the journey, the revelations—everything ended here. Her mother had recorded this so her daughter could have closure, and for that, Dana felt a gratitude and love more intense than any memory of their life together before the world had come crashing down. She loved her mother for giving her sister a chance, a chance to live, to reunite her with Dana someday. Ashley was a gift.

"Dana, just remember that parents lie, but it's because we love. It's our pain, not yours." Onscreen, Simone bounced Ashley on her knee. She looked to the side of the camera and sighed. "Okay. Did you get everything?"

A male voice murmured off-camera, "Perfect. I got it in one take, honey."

A handsome man with a ragged beard leaned in and kissed her mother on the forehead before stopping the recording.

Dana dropped the tablet and gasped.

An invisible punch to the chest knocked her breath from her. Dana's heart pounded against her ribcage, every beat pulsing faster and faster.

Dana reached a trembling hand back to the tablet. Her finger shook violently as she attempted to land it on the rewind button. She clicked it once, but she already knew the voice she heard, the face she glimpsed, one that had been gone for over a decade.

"Perfect. I got it in one take, honey."

"*Dad?*"

*Dana Jefferson will return.*


*. . . And Ashley.*


*. . . And Nick and Cher.*


*. . . And Angela.*


*. . . And Laverne and Shirley.*

# *Acknowledgements*

Thank you to everyone who participated in the journey. This book concludes the "Juggernaut Trilogy", which was written as a labor of love and healing. The death of my father and my own struggles with mental health provided the map that led me here. Finishing this book is nothing less than a tribute to everyone who has supported me along the way. I could not have done this without every single one of you, and I acknowledge that blessing every single day.

To Amy Reeve, my editor and "bad cop", you have my eternal gratitude. I will never enjoy any book for the rest of my life thanks to your critical eye and the education you have provided.

To Cleo Miele, all I can say is "wow" and thank you for all of your assistance, guidance, and cheerleading. Your professionalism has been exceptional, and I greatly treasure our business relationship. And thank you for putting an extreme amount of pressure on me to take care of Dana and Nick.

To my wife, as always, I'm sorry about the mess. Thank you for your support and patience. I don't have enough words and will never find the right ones to say how much you mean to me.

And finally,
Dana Jefferson. Thank you for showing up when you did.